"I have a message for Miss Julie Smith . . ."

The voice over the phone was low, masculine, faintly accented.

"Who is this?" Julie demanded.

"You'd be wise to tell us where you've hidden the disk." The quiet command came over the phone like a gunshot.

"I don't know anything about the disk. I was arrested by mistake," she insisted.

A harsh laugh caused her to grip the phone tightly. "We intend to get that disk, Miss Smith. If you're thinking of holding out for a better price, you're making a big mistake. The police are in way over their heads, and so are you. You have twenty-four hours to produce the disk. If you don't, you're as good as dead."

Julie stared at the phone as if she'd never seen one before. Twenty-four hours. For all the hope she had of meeting the demand, it might as well be twenty-four seconds. . . .

ABOUT THE AUTHOR

Deborah Joyce is the pseudonym of a unique mother-daughter writing team. Although they have written many romances, this is their first Intrigue. Deborah and Joyce confess that they love a good mystery, and have always hoped to write one. This proved a little difficult, because Deborah has just moved to Virginia and Joyce to Texas. But writing a book together, across the miles, has been just as intriguing as the story they've created.

Books by Deborah Joyce

HARLEQUIN SUPERROMANCE

A MATTER OF TIME
DEBORAH JOYCE

Harlequin Books

TORONTO • NEW YORK • LONDON
AMSTERDAM • PARIS • SYDNEY • HAMBURG
STOCKHOLM • ATHENS • TOKYO • MILAN

Harlequin Intrigue edition published March 1986
Second printing August 1986

ISBN 0-373-22037-5

Prologue

He was following the woman in the beige raincoat. Not that he could see much of her. The raincoat was belted tightly around her slim waist and the paisley silk scarf tied firmly under her chin effectively hid her hair. Dark glasses obscured her face, screening her eyes and blurring the shape of her cheekbones.

She had been his quarry for hours now, and he was beginning to suspect she knew he was behind her, though he had taken every precaution to conceal his presence. Despite Tokyo's rush hour traffic, she was making good time on her merry chase across the city, seemingly oblivious to the steady beeping of dissonant horns and the screeching and squealing of protesting brakes. He struggled to keep her in sight amid the Friday crowds.

It seemed he had seen all of Tokyo that day and yet he remembered nothing except that damn beige raincoat. Since late morning he had been on her trail. Yet she had kept him moving so fast, he'd not had a chance to appreciate the sights of this vast city. Tokyo was merely a jumble of quick impressions in his mind: teeming crowds of scurrying pedestrians, a concrete jungle of futuristic buildings and hundreds of beige raincoats. If it hadn't been for the paisley scarf, he would have lost her a hundred times.

He knew her name. A quiet conversation with the desk clerk at the Masuda Inn, where he had picked up her trail this morning, had provided him with that information. He had also learned that she had spent the night with a man. The man had already disappeared when he arrived at the hotel. Luckily, this woman was a late sleeper and he had managed to follow her. Perhaps soon she would lead him to his real target: the man.

They were now at Shinjuku station in western central Tokyo, a major transport stop overflowing with weary office workers and exhausted shoppers. Elderly women in traditional kimonos mingled with ultramodern business women wearing the latest fashion in a steady stream of humanity that had a pulsing, vibrant life of its own. Nearby, two tiny, doll-like toddlers grinned at him endearingly before hiding their faces behind their mother's skirt. What a marvelous place for people watching, he thought, and then realized most of the people were watching him. His height and his Western features made him distinctive, even in this teeming throng. Despite his expertise at surveillance, it would be easy for his quarry to notice him under these circumstances.

Even she, the woman in the raincoat, had been slowed down by the crowds. But eventually, she managed to push her way through to one of the ticket machines, emerging from the throng clutching the slip of paper as if it was a prize.

Sighing heavily, he noted the direction she was headed—toward the green train, the Yamanote line that looped Tokyo in both directions. For a moment, despair threatened to overwhelm him. He was going to lose her now; he knew it. In these crowds, with his own need to purchase a ticket slowing him down, he would lose her and all that she represented.

A sudden spurt of determination caused him to shoulder his way through the crush around the machines. Luck was with him. Within moments he was standing at the front of the line, grasping a thousand-yen note and hoping against hope this machine had change for larger bills.

Again, fate was on his side. He bought a basic-fare ticket, impatiently waiting for his change. Too bad he didn't know where she was going. He'd lose more time when they exited the train, paying the difference between basic fare and what he owed.

As he turned, he felt a thump against his leg and heard a shrill cry. Looking down he saw one of the toddlers sobbing quietly, and as he bent over to help, he was treated to a long, accusing stare from the weary mother. "I'm so sorry," he murmured, but she merely glared at him, uncomprehending, and he gave up. An uncomfortable silence surrounded his departure from the ticket line, and he suspected most of the people were probably dismissing him as simply another ugly American, rude and impatient.

He felt he had a personal score to settle with the woman in the raincoat now. But first he had to find her again. Soon lost in the endless surge of people, he was carried along by the momentum of the crowd. There was no chance he would find her in this crush. He could only hope to locate her once he was at the gate.

The Yamanote line was serviced by an electric train, one of several in Tokyo. It was a main thoroughfare for many of Tokyo's commuters, a fact that was working against him today. But as he reached the fringe of the crowd, he spotted her. It was the scarf. Thank God she was wearing that scarf.

He maneuvered to stand close to her once they were on the train. Despite the pushing and shoving of the wearily impatient passengers, he didn't manage too badly. She appeared to be unaware of him, but it was difficult to be sure. Behind those glasses she could be noticing everything or nothing.

An old woman clad in a sky-blue silk kimono pressed close beside him, dropping a heavy shopping bag on his foot. *Sumimasen,* she murmured and then, seeing his Western face, added in halting English, "Excuse me."

Cursing inwardly, he managed a polite smile before carefully pushing the bag off his foot. Fortunately, the woman seemed satisfied he was unharmed and turned away. He didn't need any unwanted attention that might alert his quarry to his presence.

After a seemingly interminable ride and several stops, the train pulled into Shimbashi station. The woman in the beige raincoat moved abruptly and he was instantly alert. Sure enough, she was getting off. Scrambling madly, he managed to exit the train before it pulled out again in a burst of energy. Now where, he wondered, as she paused to decide which direction to take. While he waited for her to move again, he edged out of sight, and fished in his jacket pocket for a cigarette. Pulling out a heavy silver lighter, he prepared to light up, but paused as a passing official of some kind eyed him sharply and pointed at a nearby no-smoking sign.

So he was to be denied even the smallest of human comforts, he thought, feeling disgruntled and vaguely angry. He glanced idly at the lighter and then tensed, remembering the woman who had given it to him. Although it was too ornate for his tastes with its heavily embellished initials and scrollwork, he kept it as a reminder. A reminder of a time when his instincts had been wrong.

Shoving the lighter back in his pocket, he noticed the woman was moving again. As he expected, he wasted moments he could ill-afford to lose paying his fare difference. Without waiting for his change, he caught up with her as she left the eastern exit, passing the steam locomotive displayed outside with only a quick glance. There wasn't time for sightseeing today. This woman knew Tokyo well; of that he was sure. He had a grim premonition that if he followed her for much longer, he was going to become familiar with it himself.

The area outside the station was hectic and wet. Rain was falling softly as dusk neared, making the streets gleam darkly and obscuring the store windows they passed. Surely she would remove those sunglasses now. Oblivious to the rain, she continued on her way, and he restrained an urge to remove the glasses himself.

Still he followed her, his stomach knotting with hunger as the pleasantly unfamiliar odors of the Japanese dinner hour assailed his nostrils. They were moving north now, into the department-store area. He realized they must be in the famous Ginza district.

A canopy of umbrellas had sprouted under the gentle rain. Noisy traffic tore up and down the streets while the sidewalks swarmed with foodstalls and shoppers. As he passed a street vendor, rice straw crackled wildly, sending a burst of fragrant steam into the air around him. Even as he watched the woman ahead, he perceived the dramatic contrasts between Tokyo's feverish, Western-style prosperity and Japan's timeless traditions.

If it was possible, the streets grew even more crowded as night fell. In the rainy haze the brilliant neon lights seemed to swirl crazily, a kaleidoscope of endless dimensions. He wished he could stop to explore, yet he knew his pursuit must remain relentless. He couldn't lose her now. Too much was at stake.

At last she slowed and he realized she planned to cross the street. Glancing in that direction, he glimpsed the solid bulk of the Imperial Hotel. This was a landmark he could recognize, Tokyo's most distinctive older hotel.

She darted across the street and he followed at a safe distance, more mindful than she had been of the remorseless traffic. Heading for the entrance of the hotel, she quickened her pace and he felt a surge of relief. Perhaps at long last she would make contact with her partner.

He paused by a newsstand and allowed a few moments to pass before he followed her inside, in case she had become suspicious.

Once in the building, he groaned audibly. There were at least a dozen raincoats in the lobby and from the pile of expensive luggage near the doorway and the familiar American accents, he surmised a tour group must have arrived only minutes earlier.

What was it about women that they so loved beige raincoats? Was it some fad this year he didn't know about? Until today he hadn't realized they manufactured the garment in such a plethora of sizes and shapes. He glanced around the room, his gaze sharp and quick, but was unable to pick up the trail of his quarry.

Then he remembered. The silk scarf, of course. Now that was more easily located. Three complete circuits of the room finally convinced him there was no paisley scarf; at least none of the women in this room was wearing one. Damn, where was she? She had to be here.

Ten precious minutes passed while he searched for her, minutes in which she might have slipped out a back exit or taken an elevator to an upper floor or ducked into one of the myriad shops in the Imperial's shopping arcade. Suddenly he had an idea. It was an old trick but it just might work.

Looking around, he located an information desk. The clerk, a young woman with gorgeous, heavily made-up eyes, smiled at him when he approached. "Yes?" she inquired.

"I seem to have lost my girlfriend," he explained with just the right touch of humble apology. "Would you mind paging her?"

"Certainly, sir. Her name?" She was already reaching for the phone, dialing the number that would connect her with the lobby intercom.

"Julie Smith," he said, adding hurriedly, "When she comes over, tell her I'm waiting in the coffee shop with mother." A quick invention, a neat lie, but it might locate her. Too bad it might also confirm to her that she was being followed.

"Of course," the clerk replied smoothly, and as he moved quickly out of sight, he heard her announcement. "Julie Smith. Please. We are paging Julie Smith. Please come to the information desk as soon as possible."

His heart raced uncomfortably as he waited. If this didn't work, he would have a lot of explaining to do. Eventually, a woman approached the desk, and he moved farther into the shadows behind a conveniently large palm.

A frown creased his brow. Was this her? If so, she had managed to get rid of the beige raincoat. As the woman approached, he memorized her features.

She was younger than he had expected and very attractive. Soft blond hair fell in a smooth bell to her shoulders, swinging with a healthy bounce as she walked. Honey gold and faintly streaked with sun, it appeared even lighter against her golden tan. A relaxed smile curved her mobile, expressive mouth, and as his gaze narrowed on her lips, he felt a sudden primitive throb of desire pulse through him.

For a moment he forgot his purpose and was simply a man reacting to a beautiful woman. Her walk was smooth and sexy, her hips moving in a discreet yet unmistakably feminine glide. Her expression was open, honest and deceptively innocent.

Nothing about her was as he had expected it to be. And nothing had prepared him for the uniform she was wearing. An airline stewardess, he realized. Of course. What could be more convenient?

The desk clerk glanced up. "Yes?"

The woman's voice was inaudible to him, but he saw her lips move and read her response. "I'm Julie Smith," she explained with a smile that would have melted a harder heart than his own.

He watched her only long enough to see the confusion that crossed her face as she listened to the clerk's message before heading in the direction of the coffee shop. Then he looked for a phone.

Now was the time to get that backup man on her trail, he decided. He felt a renewed sense of energy, a surge of power and confidence. He had found his quarry. He had seen her face. From now on it was simply a matter of time....

Chapter One

For as long as she could remember, Julie Smith had known there were two kinds of people in the world: the organized and the disorganized. Organized people had a routine, lived on a schedule and kept track of keys, tickets and their checkbook balances. Disorganized people were always just a step ahead of disaster. She was one of the disorganized ones.

No matter how hard she tried she was invariably a few minutes late, a little less than put together and a tiny bit frazzled. For a long time she had tried to change herself, embarking on massive self-improvement campaigns, suffering through two time-management courses and making hundreds of New Year's resolutions, all to no avail. At some point in the last year she had decided to accept herself exactly as she was, and that is why she found herself tearing through the Tokyo airport this Saturday morning toward a plane poised on the brink of takeoff.

She had started the day with the best of intentions, leaving the Imperial Hotel promptly at seven with the rest of the flight crew. Two taxis had delivered them to the entrance of Narita Airport's main terminal building in good time. But there the trouble had started.

Passing down the long corridors that led to the departure gates, Julie had spotted a display of gorgeous silk scarves nestled in the window of a duty-free shop. Ignoring the admonitions of her roommate and fellow flight attendant, Tricia Hyde, Julie had stopped to shop.

Now she was late, and the four scarves spilling from a bag shoved hastily into the pocket of her flight tote were mute testimony to her folly. With her bag bumping along on a wheeled cart behind her and her beige uniform raincoat and purse slung over her arm, her progress was slow. Only as she neared her destination did she feel able to relax somewhat. Slow down, calm down, she reminded herself mentally. Fixing a cool, poised smile on her generous mouth, she slackened her pace and nodded a greeting to the check-in crew.

"You're late," a woman behind the airline counter stated bluntly. "The rest are on board and looking for you."

Julie quelled the nervous flutter of her stomach and paused to straighten the slim skirt of her khaki-colored World Airlines uniform. Brushing an imaginary piece of lint off her sleeve, she smoothed the jacket over her hips and checked the bow on her silky multihued blouse.

"You look great," a male voice murmured reassuringly, and Julie turned to face the pilot, Bob Reed. There was indulgent admiration in his eyes as he surveyed Julie's fresh glowing skin, sunny smile and free-swinging shoulder-length blond hair. "Enjoy your last-minute shopping?" he asked, and she relaxed under his tolerant smile. Bob was an older pilot, one of the airline's best, and since joining the company she had grown close to him and to his wife, Carol.

"I always do." In her relief at having escaped a reprimand from him, Julie let her enthusiasm show. "Somehow I never decide what I want to buy until it's time to leave."

"Just make sure you keep your receipts for customs," warned the woman who had spoken earlier.

"Thanks for reminding me," Julie replied, smiling. Noticing that Bob was eyeing his watch anxiously, she headed for the plane.

Tricia was waiting inside the door. As usual, Tricia's sleek brown hair was smoothed back in a flawless chignon, her delicate face carefully made up and her uniform spotless and unwrinkled. Tricia was one of the organized people of the world. But although Julie had shared a condominium in Honolulu with her for the past two years, none of Tricia's good habits had yet rubbed off. "Where have you been?" Tricia said in a loud whisper. "I've been covering for you, but you scared me to death."

"Look." Julie reached into her flight tote. "These scarves are fantastic. I got one for you."

Tricia spared the scarves the briefest of glances. "Never mind that now. But thanks."

Soon Julie was caught up in preflight procedures. Tricia and she made a good team. The other woman's tall, serene presence seemed to reassure the passengers, instilling them with confidence, while Julie's high-spirited, extroverted style drew out even the most reserved and shy ones.

Today the plane was more crowded than usual, though there were a few empty seats in the first-class section where Julie and Tricia were stationed. The passengers were restless, shedding raincoats and umbrellas and searching for space for their carry-on baggage. June was the height of Tokyo's rainy season, and the cabin was filled with the faintly musty odor of damp clothing.

Julie liked to spend the few moments before takeoff getting to know her passengers. They seemed to appreciate her friendliness, especially those who were nervous about flying. Moving slowly along the aisle with an open smile, she answered questions and poured glasses of complimentary champagne. Today's flight held the usual mix of business travelers and tourists. She could usually guess which were which, not only by their style of dress but also from the questions they asked.

Turning to the second row, she saw a familiar face. A young woman in the aisle seat was reading a magazine, her fingers gripping the pages so tightly that her knuckles were turning white. She was dressed in a crinkled cotton jumpsuit, and a mink jacket was slung casually over her shoulders. "Hello there," Julie greeted her softly.

The other woman looked up abruptly. For a moment her anxious blue eyes registered what seemed to be shock. Then her expression went blank.

Julie wasn't daunted. "You were on my flight over, remember?"

"I...I didn't notice," the woman replied finally, her long lashes veiling her eyes.

She certainly put me in my place, Julie thought. She forced herself to smile and offered the woman some champagne.

"No, thanks. Not now." The woman's voice cracked, and she turned a page, clearly hoping Julie would regard this as dismissal.

"Nervous about flying?" Julie persisted. "The forecast promises excellent flying conditions today, so you can relax and enjoy yourself."

"Yes, of course." The woman's voice was toneless. Julie studied her pale face, noting that dark shadows under her eyes seemed to indicate at least one sleepless night. As she sat, twisting nervously at the magazine now rolled in her hands, obviously impatient for Julie to move on, the woman's breathing quickened. That was not at all how she had acted on the flight over, Julie reflected. Then the woman had seemed excited, as if enjoying every moment of the flight.

On impulse, Julie returned to the galley. Tricia was checking the breakfast supplies. "Did you notice the woman in row two, aisle seat left?" Julie asked.

"What?" Tricia replied absently before looking up and adding, "You mean Miss Clark?"

"Is that her name?"

"Brenda Clark. I checked her off on the manifest. She was on our flight coming over. I remembered her as soon as I saw her. You can't forget a mink like that."

"She seems a bit jumpy today. Perhaps she's nervous about flying. Do you think I should mention her to Bob and have him speak with her?"

"Nervous?" Tricia echoed. "Oh, I don't think so. Not Miss Clark. She told me she's made this trip several times. We talked a lot on the flight over on Thursday. I told her we were staying at the Imperial, and we compared notes on restaurants in that area."

Rummaging through the supply cabinet, Tricia frowned. "Something's not right," she mumbled, and Julie hurried away before she could continue. Tricia was always this way before a flight, meticulously checking and rechecking everything a dozen times. Julie often

wished her friend was more relaxed but she knew that
thanks to Tricia's compulsion about being organized the
two of them had a flawless record.

Miss Clark was still assiduously reading her now-
wrinkled magazine, and Julie didn't attempt a conversation. The woman puzzled her, though. She was agitated about something, and Julie made a mental note to
keep an eye on her.

The moments before takeoff ticked away quickly as
Julie acquainted herself with the other passengers. Most
of them were friendly, eager to talk about Tokyo or
discuss what they planned to do in Honolulu. Julie dispensed information as freely as champagne, happy to
share her enthusiasm about Honolulu, her adopted city.

She was approaching the fifth row when she saw him.
Actually she felt his presence before she saw him, as a
slow heated warmth that curled through her body and
darkened the blue of her eyes to cobalt. A strange excitement gripped her, an odd sensation of premonition
that caused her to turn deliberately, knowing even before her gaze settled on him exactly which passenger was
eliciting this response.

The man's presence was absolutely mesmerizing. She
stood still, rooted to the spot, only her hands moving as
they automatically released the champagne bottle back
onto her tray and made unnecessary adjustments to
napkins and glasses. He was seated in row five, next to
the window, the aisle seat beside him unoccupied. His
face was turned toward her. His expression held a curious blend of strength and vulnerability, and his compelling but enigmatic gaze caught and held her for what
seemed an eternity before she managed to slowly release the breath she had been holding.

Sunlight filtered through the window, throwing his face into shadow and spraying copper glints through thick, dark hair that tapered to graze his shirt collar. Even seated he had the presence and dignity of a tall man, his dark business suit and crisp salmon shirt emphasizing a smooth expanse of broad, well-muscled shoulders.

Something was different about this man; she knew that at once. Not that she could pinpoint exactly what that difference might be. No, she simply felt a change in the atmosphere, a subtle heightening of awareness that put her instantly on guard. Instinctively she felt a flash of resentment against him, without knowing exactly why. She had seen many dynamic and virile men during her two years as a flight attendant on the Tokyo-Honolulu run, but none of them had quite this aura of power and assurance.

His expression suggested that he was intimately acquainted with everything about her—and didn't quite like what he knew. Trapped by the penetrating depths of his gaze, Julie found it impossible to look away. His eyes were a deep gray, an unusual color that seemed now to be cold and off-putting despite his superficially friendly demeanor. Yes, there was something about his eyes, she realized, something that didn't match the rest of him, something watchful and wary.

As she managed to break the eye contact at last, she realized Tricia was observing her crossly from the galley. Marshaling a reasonably calm smile, Julie said quietly to the man, "Good morning." She followed the greeting with a cool but she hoped professionally friendly nod of her head.

"Hello, Julie," he added, glancing at her name tag and then treating her to a slow, warm smile that didn't quite reach his eyes. It was a remarkably sexy smile, melting her resistance like a spring sun after a long winter of snow. Her unwilling surge of response irritated her and froze the answering smile that normally would have formed on her own lips.

An alarm went off in her head and she trembled slightly. With one of her flashes of insight, she had a sense of impending doom. Suddenly the day didn't seem quite so bright, or the future so rosy. It was as if on some primitive level they were communicating, and he was warning her to watch out, be careful, stay alert.

As suddenly as the feeling had come it was gone, and he was simply a passenger again. Assessing him deliberately, she pegged him, perhaps unfairly, as a man on the prowl. Practiced flirts bored her. She met them in droves in her job: married men, single men, unhappy men, men who felt they had something to prove by making a conquest of every attractive woman they met.

An instant prickling resistance to this particular passenger formed in her mind. His expression was too smooth, too friendly, too self-assured. She felt an urge to ruffle that confidence, to prove to him that his charming manner failed to impress her.

Probably married, she thought critically. He'll soon be telling me some story about how no one at home understands him. Sneaking a surreptitious glance at his hands, she noted the absence of a wedding band. Strong, well-shaped and tanned, his hands were bare of rings of any sort. But that meant nothing these days. He must be in his mid-thirties, and he was far too attractive to spend much time alone.

"Champagne?" she asked coolly. "With orange juice, if you prefer." Reaching for a glass she prepared to pour.

His voice arrested her hand in motion, as it surely must stop any woman whose attention he was seeking. "Nothing, thanks. I can't look at anything except coffee this early."

Although it was inconvenient, she could have prepared him a cup of coffee before takeoff. Instead, something churlish and antagonistic inside her decided to make him wait. "We'll be serving breakfast once we're airborne," she replied briskly. "You can have coffee then." Before he could trap her into further conversation she moved to the next row of seats.

Aware of his presence even after she was past his seat, she made a quick decision to avoid him until the flight took off. She gave her full attention to a fractious elderly man who insisted on changing seats three times before he was satisfied. Things began to go downhill after that. Tricia flew into a minor panic when she discovered no diet sodas had been stocked in the first-class galley and, to stay out of her way, Julie scurried to the rear to locate a bottle of gardenia scent for the warm, wet towels they always dispensed.

"Your turn to demonstrate the emergency routine," Tricia whispered in her ear as they passed each other.

Julie made a face at her. Ordinarily she didn't give it a thought, but today she had no desire to display herself before at least one of the passengers. Slipping to the front of the cabin, she began gesturing in sync with the taped announcement concerning safety procedures.

That dark gaze never left her. Now his eyes were warmer, a lambent smoky gray, intent and hypnotic. She found his steady regard extremely disconcerting and fumbled when she reached for the oxygen mask, causing a sprinkling of laughter to ripple through the cabin. He didn't laugh.

Instead she caught a sympathetic softening of his gaze that irritated her more than if he'd made fun of her. Seldom could she remember being as put out with a passenger as she was with this one and never with a personable, attractive male who had done absolutely nothing objectionable that she could put her finger on. In the end she blamed her antipathy to him on the very fact that she did find him attractive and resented the fact that he seemed to know it and be enjoying it.

After takeoff, when the plane had leveled off out of the steepest part of its climb, the captain's voice drawled overhead, "Flight time to Hawaii will be approximately seven hours and ten minutes. The temperature in Honolulu right now is seventy-eight degrees, and for those of you who are dreaming of the beaches you'll be happy to know the skies are sunny and clear."

An appreciative murmur rose in the cabin, a contented sound that was music to Julie's ears as she hurried to the galley to prepare the breakfast buffet cart. Tricia was already there, opening cartons of fresh, presliced pineapple and mangoes. "Everyone settled?" she asked.

Julie reached for a crystal bowl. "At the moment." Striving to appear casual she asked, "Do you still have the passenger list handy?"

Tricia smiled knowingly. "His name is G. D. Stafford."

"Whose name?"

"As if you didn't know," Tricia admonished. "He hasn't been able to keep his eyes off you since he boarded. Now *he's* what I call attractive."

Julie shrugged her shoulders slightly, arranging sprigs of fresh mint around the fruit bowl. "Yes, I've seen him. Honestly, Tricia, how do you manage to remember everyone's name?''

Tricia refused to be diverted by Julie's flattery. ''He's not bad, right?''

''Okay, but not really my type.''

''Has he already moved in on you?''

Julie shook her head slightly. ''No, just friendly. Are the croissants warmed?''

Tricia took the hint and dropped the subject. The two women worked well together in the confined space, piling the cart with fluffy omelets, breakfast meats and rolls and an assortment of jams, jellies and cheeses. No plastic trays or food that tasted like dried leather for those World Airlines passengers who could afford first-class tickets.

''Will Tony be waiting for you at the airport?'' Julie asked.

''Yes. At least I hope he'll be able to make it.'' Tricia's eyes softened dreamily.

Julie turned from the coffeemaker. ''Something tells me I'm going to need a new roommate soon.''

''Maybe. Perhaps you should consider a male roommate this time. I hear it's much cozier.''

''Did you have a candidate in mind for me?'' Julie asked dryly. Since Tricia had started dating Tony, a medical resident at a Honolulu hospital, she had developed the maddening habit of seeing the whole world in terms of couples.

''Not Dan or whatever his name was you dated last week.''

Julie groaned. ''I told you I only agreed to go out with him as a favor to a friend. Actually, he wasn't so bad if you shared his passion for the molecular structure of cells." She checked to see if the tea bags were on the second shelf of the cart. "Ready to roll?"

Tricia hesitated, taking time to straighten the cups so all the handles were lined up neatly. Fascinated, Julie watched. "You amaze me, Tricia. People like you keep the whole world organized. But would anyone have really noticed that the cup handles weren't perfectly aligned?"

"I would notice," Tricia replied evenly. "Shall I serve the beverages? You handle the food this morning, and we'll reverse for dinner."

Julie assiduously kept her eyes away from the fifth row as she dispensed generous portions on the china plates that were a feature of her airline's first-class service. "Yes, the omelets are made with fresh eggs," she assured the woman in seat 1A. "Our sauces are also made only with natural ingredients."

Tricia grinned at her quickly as they pulled up in front of the row where G.D. Stafford sat. "Can you handle this by yourself a moment, Julie?" she asked. "I just remembered something."

Julie bit back a sharp retort as Tricia departed; she was acutely conscious of the watchful gray gaze on her back. Reluctantly she turned and, with her professional smile firmly in place, said, "I didn't forget your coffee, sir."

He was smiling, a half smile that she found oddly likable. "Smells wonderful," he said, his manner faultlessly correct. "I'll take a little of everything on my plate. I'm starving."

Julie's hands trembled slightly as she scooped fresh fruit and slipped it into a bowl. Aware of his intent regard, she found it increasingly difficult to resist looking at him. Incensed with herself for not retaining her usual poise, she piled his plate high and set it squarely down on the tray in front of him.

"You know, I think I've seen you before."

Julie smiled grimly, knowing exactly what was coming. She had heard it so many times before. Still, it was disappointing he hadn't thought of a more original way to show interest. He had seemed like a man with imagination. "Really?" she said dismissively, starting to push the cart away.

"No, wait a moment," he urged, detaining her with a light pressure on her arm. His fingers burned against her skin. Inwardly cursing her betrayingly fair complexion, she felt a blush mount in her cheeks. "I'm sure I saw you in Tokyo yesterday." His expression was serious.

"Small world, isn't it?" she said flippantly. Jerking her arm away she moved to the next passenger. "And what would you like this morning?"

When Tricia returned a short time later, Julie muttered under her breath, "Thanks a lot."

"What did he say?"

"The usual. Men continually amaze me with their predictability. You think they'd come up with a new way of introducing themselves."

After breakfast was over and the trays had been removed, Julie started down the aisle with earphones. G.D. Stafford's eyes were closed. It was tempting to linger a moment and admire the hard lines of his face; there was a controlled strength there that didn't vanish even in his restful state. He was the sort of man she'd want on her side in a fight, she found herself thinking, though she had no idea why such a thought should pop into her head.

Carefully she leaned over to place the complimentary earphones in the pocket of the seat fronting his. "Mmm, I like that perfume," his deep voice murmured.

The sweep of Julie's sleek, bluntly cut hair swung forward to shield her expression as she straightened. "The movie this morning is an adventure film, starring Clint Eastwood. There's a rundown on it in the flight magazine in front of you. It starts in fifteen minutes."

The corners of his mouth quirked. "Do you recommend it?"

"It depends on your tastes."

"Not too enthusiastic about it, are you?"

"It's difficult to remain enthusiastic when you've seen a movie at least a dozen times," Julie replied crisply. This man was managing to make her appear rude without half trying. "I'm sure you'll enjoy it," she added with as much friendliness as she could muster.

When she had completed her rounds and started toward the front of the cabin, she glanced over one shoulder and saw that he had resumed his scrutiny of her. His attentiveness was flattering, she was forced to admit. Making no effort to conceal his interest, he let open admiration show in his eyes. Perhaps she really had reminded him of someone he'd seen in Tokyo. But that shouldn't be so intriguing. She was an ordinary enough person, so there were plenty of women who might resemble her on casual observation.

She knew she was attractive, but there was no reason she could see for Mr. Stafford's unwavering absorption in her every movement. Again she fought down a surge of foreboding. Good heavens, was she becoming fanciful? Since that strange incident at the hotel last evening she had felt vaguely uneasy. Suddenly eager to talk to Tricia, she turned back to the cabin and hurried to complete the premovie routine.

With the passengers settled and the shades drawn so that the movie could be viewed, Julie sank down into a seat beside Tricia. "I shouldn't have stayed up so late last night. I'm exhausted."

Tricia looked her over critically. "You do look terrible, Julie. The circles under your eyes are enormous. I bet you're going to collapse into bed the minute you get home."

So much for the possibility that she was looking exceptionally attractive today. Tricia had a knack for deflating one's ego, albeit in a very kind manner. It was just that she was so precise. No, Julie decided, she was glad she had settled for being slightly disorganized and off balance. But Tricia did make a great roommate. You could always count on her. "Don't let me forget to set the alarm so I can call my mother later. The doctor is supposed to tell her today if she's going to need more surgery."

Tricia was instantly concerned. "It's difficult having your mother so far away. Why don't you get her to move to Hawaii? She'd love it, I'm sure. There are lots of retirement villages there."

"She loves Los Angeles. Anyway, Aunt Rose would never leave, and you know how devoted those two are to each other, especially now that they're both widows. If Mother needs surgery, I'll take leave so I can be with her."

Julie leaned back against the seat and closed her eyes. If there was one area she could always count on gaining Tricia's sympathy, it was where her mother was concerned. Tricia's mother was a demanding woman who expected Tricia to dance attendance on her, while Julie's mother was as easygoing as Julie herself.

Julie had been an unexpected dividend for her parents. Both had been in their early forties and, after twenty years of a childless marriage, they could hardly believe the news that Mrs. Smith was pregnant. When Julie was three her father had died and, although she and her mother were far from well off, they'd spent some good times together. It bothered her now that she was so far away as her mother grew older, but the other woman insisted she was content with the arrangement.

"How was your dinner last night?" Tricia interrupted her thoughts.

"Delicious." Julie sat forward. "Afterward, Marge came to my room and we talked for hours. This was the first time I've seen her since we were in school together, so we had a lot of catching up to do. Her husband's engineering firm just transferred them to Tokyo, and she's finding it difficult to adjust."

"No wonder you look so tired, Julie," Tricia reproved.

"Actually," Julie said slowly, "there was another reason I didn't get much sleep last night. Something odd happened." She paused, not knowing why she felt she had to tell Tricia. Perhaps mentioning it to someone else would help put the incident into perspective.

"Well, what happened?"

"I was in the lobby of the hotel last night waiting for Marge. The desk clerk paged me, and when I went to the information desk, she told me some man was waiting for me in the coffee shop with my mother."

"You're kidding."

"No, honest. It was the strangest thing. I even went to the coffee shop and peeked inside, but of course she wasn't there."

"They must have mistaken you for someone else," Tricia soothed, always practical. "I wouldn't worry about it. After all, Smith is an ordinary enough name."

"I know," Julie acknowledged, but the sense of unease she had felt since last night refused to dissolve completely. Her disquiet increased when she became aware that someone was standing in the aisle beside her. "Yes, may I help you?" she whispered when she realized it was Mr. Stafford. Her long lashes swept down to hide the annoyed reaction that surely would be reflected in her eyes.

He pushed aside a magazine that cluttered the seat facing them. "The movie isn't my type. May I join you for a minute?"

"Please do," Tricia said brightly with a sidelong glance at Julie. "I was just leaving to make a fresh pot of coffee for the crew. I'll bring us some when I'm finished." She moved past him without acknowledging Julie's pleading gaze.

"Sounds great," he replied, his gaze on Julie as he sat down across from her. He gave her a quick, unreadable smile. "How about you, Julie? Do you like coffee?"

She slid her knees to one side so they wouldn't touch his. "I prefer tea."

His glance followed Tricia as she moved down the aisle. "Your friend intimidates me," he said abruptly.

Julie couldn't restrain a smile. While she dearly loved her roommate she did find her efficient manner unsettling at times. "In what way?"

"She reminds me of a friend of mine who lives by a rigid schedule. Great woman. Everyone relies on her to keep them in line, but I always feel a little inept around that type."

"Me, too. Tricia's my roommate and you've described her perfectly." Julie thawed slightly. "You're quite perceptive, Mr. Stafford."

His eyebrows lifted at her use of his name. "Greg," he said, removing a business card from his pocket. "I'm an attorney. From Los Angeles."

Julie glanced at him cynically. Now came the old routine. Men flirting with flight attendants frequently tried to impress them with their success stories. Attorneys usually had a line about being involved in a spectacular court case.

"Where are you from?" he was asking.

She fingered the card, wondering whether to return it or slip it in her pocket. "Same as you. Los Angeles." Deciding against keeping it, she held it out.

"Keep it," he urged, lounging back against his seat. As she hesitated, he added, "You might need a lawyer some time."

"I doubt it. I'm a very law-abiding person." Julie forced him to take the card back.

He pocketed it, and silence stretched between them for a long moment. Julie was embarrassed, angry at herself for making such a big deal out of a simple business card. It was just that he was disappointing her. Somehow she had wanted him to be different, to be above the worn-out ploys of the lonely male business traveler. "Why did you travel to Japan?" she asked at length.

"Business for a client."

"So you'll be catching a connecting flight to the mainland?"

"Not for a week or two. I couldn't pass up the chance of a vacation in the islands."

Once again she tensed, waiting for the seemingly inevitable suggestion that was bound to come. Dinner, dancing, sightseeing or some similar activity that was meant to end in only one place. Instead he surprised her. "What did you do with your free time in Japan, Julie?"

"Oh, just the usual," she replied. "This time I stayed up too late visiting with an old friend."

For a moment his eyes narrowed, but his voice was calm and relaxed when he spoke. "You don't look tired. You act as if you love your job."

"I do. I didn't get to travel much as a child, and I always dreamed of it. Someday I'd like to open my own travel agency. This job is a perfect education for that, and I enjoy most aspects of it." She wasn't quite sure why she was telling him all this. Perhaps because it was a subject dear to her heart. Owning her own agency was more than a dream. It was a goal she was working hard to achieve by taking evening business classes during the winter months and honing her language skills.

"But not being pursued by men?" he commented, and she stared at him for a moment until she realized what he was asking.

"No, I hate that part of my job," she admitted. "Most of our passengers are married men looking for a little excitement. I don't see myself providing that."

The silence between them grew tense, and she looked back at him, surprising a spark of some curious emotion in his smoky eyes. His features had hardened and his mouth was firm, devoid of laughter. "I'm not married,'' he said curtly before standing up and walking away.

THE REST OF THE FLIGHT went smoothly. Greg was back in his seat when Julie answered the summons of another passenger. Although she was friendlier with him, he made no attempt to ask if he could see her again. She was slightly disappointed, but relieved at the same time, for she didn't know how she would have answered. With little difficulty, she parried Tricia's questions about him as they prepared lunch.

Tricia grimaced expressively at Julie as they passed the row where Brenda Clark was seated. The woman appeared to have recovered her poise. She had maintained a cool and haughty manner throughout the flight, becoming increasingly difficult and demanding as they neared Honolulu. Julie noted, however, that Ms Clark's ringless hands were still twisted tightly in her lap and her eyes were shadowed with anxiety. Something was seriously worrying the poor woman, and despite her irritation at having to answer her numerous summonses, Julie couldn't help feeling a twinge of sympathy.

''Sorry I snapped at you about being late,'' Tricia apologized as they wheeled the dessert cart down the aisle at the end of the meal.

''Forget it.'' Julie was surprised that Tricia was still worried about something so trivial.

''What about those scarves you mentioned?''

Julie's blue eyes twinkled. Scarves were a passion with Tricia. ''I thought you'd get around to that eventually. They were a fantastic bargain. I got four, one each for you, Mother, Aunt Rose and myself. You get first pick, since I may have duplicated ones you already have.''

"You're making me feel like a beast now," Tricia said. Turning once again to Brenda Clark, she offered more coffee before saying to Julie, "Did I see a paisley one peeking out of the bag? It looked fabulous."

As Julie smiled her agreement, she glanced at Brenda Clark. Brenda's eyes were open wide, the earlier anxiety replaced with an emotion Julie couldn't quite define. Disbelief? Amazement? No, shock was a better word. She felt compelled to say something, anything, to snap the passenger out of her trance. "How about you, Ms. Clark? Do you like paisley? I understand it's going to be extremely popular this year."

Brenda Clark seemed to be fighting to draw a deep breath. When she spoke at last, her voice came out husky and thin. "No," she said quickly, emphatically. "I've always abhorred paisley."

Chapter Two

The passengers seemed exceptionally slow deplaning. One woman insisted the beige raincoat Julie handed her was not the one that belonged to her. It wasn't until Julie pulled out a package of gum from the pocket that the woman admitted she was mistaken. Finally, only the beige uniform raincoats belonging to her and Tricia remained in the small coat closet. Tricia was having similar difficulty helping a young mother locate her infant's favorite teething ring, and the two of them exchanged weary glances several times.

Julie watched from the corner of her eye as Greg Stafford leisurely allowed the other passengers to precede him down the aisle, and she was positioned at the door by the time he walked past. "I hope you had a pleasant flight and will fly with us again, Mr. Stafford," she said in a voice she hoped struck the right blend of friendliness and formality.

"I'll look forward to it," he answered, and the warmth underlying his words made it seem almost a promise rather than the polite banality she knew it must be.

As the last passenger made his way out of the plane, Julie began to gather up her things. Her flight tote wasn't in its usual storage spot, and she frowned, trying to think where she might have put it during the mad dash aboard in Tokyo. It was at times like this that she hated her lack of organization. She began to scan the area frantically, anxious to get off the plane and home to a long, restful nap.

"Ready?" Tricia asked, her raincoat and flight tote neatly aligned beside her.

Still puzzling over where she could have put her bag, Julie answered, "Not quite. I'll be along in a moment. You go ahead. Tony will be waiting."

Tricia nodded, her mind already shifting to thoughts of the man in her life. When she was gone, Julie hastily pulled open the cabinets where the employees stowed their luggage and then remembered she'd shoved the bag in a drawer, instead.

Triumphantly retrieving it, she slung it over her shoulder. She was the last to leave the plane, and the long carpeted corridor was deserted as she hurried toward the terminal building. Her mind switched to the evening ahead. A long nap was in order, and then perhaps dinner out with a friend.

She was naturally friendly and outgoing, and never needed to spend an evening alone unless she chose to. Although she wasn't involved with any particular man at the moment, she dated often and frequently did the inviting herself.

Pausing to rest a moment, she searched her handbag for a cigarette. She was an infrequent smoker but, although the airline generally frowned on employees smoking before they cleared customs, today she felt a need for something to steady her nerves. As usual her fingers encountered a tangled mass when she rummaged through the bag's contents. At length, she located a bent cigarette and placed it in her mouth before continuing the search for her always-elusive lighter.

"Here, let me help you," a deep masculine voice murmured.

Julie caught her breath and looked up, to find the warm fire of Greg Stafford's gaze pinning her down with the same intensity that had unnerved her earlier. He withdrew a heavy silver lighter from his pocket and it flared to life.

Moving closer, his long fingers cupped the flame as he offered it to her. A flare of heat curled deep within her as she drew in a long breath and tried to ignore his clean, powerfully evocative male scent. Her eyes were level with his crisp shirt collar and she focused on the smooth, hard column of his neck, watching in fascination as the pulse beating firmly in his throat quickened its pace. So he was affected by her presence, as well. The thought gave her such intense pleasure it shocked her.

Her cigarette momentarily forgotten, she glanced up into his eyes and then looked away. The lighter's flame was only half as bright as the flare in his eyes. The lighter was heavy and ornately carved with what seemed to be two initials entwined on the base. Funny. . . it was not at all the sort of lighter she would have chosen for him. She would have gone for something sleek and smooth and modern, with crisp, clean lines.

"I was beginning to think you'd vanished," he murmured, and his voice was husky.

His remark brought her back to an abrupt awareness of her surroundings. She drew a determined breath and moved back. "Did you forget something on the plane?"

He gave her a measuring glance and smiled his half-amused smile. "No, I wanted to ask your recommendations for a good place to dine this evening."

Julie knew she had been secretly wanting this to happen, yet she still sighed. Now that he was actually going to ask her out it was almost anticlimactic, and she had no idea what her answer was going to be.

Starting to walk along the corridor again, she took a quick puff on her cigarette before discarding it in a nearby ash can. Greg fell into stride beside her. "Any suggestions?"

"I'm sure the concierge at your hotel could make a better recommendation."

"You're right, of course," he conceded readily.

Too readily for someone who had been waiting at least ten minutes for her, Julie thought. She sighed uneasily. There was a hardness to Greg Stafford lying just beneath the veneer of friendliness. A man like this could hide many secrets, and she found herself wondering what he really wanted of her. She glanced edgily around the terminal building as they emerged in the waiting area, looking for a friendly face.

"It's been nice meeting you. Have a good vacation," Julie told Greg and moved quickly away from him. He raised a hand in casual farewell and headed for the immigration desks.

As Julie passed the sketchy passport inspection accorded to airline staff, she saw that the last passengers were clearing immigration and moving into the baggage area. They hovered around the moving conveyor, waiting to reclaim their luggage. A cluster of people waited outside the glass doors to greet the new arrivals, and her friends and fellow workers were pressing forward in the customs line.

Tricia was waiting for Julie. "What took you so long? You're not yourself today. Is everything okay?"

"I was looking for my tote," Julie admitted. "I was in such a rush to get to work when I boarded the plane I didn't remember where I'd put it." She reached into the bag and drew out the white plastic sack containing the scarves. "Don't let me forget to give you the paisley one."

Her attention diverted, Tricia fingered the scarf and then neatly tucked it back into the bag as she started through the channel reserved for flight personnel. It took only moments for her clearance, and she waved briskly at Julie before looking around for Tony.

"How are you, Charlie?" Julie greeted the man behind the desk with a friendly smile. After two years she was on first-name terms with all the officials who worked at this terminal. Charlie was one of the nicest. He never failed to tell her a good joke as he checked her bags. Expecting only her usual cursory inspection, she flipped her tote deftly onto the counter.

Charlie looked at her blankly, ignoring her cheerful overtures and gazing at a point slightly above her shoulder. "Open your bag, please," he directed somberly. Two men were standing behind him, men in dark suits. Both were in their thirties and wearing almost identical scowling expressions that made her think a giant cookie cutter labeled "Federal Customs Inspectors" had been used to stamp out these bureaucrats. Poor Charlie, he must be undergoing one of his annual evaluation sessions, she decided.

Quickly falling in line with his solemn expression, Julie efficiently opened her tote bag. "My only purchases were these scarves, four of them. My receipt..." Her voice trailed off as one of the men behind Charlie stepped forward. His fingers slid inside the plastic bag and pulled out the scarves. He held each up briefly, glancing across the room and letting all except the paisley one drop. Julie turned her head to see where the man had been looking but saw only Greg Stafford zipping his bag, his head down.

"The receipt's inside the bag," she said defensively. "I declared the amount I paid on my customs form. I'm certainly well under my allowance." Her eyes met the stony glance of one of the dark-suited men.

"Your passport," Charlie demanded, holding out his hand.

Julie refrained from reminding him that she had already passed immigration, and that he had known her for long enough to dispense with this formality. He flipped open her passport, studied her picture and lifted his heavily hooded eyes to give her an almost sympathetic glance.

"Julie Smith," he stated, his voice echoing loudly in the nearly deserted room.

"Is something wrong, Charlie?" Julie felt compelled to say something to get back on their usual, friendly footing. "It's me, Julie. Have I done anything to upset you?"

Before he could reply, the two men in the dark suits came from behind the counter and pinned her in, one on each side. Flashing an identification badge at her, the taller of the two said, "We're federal agents, Ms. Smith. We're placing you under arrest on suspicion of theft of government property."

EVENTS HAPPENED QUICKLY after that, confusing events, as the customs area suddenly filled with another planeload of tired passengers wielding heavy bags, attempting to pacify crying children, chattering in several foreign languages as they snaked into long lines.

Julie heard one of the men start speaking, but his voice seemed to come from a deep fog. She couldn't believe this was happening. It was all a big mistake.

"Read her her rights," the taller man ordered, and the other began speaking in a monotone that was curiously somber. "You have the right to remain silent..."

"This is ridiculous!" From somewhere she summoned the strength to voice the protest. The rest of the flight crew had cleared customs ahead of her, and she realized they were pausing at the exit, staring at what was taking place.

Bob Reed, the pilot, came toward her. "What's the problem?" he demanded. "This is one of our crew members. I can vouch for Miss Smith."

Several more men emerged from a corridor and blocked his path. "We're federal officers. We advise you not to interfere in this arrest." Bob argued fiercely for a moment, but they refused to budge.

Feeling surrounded by a sea of grim, unyielding faces, Julie demanded loudly. "What do you mean, theft of government property? I don't understand. And you can't arrest innocent people. This is a free country." Her earlier mood of shock and disbelief was turning into anger.

From across the room a tall figure strode into view. As one of the officers stepped forward to intercept him, Greg Stafford held out a card. "I'm an attorney. Miss Smith does have the right to some information about the charges against her."

Relief surged through Julie as she took in with a swift glance Greg Stafford's totally commanding presence. He confronted the two officers detaining her with a self-assurance she admired even through her fear.

One of the officers took his card and examined it carefully, his brows drawn together in a frown. After a long silence he turned to Julie. "Do you know this man?"

"Well, I ..." Julie faltered, looking desperately at Greg. Should she say yes? Her eyes asked the question, and he nodded slightly, his own gaze reassuring her and warming the cold knot of fear that had begun to form inside her.

"I do now," she said abruptly. "I just hired him as my attorney."

Apparently satisfied, the officer handed the card back to Greg. "Mr. Stafford, we're taking your client to the main Honolulu station to book her. At the moment she is being charged with suspected complicity in the theft of government property."

Julie heard his words through a haze. Even as she listened, she was minutely aware of her surroundings. The thump of her own heart seemed overwhelmingly loud, and off to her left she heard a baby crying. It all seemed so unreal. It took all her self-discipline to remain calm.

"I'll follow you there," Greg was saying brusquely, and she realized they must be talking about police headquarters. "Be advised that my client is to be treated with respect," he warned.

Directing his attention to Julie, he said quietly, "Cooperate fully with the police. I'm sure this is all a mistake."

The officer prodded Julie's arm to move her forward. As she began to move, she saw Brenda Clark hovering at the edge of the crowd of passengers and crew that had gathered to watch. It was obvious the other woman was stunned. For a moment Julie almost thought she was going to say something. The woman's mouth worked convulsively for a second, but no sound came out. Then she was gone, lost in the crowd.

There was no time for Julie to speculate about this strange behavior. She stole a quick glance over her shoulder at the rest of her fellow crew members. Tricia's face was stricken. She tried to hurry forward but was stopped by a security officer.

"Greg," Julie said hurriedly. "Please get this straightened out quickly and let Tricia know what's happening."

His dark gaze settled on her face with comforting directness. "You can count on me," he said, and in that moment she knew it was true.

A COLD, AIR-CONDITIONED BREEZE hit Julie like a breath from an open freezer as she extended her left hand to be fingerprinted at police headquarters. The ink was icy as well, but she could hardly expect the fortyish man methodically pressing each of her fingers onto the messy pad to care about that.

She scanned the room. Under different circumstances she could have enjoyed this first visit to a metropolitan police station. It was a study in controlled chaos. The space was crammed with desks and filing cabinets. Uniformed men and women called out to each other over the sound of constantly ringing phones. Shouts erupted, and Julie craned her neck to follow the progress of two men in brightly flowered shirts as they were led away protesting to a cell.

She sighed and turned her attention back to the fingerprinting process. As she looked up, her glance met that of a policewoman in a crisp uniform. The woman put down the sandwich she had been munching and smiled briefly. Julie looked away quickly. All she wanted to do was remain as anonymous as possible. Within moments Greg Stafford should be arriving, and she would be able to put this whole unfortunate incident behind her.

Thoughts of Greg Stafford took top priority in her mind. He intrigued her. On the plane she'd found her attention drawn to him with unusual frequency. Then, after the way she had brushed him off in the airport corridor she hadn't expected to see him again; but she had to admit his appearance at the moment of her arrest had been a godsend. What if he'd walked away, unconcerned about her plight? After all, she had been the one who had told him only hours earlier that she doubted she would ever need an attorney. She hadn't expected to have to swallow those words quite so quickly.

Even now this whole situation seemed like a bad dream. Any moment she would wake up and find that it had all been a horrible nightmare.

The bulky man behind the counter released her hand and pointed to a dilapidated box of tissues. Julie removed one gingerly and began scrubbing off the messy stains. So much for her last manicure, she thought ruefully.

Before Julie could finish, the stout balding police sergeant who had hovered beside her since the moment she'd arrived at the station grasped her arm more firmly than she thought necessary. "This way," he commanded.

She pulled back slightly, balking. "Obviously there's been a mistake. When can I speak to someone in charge so I can get this situation corrected?"

The patronizing smile he gave her made her blood boil. "Lady, do you know how many times a day I hear that same remark?" Smiling again, he added, "And do you know how little I actually care? Down this hall to the right."

Julie tried again. "Where are you taking me? What happens next?"

He ignored her, stopping briefly to exchange a few words with another man and then guiding her to the far end of the brightly lit corridor. In front of a pair of frosted glass doors, he pointed to a row of metal chairs. "Sit there while I check to see if Receiving is ready for you."

Feeling slightly like a puppy being enrolled in dog-obedience school, Julie sat down and exchanged stony glances with three teenage boys lounging in chairs on the other side of the narrow hallway. She pulled down her straight skirt with a quick motion and pretended to be studying a stain slightly above their heads. Too bad she was wearing her uniform. The airline company wouldn't appreciate the free publicity. A new worry entered her head. What if this little incident cost her her job?

One of the teenagers leaned toward her. "How are things in the friendly skies these days?"

Julie glared at him and shrugged her shoulders. Damn, she was getting tired of this. Where was Greg Stafford? Had he decided not to take her case after all?

When a thirty-minute wait had sorely tried her patience, Julie leaned over and stopped a passing officer, asking him to remind the sergeant she was still there. His amused look reminded her she was in no position to ask any favors.

By the time the sergeant did appear her patience was totally exhausted. He motioned for her to stand and held the door open for her. Inside the room, two women were waiting behind a long counter. "Here's your next customer," he announced. Another man entered the room behind them and thrust Julie's purse and flight tote at her.

Her relief at retrieving her personal belongings was short-lived. One of the women behind the counter, a tall gray-haired woman whose grim expression suggested she'd just been sentenced to be shot at sunrise, demanded, "Hand over your purse."

Julie clutched it against her body defensively. "It's already been searched by the customs agents."

The younger of the two women spoke up. "I've got to inventory the contents in your presence." She was obviously less sure of herself than the other one, and Julie met her friendly brown eyes with a long direct gaze of her own.

"But I'm not staying. Within a few minutes my lawyer will be here and this whole thing will be cleared up."

The old battle-ax held out her square hand, her face impassive. Julie's spirits sank to a new low. The jolt of adrenaline that had kept her going since the ordeal began was gone, and a combination of jet lag and shock was sapping her ability to resist. She handed over the purse, the full import of what was happening to her finally beginning to sink in.

This can't be real, she repeated to herself. She knew false arrests occurred, but they were things that happened to someone else, to those poor unfortunates whose names and photographs were spread across the pages of the newspaper.

Once more her hopes centered on Greg Stafford. Surely he would stride through those doors any moment with an order for her immediate release. She wasn't even sure she had enough change in her pocket to pay for a phone call. Desperately she tried to remember what they'd said when they read her her rights. She had the right to remain silent, the right to an attorney... Hadn't she heard somewhere that you were allowed one phone call?

Her thoughts were interrupted as the contents of her bag spilled out helter-skelter on the Formica countertop.Julie forced herself to listen to the toneless voice naming each item: "Two lipsticks, Raging Plum and Fresh Strawberry. A half-empty bottle of perfume, label missing. One packet of artificial sweetener..." What an incredible amount of trivia she carried around, Julie thought, cringing over the way her privacy was being invaded under the glaring fluorescent lights.

Next came her flight tote, whose contents had already been searched so thoroughly at the airport. The new silk scarves were missing, she noted. Why on earth had they triggered such an intense interest? And why hadn't her uniform raincoat been returned? The answer to the whole dilemma must be here if she could only decipher it.

"In there," the gray-haired matron ordered as she finished cataloging the last item. "Strip."

"Strip?" This was the final straw. Julie felt herself going over the edge. No way was she going to submit to a search until they told her more about the accusations against her. Things had gone far enough, and she was tired of being pushed around. Glaring aggressively, she demanded, "What's the meaning of all this?"

The younger woman patted her arm soothingly. "Don't make trouble. Things will be explained as soon as possible. We're just following standard procedures."

Her kindness pacified Julie temporarily. These women were obviously just following orders. Greg had told her to cooperate, and he was the professional. At least she hoped he was. It dawned on her suddenly that she knew nothing about the man; perhaps she'd better check his credentials when he showed up.

After a humiliating body search to which she submitted reluctantly, Julie watched in helpless indignation as her uniform, lingerie and nylons were removed from the hook where she'd draped them. "Step in the shower," one of the women ordered. "Scrub yourself. Wash your hair with the shampoo you'll find on the shelf and then towel off and dress in that coverall over there."

Bone weary, Julie stepped under the lukewarm spray. Ignoring the washcloth, she rubbed hesitantly at the small bar of antiseptic soap in hopes of producing some suds. Impatiently she wrenched the cap off the tube of shampoo and then sneezed violently at the sulfurous fumes that escaped. Any germ brave enough to survive this assault deserved to live, she decided.

To keep her sanity she tried to concentrate on what she was going to do when she got out of this place. Tricia must be out of her mind with worry. And what must the rest of the crew be thinking? As far as she knew, nothing this dramatic had happened to her airline since an attempted hijacking by a man demanding passage to Borneo a year earlier. That incident had ended well when he surrendered peacefully to the authorities. Perhaps this one would be resolved as easily.

The thought cheered her somewhat, and she reached for the thin towel, drying herself as thoroughly as possible. She slipped into the stiff, cotton coverall and buttoned it quickly. After a few attempts at taming her hair with the plastic comb she found in a pocket, she gave up in exasperation, glancing warily in a small mirror on the wall. A coldly angry face stared back at her, the face of a woman who looked determined. She had never felt so degraded and humiliated in her life. The injustice of what was happening stabbed her like a knife, and she felt a surge of strength.

"Time's up," the matron called. "Move it, sister. You're due at the photographer's."

Julie emerged from the cubicle just as the sergeant appeared through the hall doorway. "Ready?" he asked, and she realized she had no choice.

After a lengthy photo session that consisted of being instructed not to smile, to hold her head high, to turn from side to side and then face the blazing camera lights without blinking, Julie felt brutalized. "Now do I get to see my lawyer?" she demanded of the sergeant.

"You get one phone call."

So that old line really was true, Julie thought and felt an urge to laugh crazily. "My lawyer followed me to the station. I'll save my call until after I've talked to him."

"That may be a while. If you're lucky it might be this evening, but it'll probably be morning."

"Morning?" Julie echoed shrilly. Never for one moment had she visualized having to spend the night in jail. She shuddered as her mind filled with lurid scenes from old movies.

The sergeant merely turned and beckoned for her to follow.

WHEN THE STEEL-BARRED DOOR of her cell slammed shut behind her, Julie faced the fact that she was in serious trouble. She felt an overwhelming urge to grab the bars and shake them for all she was worth. Thinking better of it, however, she glanced around, sizing up her new surroundings. The occupants of the other cells appeared to be sleeping on their cots, so she subsided onto hers.

Her mind whirled with questions as she tried to analyze why she had been arrested. "Suspected complicity in the theft of government property," the official had said. Ridiculous. She had never even lifted a pencil from a post office, much less stolen any other type of government property.

Exhausted, she sank down on her back and stared at the dull gray ceiling. There was an unreal quality about the whole episode that left her dazed. She tried to figure out what time it was. It must be evening now, she guessed, wishing she had checked the time before turning her watch over to the matron. That meant it was Friday evening. The plane had left Tokyo on Saturday morning but had arrived in Honolulu on what was actually the previous day after crossing the international date line. This flight schedule had become a joke among the flight attendants. If you had a good day, you were happy to have a chance to relive it. Today was definitely not one of those days. As her thoughts whirled in confusion she gave in to the overwhelming urge to sleep, knowing that when she awakened she must be ready to fight for her freedom.

"COME ON. UP. UP." It seemed only seconds later that someone was shaking her by the shoulder. "Your attorney is here."

Julie shot straight up, blinking her eyes. Instinctively, she reached for her bag, planning to comb her hair, before she remembered that her purse had been taken from her. Cursing inwardly at having to be seen in such a bedraggled state, she rose stiffly and followed the matron out of the cell.

After traversing a confusing labyrinth of hallways they stopped in front of a door. Motioning for Julie to enter, the matron said, "You've got fifteen minutes."

The room was empty, stark, impersonal. Julie sat down in one of the two chairs in the center of the room and waited obediently. In her dazed condition, all her spark seemed to have left her. Her whole body was icy, and she felt increasingly sick. If only she had something warm to drink.

Her head turned at the sound of the door opening. Greg Stafford paused momentarily, his head almost touching the top of the frame. His tie had been loosened, and his jacket was thrown carelessly over one arm. He still looked great, though, and Julie felt the contrast between them sharply. In his hand he was holding a Styrofoam cup. "I thought you might like a cup of tea," he suggested.

"You remembered I prefer tea." Julie reached for the cup. "Thank you." She took a gulp of the hot liquid and then met his gaze. "I needed that."

He pulled out the chair directly in front of her and sat down. "Has it been terrible?" His voice was so warm, so sympathetic that a lump rose in her throat.

Taking another gulp of the tea, she fought to control her voice before replying. "It's been awful. But I can go home now, can't I?"

Reaching out, he took her cup and set it down on the floor before grasping her hands. Her skin burned at his touch and she drew back slightly. He was aware of her withdrawal; she knew that by the way his eyes narrowed slightly and darkened to a stormy gray. "I've run into a little difficulty, Julie."

At the startled widening of her eyes, he added quickly, "It's not unusual. After all, this is after regular working hours."

She suppressed a tremor of reaction. "I don't know what time it is. I'm completely disoriented."

Glancing at his watch, he replied, "It's about eleven. No wonder you're disoriented, since it's Friday again. I'm sorry I had to bother you this late, but I thought you'd prefer to know what's going on."

Moistening her lips, she forced her voice to remain calm as she looked at him steadily. "I can't stay here any longer."

His gaze sharpened. "Have you been mistreated?" A hint of steel underlay the quiet inquiry.

She lifted her shoulders. "Look at me. I've been dehumanized. They won't even let me wear my own clothes, and they've confiscated my personal belongings."

"You do a lot for that outfit you're wearing." He smiled at her in a way that made the room seem warmer immediately.

"Don't try flattering me. I know what a fright I must look. But that doesn't matter right now. Just tell me more about why I've been arrested."

He frowned and looked away. "As I said, I haven't had a lot of luck in that area. You already know that you're being accused of having stolen some government property."

Julie expressed her bewilderment openly. "But what property? And what sort of evidence do they claim to have against me? What makes them think I've done anything wrong? It's so absurd.''

From the deep frown lines creasing his forehead, she could see he didn't share her certainty. ''It's not that easy. We're dealing with something very serious, Julie. Don't make the mistake of taking this too lightly.''

Standing up, he paced the length of the room and turned back to her. ''In the morning you'll be questioned thoroughly. Perhaps we'd better run through a few of your answers.''

Rebellion stirred in Julie, a defiance fostered by a burning need to express her anger and frustration over what had happened these past few hours. She rose from her chair to confront him. ''Are you suggesting you need to coach me? I don't have anything to hide.''

He stared at her for a long moment before snapping, ''Don't be naive.''

Julie's eyes blazed. ''And don't you be patronizing.''

His brows lifted slightly. ''For someone up to her neck in trouble, you're damn brave.''

''The innocent can afford to be brave, Mr. Stafford,'' she said coldly.

Once again he watched her for a few seconds. She could almost feel the way he was weighing her in the balance. ''Touché,'' he said at last, smiling. ''Julie, I don't want to disillusion you about our system of justice, but innocent people have been found guilty.''

Julie regarded him warily. ''What's that supposed to mean?''

''It means you're in a lot of trouble, and if you don't watch out your stay in places like this could be quite lengthy.''

"I'm innocent," Julie protested. "I've done nothing wrong. If you don't believe that, perhaps I should get another lawyer."

Greg took a deep breath and a muscle twitched along his jawline. "I'll be happy to find you another lawyer if that's what you want, Julie. But for now, why don't we go over your situation calmly and see if we can make some sense out of this thing."

His voice was so reasonable that Julie felt ashamed. Greg didn't have to be here. His offer of help had been a godsend. "I need your help, Greg, I'll admit it. Please don't start by thinking I'm guilty of what the police are accusing me of doing."

"Looking at you right now, I find it difficult to believe you could be guilty of any crime," Greg said. "But don't ever lie to me."

Julie stretched out her hand to him. "It's a deal. We'll agree right this minute to be absolutely truthful with each other. Okay?"

Greg's expression tightened and his eyes grew shadowed. For a moment she thought he was going to refuse to shake her hand. Finally he reached across and clasped her hand in his. "Deal," he said huskily.

Chapter Three

So Greg did believe she was innocent. Julie refused to think too deeply about why she felt such relief at the knowledge. After all, if your lawyer didn't believe you were innocent, no one else would. It didn't really matter what Greg thought of her personally, Julie told herself; but if he was going to convince others of her innocence he'd better start by believing in it himself.

Drawing a deep, calming breath, she decided that Greg had been directing this conversation long enough. It was her turn to demand a few answers. "Exactly what have you learned about the charges against me?" she asked, her voice as cool and regal as if she were dressed in an elegant designer suit and dining at the Ritz instead of standing in this bleak gray cage clad in a grubby government-issue sack.

Greg noticed the change in her; she could tell by the way his eyebrows lifted slightly and those expressive eyes of his darkened. He motioned for her to sit down and then seated himself. "This case is a big one." He frowned as if to emphasize the gravity of her predicament. "Evidently it involves something that occurred in Japan."

"What, exactly?" Julie demanded.

"It's a bit complicated. I'm having trouble finding out all the details tonight. They've promised to go over everything with me tomorrow. Although that's Saturday, they've promised me the police captain will be here to discuss the case."

"Tomorrow." Julie felt some of her confidence ebbing as she contemplated waiting that long for answers to her questions.

"For now, let's start by discussing what you did in Tokyo," Greg suggested. "You were there two nights, right?"

"Yes, that's right."

"What did you do the first night?"

"That's easy. I did the usual. Checked into the hotel with the rest of the flight crew, ordered dinner from room service and got a good night's sleep."

He gave her an odd glance. "At the Imperial?"

"Of course. We usually stay there."

"I see," he murmured. "Did you share a room?"

"No, we all prefer our privacy."

There was a long pause. "And the second night?"

"I had dinner with a friend."

"Who was that?" Greg's question was quick, almost too quick, with a sharp edge to it that Julie didn't like.

She waited for a moment before answering, debating whether he had a right to ask such a question. But of course he did, she reminded herself. The police were probably going to ask these same questions so she better arm him with the answers beforehand. "A friend I've known for ages," she said evenly. "Marge Kelly. Her husband was transferred to Japan recently. He's an engineer. He was out of town working on a project, so

Marge came to the hotel. We had dinner and then stayed up late catching up on old times.''

He took a pad and pencil from his inside coat pocket. "Your friend's name and address? I presume this can all be verified by the hotel staff?''

"Are you doubting me?''

Greg glanced up from his pad. "You haven't said anything to make me think you're not innocent, but I'll need solid evidence for the police.''

"Of course. Marge's address is in my purse, the purse that was taken from me.''

"I'll get it. What else did you do in Tokyo?''

"After Marge left, I went to bed and got some sleep.''

"Alone?'' Greg asked casually, his pencil poised above the pad in his hand.

Julie looked at him hard, but he refused to meet her gaze. "Yes,'' she said finally, hating to have to report on her actions to anyone. Was she to have no privacy left? she wondered.

"That seems simple enough.'' Greg's frown seemed to indicate that he thought it was too simple. His next question confirmed that. "Have you left out anything? Did you meet anyone else, go any place?''

"Well.'' She thought hard. "No, just like I said. The first day I was too tired to do anything but go to the hotel with the rest of the flight crew. The second day... yesterday, I guess,'' she faltered, trying to calculate how much time had passed since this whole thing had started. "Yes, yesterday. I did some shopping in the afternoon, and then I had a little time before meeting my friend for dinner so I went for a walk.''

She might have imagined it, but he seemed to tense, and when she looked at his face, his gray eyes were boring into hers with sharp intensity. "Where?" he demanded.

She held up her hands expressively. "I don't know exactly. I know the general area, the Ginza district. I just walked around and looked in shop windows."

"In the afternoon," he probed. "But not in the morning."

"Yes, the afternoon."

"Did you ride the subway or get on a train?"

"No." She looked at him curiously. "Why? Did someone claim they saw me on a train? And what does that have to do with stolen government property?"

He didn't answer. Instead he regarded her steadily for a moment and then resumed his questioning. "Did anyone go shopping with you?"

"I went alone."

"Did you talk to anyone while you shopped?"

She surveyed him angrily, her temper rising in the face of his persistence. "I may have. I can't remember every detail. I remember admiring a baby being pushed along in a carriage by his mother, but our conversation consisted mostly of oohs and goos. My Japanese is spotty, and the baby's English wasn't too developed."

He glanced up quickly, as if measuring her mood. "Don't give those cutesy answers to your interrogators tomorrow."

Her temper soared out of bounds. "You're making it sound as if I'm on the 'Ten Most Wanted' list."

"Julie," he urged. "We need to reach an understanding from the very beginning. I'm on your side. Any advice I give you is meant for your own good."

Julie shifted uneasily in her chair. "How do I know that? Don't misunderstand me; I'm not doubting your ability."

"You're wondering about my qualifications?"

"Frankly, I'm wondering why you're helping me. I wasn't particularly friendly to you on the plane if I remember correctly."

He laughed. "I suppose I have to plead guilty to helping anyone I see in trouble, but I'm not an ambulance chaser." At her puzzled look, he explained, "I'm not an attorney who ordinarily goes seeking cases, but since I'd just met you . . ." His voice died down but his eyes darkened in a way that warmed her through and through.

"You're from California, I believe." She attempted to regain a businesslike footing. "Does that mean you don't have a license to practice law in Hawaii?"

"I'm licensed in several states," he answered quickly. "But if you have an attorney I'll be happy to contact him for you."

She felt a sudden need to pin him down. That evasive quality she had noticed might only be a result of his legal training, but it was beginning to annoy her. "I have no way of judging an attorney, especially in a criminal case. But what are your fees? My bank account is a disaster."

"Don't worry about that now. I was looking for an excuse to stay in the islands longer, and now I've got one. Anyway, this case looks interesting." Glancing back at his pad, he asked, "I'd like to verify the information you gave the booking officer. Your legal name is Julie Smith?"

She nodded as he continued to run down his list of her birth date, place of birth, address and length of employment.

When he finished he said, "Now for a few questions you may be asked tomorrow. What are your parents' names and addresses?"

"Evelyn Smith is my mother. My father is dead. He died when I was very young."

"Your mother lives in Los Angeles?" Greg's eyes were narrowed slightly and he leaned toward her, trapping her gaze with eyes that asked questions of their own.

"Yes. In a retirement village with her sister, my Aunt Rose."

"No brothers or sisters?"

"None."

"Boyfriend? Lover? Any ex-husbands I should know about?"

Now it was Julie's eyes that narrowed. "Is this really necessary?"

"I need to know who else might be involved in this case."

"No one else will be involved in it," Julie protested, "because there isn't going to be any case. I'm innocent, remember?"

"Just checking."

"No special boyfriends or lovers, and I've never been married."

Greg wrote quickly on his notepad. The silence in the room, broken only by the scratching of his pen across the paper, became more than Julie could bear. She pressed her hand against her head briefly and then leaned forward, her fingertips coming to rest lightly on the sleeve of Greg's shirt.

"Greg, I have a headache. I don't think I've eaten much today. Please, can't you get me out of here tonight. I'm not guilty of any crime. Why am I being held like this?''

For a moment Greg's face remained hard and impassive. He looked away from her, lost in thought, and Julie felt as though the silence between them had become a wall. Turning back to her abruptly, he let his lips relax into a smile, but even in her tired state she sensed that the smile didn't reach his eyes. He had very expressive eyes, and she had begun to intuit their many moods.

Placing a warm, enveloping palm over her hand, he murmured, ''Julie, I'd give anything to get you out of here.''

Shaken by his sudden tenderness, the first warmth she had felt from another human being since she had been brought to this place, her eyes filled with threatening moisture. She removed her hand slowly and leaned back, attempting a shaky laugh. ''I'm sorry. Of course none of this is your fault, and I know you're doing all you can to help me.''

For a second she thought his face was going to close down again, as if he was withdrawing from her even while he smiled. But his words were friendly enough. ''Perhaps I can talk the matron into letting me bring you something to eat.''

''No, I'm okay. It's late. Will I get breakfast in the morning, though?''

''Nothing like you served me.''

''Was that only this morning? I feel as if I've spent days here already.''

''Actually, it was tomorrow morning. Crossing the international date line is enough to throw anyone off balance.''

"Especially when the second time around turns out to be such a disaster."

"You'll feel better when you've had some sleep." He glanced at his watch. "Our time is almost up."

Julie stood reluctantly, unwilling to see him leave. He was her only link to the outside world and she wanted to cling to him, to beg him not to leave her.

He rose and towered over her, his expression softening with concern. "Try to get some sleep. First thing in the morning I'll be knocking down that judge's door to get you released."

He was so close, and his clean masculine essence contrasted sharply with the musty odors she had begun to associate with her stay in this building. She swayed toward him involuntarily, seeking his warmth and comfort like a moth searching for a flame. His hands came out to steady her and then stayed, close and burning, on her shoulders.

"I knew we'd see each other again, Julie."

"But I'm sure you didn't expect it would be in quite these circumstances."

He was quiet so long she was forced to look up at him. His face was close, so close she felt the brush of his breath against her forehead. She could read nothing from his expression; his eyes were concealed by the curve of lashes that were surprisingly long on such an intensely masculine man. His hands left her arms slowly, traveling up to cup her face and tilt her head backward.

Moving deliberately, he pulled her against him with a gentle force she could not, did not want to, deny. Then his lips were on hers, and she gave herself up to the moment she had known was inevitable since she had encountered him on the plane.

She had wanted this to happen, unconsciously and unadmitted even to herself. The scent of his woodsy cologne, the firm strength of his body as it pressed against hers, the taste of his warm, enticing mouth, awakened a longing that suddenly surged to life and begged for release. For the moment she couldn't think, nor could she even remember why she needed to think.

When he stepped away from her she kept her gaze lowered until she could bring her pulse back under control and steady her breathing. Greg's crisp, clean scent filled her nostrils, and she still felt the heat of his body on her skin. He didn't speak.

"Is this how you say goodbye to all your clients?" she asked finally.

"I wasn't saying goodbye, Julie, only good-night."

What she could have answered, she didn't know. Fortunately, the arrival of the matron eliminated the need for any reply.

GREG STAFFORD STOOD IN THE CENTER of the hallway, watching as the matron led Julie away. She didn't turn to look back at him, and for that he was glad. He hadn't meant to kiss her, but he couldn't deny that she attracted him on a very personal level. Damn, he couldn't afford any complications. Not at this stage of the game.

A young man came out of a nearby room and held up a tape. He was grinning. "I got most of your conversation. Sounds like your plan is working."

Greg's eyes grew steely as he reached for the tape and pocketed it quickly. "Where can I use the phone without being overheard?"

"The chief's office would be best. He said to give you free run of the place."

Greg strode away without answering. He entered the office, reached for the phone and punched out the numbers with savage force. When a voice he recognized answered, he spoke without preamble. "Everything's on schedule."

"Great. I knew you could handle this. Do you have her trust?"

"I said everything's on target."

There was a long pause on the other end of the line before the gravelly, knowing voice asked, "Any difficulties?"

Greg grimaced. He should have known he couldn't keep anything from this man. They had been working together too long, and they understood each other almost too well. For the first time, Greg was less than honest with him. He couldn't pinpoint a reason for his evasiveness, but he felt he had to be cautious.

"She's very convincing." Greg chose his words carefully. "If I hadn't personally been the one to follow her in Tokyo, I'd believe we had the wrong person."

"You don't make mistakes like that, Stafford. Has she been thoroughly questioned?"

"The local police have agreed to handle her interrogation tomorrow morning."

"You know how important this thing is. We're depending on you." The words ended on an up note, as if they veiled a question.

Greg didn't answer. He didn't need to say anything. There was no doubt where his loyalties rested. Finally he spoke once again. "You can count on me."

When he replaced the receiver, he heard a movement behind him. Turning swiftly, he saw Captain Denis Lonergan standing just inside the doorway.

"Talking to your boss?" Lonergan's mouth twisted into a semblance of a smile as he settled his heavy body into the room's only chair.

"It was a private conversation." Greg refrained from making further comment, but he was angry. The police captain had obviously been eavesdropping.

Greg had just met the captain, but his first impressions weren't encouraging. "Was there something you wanted to talk to me about?" He tried to phrase the question politely.

"I need more information about Smith."

"I thought your men were checking on her background for us," Greg countered.

"We're finding out what we can. But we could use some more cooperation from your federal people."

"You feel we're not cooperating?" Greg assessed the captain warily.

Captain Lonergan held up a protesting hand. "Now, don't get your back up. We want to work with your agents, give you all the help we can. But we don't want you running the whole show. My officers are good people. They know what they're doing."

Greg understood what he was driving at. It was an attitude he encountered frequently when he worked with local authorities. As an agent for the DIA, the Defense Intelligence Agency, Greg was familiar with this initial jockeying for position. The captain was used to being the boss, and it probably wasn't easy for him to play a lesser role. Greg considered his next words carefully. "This is a very important case, Captain, and to be frank, I'm going to need as much help as you can give me."

Captain Lonergan relaxed visibly, and a small smile played about his lips. "I've had a lot of experience, Greg. May I call you Greg?"

"Of course, Denis." Greg tried to keep from grinning.

"I think you've got the right girl," the captain announced. "From the reports I've glanced at, she's obviously guilty. But I guess you know that; you're the one who followed her to the Imperial. Guess that's when you found out she's an airline stewardess."

"Yes," Greg agreed, resigning himself to a lengthy rehash of the facts. "She was wearing her uniform when I had her paged to the information desk."

"Smart thinking, to have her paged like that." Denis leaned back comfortably in his chair. "But I'm not sure that's how I would have handled it."

"No?"

"How long have you been with the agency?" Denis pulled out a cigar and lit it, taking a deep puff and exhaling a cloud of smelly smoke.

Greg groaned inwardly. Outwardly, he managed a polite facade. "About ten years."

"I've been with the force twenty-eight years. They've been tough but good years." Sitting up abruptly, he looked at Greg intently over a cloud of smoke. "Heard you had some trouble a few years back."

Greg was instantly wary. "Oh?"

"Don't worry. I'm not the type to carry tales. But you can't hide that sort of thing, you know."

"What sort of thing?" Greg decided to take the offensive.

"Your trouble with that woman, the double agent."

"Where did you hear that old story?"

The captain grinned and leaned back. "Told you I was a good cop. I've got my ear to the ground. Nothing slips past me."

"My past has nothing to do with this case," Greg said icily. He moved toward the door, anxious to make an exit. "I'm going to my hotel now. We'll get together in the morning."

Captain Lonergan stood up, taking a step toward Greg. "I'm going to nail that girl, Stafford, so don't let a pretty face spoil things this time."

"NOW THEN, MISS SMITH, we want to ask you a few questions."

Julie folded her hands carefully on the battered table in front of her and tried to assume an air of quiet dignity. The policewoman sitting across the table from her was acting friendly, but Julie didn't trust her. As a matter of fact, she didn't trust anyone this morning.

She had been awakened at what had to be the crack of dawn by the rude comments of the woman in the cell across from her. By the time she had managed to get her eyes open, she had received an education in a side of life she had never even known existed until now.

Never before had she appreciated the wonders of her own life. Like having a bathroom with a door that could be used to shut the world out. And being able to take a shower and use a blow-dryer on her hair and select from an array of cosmetics and clothes. If she ever got out of here she would never take such luxuries for granted again.

Now she was closeted in a small windowless room with two police officers, a man and a woman. The woman had just identified herself as Lieutenant Massie. "Anita," she had said with a smile that Julie didn't trust. Julie remembered seeing her the evening before. The other woman had seemed friendly then, too, but perhaps she was that sort of person. At any rate, as long as she was locked up in this place, Julie wasn't going to trust anyone.

The other police officer, the man, hadn't spoken yet. He was pacing back and forth across the room behind Lieutenant Massie, pausing to glower at Julie every now and then. "Let's get on with it," he mumbled at Anita, and she smiled again at Julie. Julie didn't smile back.

"Why don't you start by telling us about your boyfriend," Anita suggested.

"My boyfriend?" Julie lifted her eyebrows slightly for emphasis. "I have a number of friends who are male, but they're all men, not boys."

Anita took a deep breath and tapped one manicured nail against the table. "I'll rephrase the question. How well do you know Jon Derickson?"

"Who?"

Anita eyed her sharply but repeated the name carefully. "Jon Derickson."

"I've never heard that name before."

Anita's patient smile faded rapidly, and the atmosphere in the room grew tense. The man spoke to Julie directly for the first time. His voice was gruff, harsh. "We're not playing games here, missy. You better settle down and answer our questions." The scowl on his lined face deepened, and his thick, heavyset body leaned over the table threateningly.

Julie gave him a measuring glance, intended to show that she was not frightened by his manner. After all, this was the United States and she had her rights as a citizen. An innocent citizen, she added mentally. "We haven't been introduced," she said quietly.

He straightened up, clearly taken aback by her calm attitude. Anita intervened. "This is Denis Lonergan, Julie. Captain Lonergan. He's in charge of your case."

"If he's in charge, perhaps he'd better tell me exactly why I'm being held in this jail. What are the charges against me? You can't hold me without informing me of the charges."

"We have told you the charges, Julie. You are suspected of having a part in stealing some property that belongs to the government." Anita's voice was still soothing and friendly.

"What property?" Julie asked flatly.

"A computer disk." Captain Lonergan bit the words out curtly. "A disk stolen from a U.S. Navy ship while it was in port in Japan. A disk containing some highly sensitive, classified material."

"I've never even been on board a navy ship," Julie protested. "How can you think I've stolen this disk?" Trying desperately to make sense out of this mess, she realized they must have a certain amount of evidence against her. Otherwise, how could they have arrested her? "Do you have any evidence?" she asked warily.

Captain Lonergan pounced on her question, seemingly taking it as some sort of admission of guilt. "Evidence? Of course we have evidence, Ms. Smith." Coming around to her side of the table, he leaned over until his face was only inches from her own. "So you better start talking now, missy. You better sing like a bird, because if you don't you're going to be in more trouble than you can handle."

"Now, Denis," Anita said placatingly. "I'm sure Julie is going to cooperate with us. Just give her a few minutes."

Captain Lonergan leaned back reluctantly, and Julie breathed a sigh of relief. She didn't care for him at all and, despite Anita's facade of friendliness, Julie didn't trust her, either. She had watched enough television drama to know what game they were playing. Anita was being the "good guy." Captain Lonergan was the "bad guy." Apparently his job was to scare her so badly that she would run to Anita's comforting protection and tell all.

"Where is my lawyer?" Julie asked suddenly. "I want to talk to him before I answer any of your questions."

The other two exchanged a knowing look before Anita replied, "Mr. Stafford will be in later. Right now, you must answer our questions."

"I am answering them," Julie said shortly. "I don't know this man you're talking about. I've never been on a navy ship. I didn't steal any computer disk—or anything else for that matter. I have no idea why I'm here or what makes you think I had anything to do with this, but I'm tired and I'd like to go home."

Anita leaned forward across the table. "If you are really innocent, Miss Smith, you'll be able to go home quite soon. All you have to do is talk to us. Otherwise, we have no way of finding out if you are innocent or guilty."

"What more do you want to know?"

"Let's start by discussing what you did in Tokyo," Anita suggested.

"I arrived in Tokyo on Thursday with the rest of the flight crew," Julie explained. "I went to the hotel, checked into my room, had dinner and went to bed early."

"What hotel was this?"

"The Imperial. That's one of the hotels we stay at when we're stopping over in Tokyo."

"You didn't leave the hotel at all that first evening?" Anita's gaze became sharp, pinning Julie down and demanding an answer.

"No."

"So, you got up the next morning and went out," Anita said, leaning back in her chair and adopting a studiedly casual pose.

"I got up late," Julie said. "I missed breakfast. The others met in the coffee shop for breakfast, but I overslept. By the time I went downstairs, the rest of the flight crew had left the hotel, so I went out shopping."

"What time was this?" Captain Lonergan spoke again, his impatience evident in the snap of his voice.

"Around one, I suppose." Julie frowned, trying hard to remember exactly when she had left the hotel.

"You didn't eat breakfast or lunch?" Anita probed.

"I stopped at a street stand and ate a bowl of *yakisoba* noodles."

"Where did you go shopping?"

"I walked around the area near the hotel, mostly in the Ginza district. There are a lot of big department stores there, and I simply wandered around."

"Did you buy anything?"

"No."

"So no one can really verify that you were out shopping all that time?"

"Perhaps the street vendor who sold me the noodles?" Julie suggested.

"Ms. Smith," Captain Lonergan drawled wearily. "Do you have any idea how many street vendors there are in a city the size of Tokyo? I'm afraid that's not much of an alibi."

"You mean you don't believe me?" Julie protested hotly.

Captain Lonergan mumbled something, but Anita stopped him, smiling patiently at Julie all the while. Where had she learned to smile like that? Julie wondered. "These are routine questions, Julie, so please cooperate with us."

As far as Julie was concerned nothing about any of this was remotely routine, but she forced herself to remain calm. Soon Greg would be here, and she would be going home.

"So you didn't buy anything while you were out shopping," Anita questioned.

"No. My budget is already strained this month."

The two officers glanced at one another again as if she'd said something significant, but Anita's voice sounded the same as she continued. "Now, you were supposed to have breakfast with the rest of the flight crew."

"It wasn't anything official," Julie explained. "But Tricia and I usually breakfast with the others if we're not too tired."

"Tricia?"

"Yes, Tricia Hyde," Julie said. "She's my roommate. We share a condominium here in Honolulu, and we're frequently assigned to the same flights."

Anita looked up at her. "A condominium? You lease it?"

"No, I own it and Tricia pays me rent." Julie smiled. "Actually, the bank owns it. I make payments on it every month, which explains why I can't do too much shopping."

"Are you saying you're a little short of money?" Anita asked carefully.

"Isn't everyone?" Julie quipped, but she could see that no one else found her statement the least bit amusing. "I don't have any big money worries," she added at length. "As long as nothing unexpected comes along I'll make it with no trouble."

"Unexpected?" Captain Lonergan demanded. "What does that mean?"

"Illness. Loss of a job," Julie explained patiently. "My mother may need surgery soon, so I'll probably have some additional expenses then."

He leaned forward, a triumphant gleam in his eyes. "Your mother is ill and you need a little money to pay for her surgery? Your boyfriend offered you some money to help him and you couldn't say no. Is that what happened?"

"No."

"Better tell us the truth," he warned.

"I am telling you the truth. You just refuse to believe it."

The captain pushed back his chair and began pacing the room again. Anita placed her hand on Julie's. "Let's get back to your day. You're sure you didn't buy anything at all?"

"Only the scarves at the airport as I was leaving."

"Yes," Anita murmured. "We'll get to the scarves in a minute."

Captain Lonergan stopped his pacing to shoot a question at her. "What were you wearing when you went shopping?"

Julie glared at him but thought carefully, trying to remember. "Jeans. Black jeans and a shirt."

"What color shirt?" Anita asked.

"Pink, pale pink. One of those big shirts. Almost like a dress, actually."

"Wasn't it raining? Weren't you wearing a rain-coat?"

"No," Julie said slowly. "I mean yes, it was raining, but I took an umbrella. I seldom wear my raincoat except when I'm on duty."

"What color is that raincoat?"

"Beige," Julie said, looking first at Anita and then at Captain Lonergan. Both of them seemed to tense at her answer. "My raincoat is a basic beige, part of my uniform for the airline. There's nothing particularly special about it. You'll see them on half the women in the world on a cool rainy day."

"What time did you return to the hotel?" Anita asked.

"At six. I remember the time exactly because I looked at the clock in the lobby when I came in."

"You don't have a watch?"

"I have one, but it was back in the room. I forgot to put it on before I went out. I'm always forgetting my watch," Julie explained. She felt trapped by the oppressive atmosphere in the room, but when she attempted a smile to lighten the mood she received only blank stares in response.

"What did you do then?"

"I went up to my room and showered and changed clothes. At seven-thirty I went down to the lobby and waited for a friend who was meeting me for dinner."

Captain Lonergan seemed almost to leap across the room as he said, "Jon?"

"I'm tired of telling you I don't know anyone by that name. The person I had dinner with is named Marge Kelly. She's an old friend from college who lives in Japan now. My lawyer can give you her address, and you can check with her."

"Don't worry, we will," the captain said shortly, and his dark gaze seemed to cut right through her. "And you wore your uniform to meet her?"

Julie glanced at him. "Why yes. How did you know? The only dress I brought with me got wrinkled, so I decided just to wear my uniform."

"What time did Marge leave?" Anita asked.

"Around midnight, I think. We talked in my room after dinner."

"Where did you go then?"

"To bed," Julie said. "I had an early flight the next morning."

"Did you go to bed at the Imperial?"

"Where else would I go?"

"Well," Anita said, "perhaps you went out to meet Jon, at his hotel."

"This is ridiculous," Julie almost shouted. "I don't know any Jon, I've never known a Jon, and I certainly didn't sneak out of my hotel at midnight to rendezvous with him somewhere in Tokyo."

"That's interesting you used the word sneak," Anita murmured softly. "I didn't suggest that you were sneaking around. Why use that word?"

Julie looked at her helplessly. "I don't know anyone named Jon," she repeated at length. "I went to bed, alone, at midnight. I got up the next morning, alone, and I went to the airport with the rest of the flight crew. I bought some scarves and almost missed my plane, and then I landed here in Honolulu and you arrested me."

"Yes, the scarves." Anita looked at her speculatively. "After shopping for a whole afternoon and buying nothing you suddenly risked missing your plane for some scarves."

"The sign said they were on sale for half price," Julie said defensively. "I'm what's known as an impulse shopper. That reminds me. Where *are* my scarves? You'd better make sure I get them back."

Anita ignored her, looking down at the table while Captain Lonergan made two complete trips around the room pacing nervously. "Do you like paisley, Miss Smith?" Anita asked finally.

"Paisley? Oh, you mean the paisley scarf I bought at the airport."

"I mean the paisley scarf you had in your possession at the time of your arrest," Anita said carefully. "I don't know where you bought it."

"I bought it at the airport," Julie said dryly, " and I have the receipt to prove it. Do you think that I've somehow hidden this computer disk in that paisley scarf?"

Captain Lonergan turned sharply and, despite Anita's protests, leaned toward Julie menacingly. "Yes, let's talk about the disk now, Ms. Smith. Where is it? What have you done with it?"

"Nothing."

"Nothing?" Captain Lonergan's eyes leaped with an inner fire. "If you haven't done anything with it, then why wasn't it in your possession when you landed?"

"The answer to that is quite simple," Julie said. "I don't have it. I never have had it. I don't even know what you are talking about. If you think I've stolen this disk you must have some sort of evidence. If you don't, you have to let me go."

Anita and the captain both looked at her for a long time, but Julie sat composedly under their scrutiny.

"We'll find that disk, Miss Smith," Anita said at last. "If you had anything to do with stealing it, you'll spend the rest of your life behind bars."

Chapter Four

Greg Stafford turned away with a frown from the one-way window that revealed the room where Julie Smith was being questioned. He met the gazes of the other two men who had watched the interview with him. They had arrived separately only minutes earlier, and this was their first chance to discuss the case in person.

"I'll grant you she's convincing." The man who made the statement was older than Greg by about ten years, a tall, thin, curiously nondescript man whose nonchalant demeanor could be deceptive. His gravelly voice, the result of years of heavy smoking, imparted a wealth of hidden meaning to the simple question. "Still certain she's the one you followed?"

"I think she's the courier." The third occupant of the room spoke. He was younger than Greg, only recently out of college, new to this game. His eagerness was revealed by every word he spoke, every expression that passed across his face.

"I don't see how I could have made a mistake," Greg said tersely. His tone implied he wished he had. Most of his career he had relied on a nearly infallible internal sensing process that always told him when he could trust his instincts.

Only once had his instincts been wrong. While investigating his first case, he had been duped by a female double agent. The incident had badly shaken his professional confidence, but more than that, it had affected him personally. He had trusted the woman, and he had grown to care for her with a feeling he supposed was love. It had devastated him to find he had been so wrong, but he had learned from the experience. Now he was seldom fooled by anyone.

Usually he could tell by a simple gut reaction whether someone was guilty or not, but Julie was different. She seemed so open and innocent and honest. Yet he was the one who had personally compiled the evidence against her. As far as he could tell, she had to be the one they were looking for.

Still, he hesitated. He turned again to the window and watched as a matron arrived to lead Julie from the other room. Her blond hair swung softly against her shoulders, tangled and slightly wavy, but still shining with health and youth. The shapeless garment provided by the jail failed to hide her lithe figure and energetic walk. His eyes softened as he noted the dejected slope of her shoulders this morning.

He knew instinctively that she was thinking of him at this moment. She was depending on him to get her out of here. How ironic, when he was the man most responsible for her being here in the first place. He hated deceiving her. It wasn't his style. At least he'd been honest with her about being an attorney. He didn't actually practice law now, but he had once had a partnership with his brother in Los Angeles until the lure of adventure and a strong sense of patriotism had led him into his present line of work.

He could avoid the discussion no longer. Turning to the other two men, he said, "Let's consider the facts as we know them. Why don't you give us a rundown, Keith?"

Keith Parker, a stocky blond man of medium build who had come to this work with a degree in criminal justice from a Texas university, was ready to speak. "Julie Smith," he said, glancing down at a sheaf of papers in his hands. "Age: twenty-nine. Flight attendant for World Airlines. No known political affiliations. No long-term lovers, although she dates frequently and seems to have many friends. She takes evening classes in business administration and is currently studying languages with several private tutors."

"Sounds like the type of woman Derickson would find useful," the older man said. In his forties now, Walt Osborn was in charge of this operation. After Greg's disastrous first case, the agency had assigned Walt to be his partner.

Their first case together, breaking a theft ring responsible for stealing spare parts from a sensitive military-weapons system and selling them to a third world country, had netted them both a promotion. There had been many successful cases since then, earning them the respect of their fellow agents in this, the most secret and highly effective defensive intelligence organization.

They were civilians, both of them. Walt had at one time been an officer in the navy, but Greg had come to this work after obtaining a degree in criminal law. Perhaps the difference strengthened their partnership, giving it balance.

"This girl—this Julie Smith," Walt continued. "Do you think she might lead us to Derickson?"

"Our Tokyo connection really flubbed when he lost him," Keith agreed.

"He's a wily enemy." Walt's expression was sober. "Wanted in at least five countries for espionage. He's a spy at large. Since he's a master of disguise, he's especially difficult to track. He's an American, born in California, but he has no loyalties to this country or to any other. He is constantly searching out secret or sensitive information, which he sells to the highest bidder."

"This time he must not succeed." Keith leaned forward, eyeing each man intently as he spoke. He was eager to make their partnership a trio, a fact that both amused and touched Greg and Walt.

"Right. That computer disk contains the complete details of a meeting planned by our chief of staff with a newly emerging Asian power. If word of that meeting leaks out to the world press prematurely, the other country will back out. We'll miss a crucial opportunity to stabilize international relations in that part of the world."

"Any idea who is planning to buy the disk from Derickson?"

"Nothing definite. Our guess is an Eastern Bloc country. They'd pay a lot to sabotage our negotiations. If our chief of staff successfully conducts this meeting, it could tip the whole Far Eastern balance of power in our favor."

"Wonder why Derickson stole the disk itself? Why not just sell the information?"

"From the reports I've seen, it appears he had plenty of time to take whatever he wanted," Walt explained. "Security was lax. The navy is conducting a real shakedown aboard that ship. Apparently Derickson was aided by his cousin, a young sailor who worked in the ship's communications center. Derickson had been paying the boy for information since he went aboard. When the Pentagon alerted the ship, for routine security purposes, about the chief of staff's visit, the boy tipped off Derickson. All classified information aboard the ship was stored on disks, and since the sailor had top-security clearance, he had full access to all the facts."

"You'd think he would have been able to give Derickson all the information he needed without actually taking the disk."

Walt shrugged and stuck his hands in his pockets, pacing a few feet. "Apparently Derickson wanted to see for himself. Maybe he didn't trust the boy to get the facts straight. Besides, having the disk as proof makes it easier for the buyer to feed the story to the press."

"That's right," Keith agreed. "Lucky for us we found out about it before it's too late."

"It was a simple enough matter for the sailor to get Derickson aboard while the ship was in port. Derickson walked off the ship with the disk. We wouldn't have known who had it, except the cousin got scared and confessed when it was reported missing. It was either that or face a court-martial. He led us to the Masuda Inn and told us Derickson had planned to meet his girlfriend there."

"That's the inn where Greg picked up Miss Smith's trail?" Keith asked.

"The same." Walt faced the others. "So there we have the situation. The disk is gone, stolen by Derickson and known to have been in his possession when he checked into the Masuda Inn on Thursday night."

Greg had remained silent throughout the interchange. He didn't need a review of the facts. He had sorted them endlessly throughout a long and sleepless night. "Derickson's usual pattern is to use couriers to deliver the merchandise. That way, he keeps his own hands clean."

"And since Smith shared his room that night, it makes sense that she's the courier," Keith summarized eagerly.

"It makes perfect sense," Walt agreed, frowning and smacking his hand against a nearby desk. "Yet she didn't have it on her person when she arrived, and she denies any knowledge of its existence."

"So either Derickson still has the disk or Ms. Smith got rid of it in Tokyo." Greg paused and then added, "Assuming Ms. Smith is who we think she is."

"Right now, this woman is the key," Walt insisted. "If Derickson still has the disk, we have to find him, and right now our only lead is Smith. Even if she didn't transport the disk, she may hold the answer to his present whereabouts, perhaps even subconsciously. A phrase he let slip, a place or name mentioned when his guard was down. Such a detail would be meaningless to her, but to us it could be vital."

"And if Derickson did give the disk to Ms. Smith?"

"Then she's in this right up to her neck," Walt said grimly. "In fact, she may be playing a deadly game herself, hiding the disk and hoping to raise the price, or keeping it for Derickson while he puts pressure on his buyers to up their price."

"Our man in Tokyo is checking out Julie's story." Greg pulled a notebook out of his pocket.

"He called me this morning," Walt interrupted. "The Imperial verified part of her story. She checked in

Thursday evening with the others. The clerk at reception heard her telling them she had a headache and was going straight up to bed. Hotel records indicate she ordered room service around six. No one remembers seeing her again until the next evening. That's when she answered your summons to the information desk.''

"It's obvious Smith had every opportunity to muss up her bed, slip out to the Masuda Inn and not show up until the following evening," Keith interjected.

"The maid at the Imperial reports that her bed appeared to have been slept in," Walt agreed. "Yet no one actually saw Smith after six on Thursday. The clerk at the Masuda Inn tells us that a woman went up to Derickson's room around seven. She later called down to the reception desk, gave her name as Julie Smith and asked that any telephone calls for her be put through to Derickson's room."

"The timing fits perfectly," Greg mused. "A taxi could easily cover the distance between the two establishments in well under an hour."

"Did our agent check with the cab companies?" Keith was adding to his notes as they talked.

"In Tokyo?" Walt laughed grimly. "Of course he'll try, but there must be hundreds of taxis in a city that size."

"But not that many blond American women," Greg countered.

"The clerk at the Masuda says she was wearing that same raincoat and scarf when she arrived to meet Derickson. Smith speaks several languages, so she could have assumed another nationality."

Greg consulted his own notes. "This Marge Kelly agrees she had dinner with Julie on Friday evening."

"Yes," Walt agreed. "The agent who took over from you at the Imperial says they ate in the hotel dining room and then went to Smith's room. Kelly left a little after midnight, and no one else entered or left the room. The next morning Smith went to the airport with the other crew members."

"How about any of them? Could they be in on this?"

"We have people in Tokyo watching Kelly, and the police here are running checks on the flight crew. But so far we haven't turned up anything. We'll keep an eye on Smith's roommate, this Tricia Hyde."

"We haven't got much time," Keith reminded them. "The disk could be anywhere now, and Smith is our only lead. The police found nothing when they searched the plane last night."

"Since the arrest didn't turn up the disk, we'd better switch to Plan B now," Greg said slowly. "I've already set things in motion for that plan by gaining Julie's trust."

"Yes, Plan B," Walt agreed, rubbing the darkening stubble on his chin and resuming his aimless pacing. "I hate to let her go. We're taking a risk in letting her walk out. But with any luck, she'll turn to you, Greg. Your job is to keep by her warm side every second until we find Derickson."

"And I'll see that the news of her arrest and subsequent release is carefully fed to newspapers both here and in Tokyo," Keith said. "If Derickson sees that his girlfriend has been arrested, he may panic about the disk and try to contact her."

"Perhaps," murmured Greg, but he turned away so the others wouldn't see the mixture of emotions he was sure were playing across his face. He wasn't yet ready to condemn Julie. Something about this situation didn't ring true, didn't mesh properly in his own mind. Some vital piece of the puzzle was missing, but he wasn't quite able to pin it down.

Walt spoke again, and Greg realized that the older man sensed his ambivalence. "We only have a week, Greg. The meeting is scheduled for next Saturday, and every minute that passes is a minute too many for what we have at stake. Even now, the disk could be falling into the wrong hands." Unable to contain his frustration, Walt smacked one fist against a palm and gritted out his next words. "Do anything you have to do, Greg, but force her to tell us what she knows."

"Keep her away from her condo long enough for us to search the place," Keith added. "If her roommate is in on this thing, she may well have carried the disk for Smith and stashed it there."

"We'll have to be careful," Walt reminded them. "We have little enough evidence against Smith. I can't even get clearance to put a tap on their phone." He turned to Greg and put a hand on his shoulder. "Do the best you can. I know it isn't going to be easy."

"This job never is," Greg replied quietly. The discussion had increased his inner turmoil. His instincts were telling him they were on the wrong track, yet he had no alternative ideas. For now, he would simply have to follow orders.

JULIE WAITED ANXIOUSLY in her cell for Greg to appear. He had promised to visit her this morning, and she had hoped that by now she would be released. Instead, there had been that session with Massie and Lonergan. Even now, it hurt to remember the suspicion and distrust she had seen in their eyes.

As a little girl she had once been accused unfairly of stealing a neighbor child's toy. Eventually the toy had been found underneath some low bushes where its owner had carelessly dropped it. But by then the damage had been done, and it had taken days for Julie to shake the hurt and frustration that had come from being thought guilty.

She had been miserable then; but to be accused falsely of a crime—of treason, actually—and to be arrested, held in a jail cell, was incomparably worse. The tension that had been building inside her all morning was threatening to break its bounds and overwhelm her completely. She made a valiant effort to think of other, more pleasant, thoughts.

Like Greg, for instance. He was a pleasant subject. She closed her mind, savoring for a moment the memory of their shared kiss the evening before. Never before had she met a man who could communicate such strength and compassion in a single kiss. In the present circumstances, it was hardly surprising that she admired Greg's toughness and assurance. But though she knew how much she needed him, it was not a position she relished. She liked to think of herself as self-reliant, dependent on no one. She sighed. It was a difficult attitude to maintain in jail, but there must be something she could do to help herself.

There was still her one phone call, she reminded herself. But who should she call? She needed to find out what was happening to her mother, but it was doubtful the police would approve a long-distance call, and if she phoned collect her mother would wonder why. Tricia was the logical person to call. She could check on Julie's mother, and she might be able to locate Greg.

It was almost lunchtime, a fact announced by the clatter of keys and the arrival of meals on trays farther down the hall. Julie waited for one of the matrons to pass, determined to demand her right to a phone call. She was about to start banging on the bars and shouting for attention when Tricia appeared.

"Oh, Julie," Tricia moaned as she hurried down the corridor. "They've really got you locked up in a cell. How awful. I've been so worried."

"Ten minutes," the matron who had accompanied her said warningly as she allowed Tricia to move closer to the bars.

"Can't I go inside and talk to her?" Tricia demanded.

"You can talk fine right where you are. I'll be back when your time is up."

After she left, Tricia moved closer. "Julie," she half whispered. "Why are you still here? What's going on?"

Julie shrugged. "I don't know. Greg promised me he'd try to get me out of here today, but I haven't seen him yet."

"He called me last night," Tricia explained. "That's how I knew you were still being held. He didn't tell me much."

"No one has told *me* much, either. I'm worried about my mother. Did she call last night?"

"Yes, soon after I got home. I told her a little white lie and said you'd stayed in Japan for another assignment."

"Thanks, Tricia. How was she?"

"She sounded fine. The doctor said she doesn't need that surgery. I told her you'd call in a few days." Tricia glanced behind her and then turned back to Julie. "Tell me what's going on."

"All I know is that they seem to think I've stolen some sort of computer disk or something. It must be some military secret because they say I've stolen it from a navy ship."

"A navy ship?" Tricia exclaimed. "That's absurd. Why, you've never even been on a ship. In fact, you wouldn't even date that nice naval officer whose ship pulled into Pearl Harbor last spring. What could you possibly have to do with the navy?"

"Beats me," Julie said. "But they seem to think I'm a spy or something."

"A spy...? Whatever are you going to do? What can I do to help?"

"Don't worry, Tricia. Greg's going to help me. I've hired him as my attorney."

Tricia looked doubtful. "I hope he can help you. But if you need anything, Tony and I are here." Holding up the plastic sack in her hands, she added, "Look, I've brought you some makeup and underwear. Greg told me I could. I tried to bring your curling iron, but the matron wouldn't let me. I guess she thought you'd try to break out of jail with it."

"Thanks, Tricia. You're a great ally."

"Would you believe I had to be searched to come in here?" Tricia complained. "And they opened all the makeup and looked at everything."

"They have to, I guess," Julie said wearily. "I can certainly see why people would be willing to do almost anything to get out of jail. I've had it already and I've only been here a few hours."

Footsteps sounded in the corridor, mingling with the clattering of trays and silverware as the other inmates settled down to their lunches. "Time's up," the matron called, and Tricia shot an angry glance in her direction before turning back to Julie.

"Maybe you'll be home by tonight," she said hopefully.

"That's a promise." Julie forced a confident smile.

After Tricia left, the matron brought Julie a lunch tray, but she pushed it away. The knowledge that another mealtime had come and gone without her release had ruined her appetite.

Even without her watch, she realized that time was passing quickly, and her impatience to know what Greg was doing increased rapidly. When the trays had been removed and quiet once again reigned along the women's corridor, she stretched out on her own cot.

She had no way of knowing how much time had elapsed when the matron next returned to her cell. "Come with me," she ordered crisply, unlocking the door and waiting for Julie to follow.

"Where are we going?"

"Your lawyer wants to see you."

Julie's heart raced uncontrollably. So Greg hadn't forgotten her. Her fatigue fell from her like a discarded garment, and she felt vibrant with life and hope again.

He was waiting in the same room where they had talked the night before. As she entered he rose quickly from the table where he had been writing something and held out his hands to her.

She grasped them eagerly, sensing that he had good news for her. His grip was warm and enveloping, reassuring and intense. For a long moment she concentrated on his hands, enjoying the contact, the rough, masculine texture of his skin, the firm pressure of his fingers against hers. For someone who probably worked in an office all day, his grip was amazingly strong. But then his broad muscular shoulders and athletic build had already told her he was a man who kept himself physically fit.

"Hello, Julie," he said warmly, and his mouth widened in a smile that did strange things to her pulse rate.

"I'd almost given up on you." She softened her comment with a smile.

"Would you forgive me for taking so long if I tell you that you're free to go home now?"

"Fantastic!" Julie said, tightening her grip on his hands and then releasing them abruptly when she realized what she was doing. "You mean I'm actually free now?"

"Yes, you've been released. You can leave here within the hour," Greg said as he pulled out a chair for her. "Of course, you'll have to observe the formalities. You'll need to sign some forms, and then your belongings will be returned to you and you can dress in your own clothes again."

"That's the best news I've ever had." Julie's body went limp with relief and she sagged into her chair, feeling faint now that she was almost free. "However did you manage it?"

Greg looked down at the notebook before him on the table and appeared to be concentrating on it carefully. "Actually, I didn't have much to do with it, Julie. They realized they don't have enough evidence to hold you, and so they're going to let you go."

"As simple as that?"

"Basically, yes."

Julie sat silently while Greg doodled idly with a pen on the paper in front of him. Her relief was rapidly changing to anger. Anger over the way her rights had been violated over the previous twenty-four hours. Anger at the waste of her time and the humiliation she had been forced to endure. "You mean that's it? After holding me, robbing me of my rights as a citizen and stripping the very clothes from my back, they're just going to wave me out of here and act like nothing happened?"

Greg looked up at her, his gaze narrowing in surprise as he noted her taut and angry face. "It happens, Julie. They thought you had committed a crime, and they thought they had some evidence against you. They just didn't have enough evidence, apparently."

"What evidence are you talking about?"

Greg was silent at first, as if considering his answer. He spoke at length. "The person who is believed to have the computer disk was wearing a beige raincoat and a paisley scarf. You had both in your possession when you landed."

"That's it?" Julie said incredulously. "They based their whole case on a raincoat and a silk scarf?"

"I'm sure there was more to it than that, but it's not important. What is important is that you're free to go home now."

"I think it's important." Julie stuck her chin out stubbornly. "I think it's pretty damn important, and I think they owe me an apology."

Greg's head shot up and he eyed her with apparent new interest. His gaze assessed her sharply, and his eyes darkened to that steely gray she was growing to know meant he was thinking hard about something. "Most people in your predicament would be eager to get the hell out of here."

"Of course I want to get out of here. That doesn't mean I'm going to pretend this didn't happen. You're my lawyer now, aren't you? I expect you to do something about this. Make sure we raise a big enough fuss that they think twice before arresting some other innocent person.''

''Quite the crusader, aren't you?'' Greg murmured. ''This is a new side of you. I hadn't realized . . .''

''There's a lot you don't know about me, Greg,'' Julie pointed out reasonably. ''After all, we've only just met.''

Greg's gaze darkened and he looked troubled, as though haunted by some deep inner fear. ''You're right. I don't know much about you.''

AN HOUR LATER, Julie was again a member of the human race, a citizen with the right to come and go as she pleased, a person entitled to privacy and freedom. Her beige uniform was slightly wrinkled, but it looked good to her. She smoothed it carefully over her hips and then attempted to bring some order to her tangled hair.

With makeup neatly applied and wearing her own clothes again, her confidence returned, and she felt more and more sure of herself with each moment that passed. Before she left, she intended to have a word with that Captain Lonergan. He was in charge of her case, after all, and he owed her an explanation. No one should be allowed to get away with arresting and accusing a person on such flimsy evidence.

Her purse was returned to her, along with its contents, and she signed the chits with angry, stabbing strokes of the pen. Moments later, she repeated the same procedure for her flight tote. But when she opened the tote, the scarves weren't inside.

Now she had the perfect excuse for seeking out Captain Lonergan. The matron seemed surprised when she asked for the location of his office, but she gave the directions politely. Once more a part of the respectable portion of society, Julie relished the heady exhilaration of being treated with respect, as if her feelings and opinions counted with someone.

Anita Massie was seated in Captain Lonergan's office when Julie knocked on the frame of the open doorway. "Come in," the captain called, and when Julie entered both of them looked up and smiled politely.

"I've come for my scarves," Julie said without preamble. "I told you I wasn't leaving here without them and I meant it."

Captain Lonergan's smile faded somewhat, but Julie had to hand it to him; the man's self-control was impressive. "Certainly. No problem. Would you like some coffee?"

"No coffee. Just the scarves."

The captain picked up his phone and spoke into it briefly in low tones. It sounded as if he was arguing with someone, but when Julie looked at him inquiringly, he smiled back soothingly. "They'll be here in a moment," he stated after replacing the receiver.

It was quiet in the office; only the muffled sounds of a typewriter being worked hard somewhere outside the room broke the silence. Neither Denis nor Anita seemed inclined to meet her eyes so Julie waited with as much composure as she could muster.

A few minutes later, the scarves were brought in by a young man who eyed Julie curiously before leaving the room. "Here you are." Captain Lonergan passed the scarves to her.

"Are you going home now?" Anita asked.

"Yes," Julie answered firmly. "After twenty-four hours of being locked up like a common criminal, I'm looking forward to getting home—where I should have been all along."

"You sound angry."

"You're damn right, I'm angry," Julie exploded. "Wouldn't you be angry if you'd been arrested unfairly?"

"Are you sure the arrest was unfair?"

"What do you mean? You're letting me go home now, aren't you?"

"We're releasing you because we don't have enough evidence to hold you."

Julie regarded them steadily, her head beginning to pound. "You still think I'm guilty, don't you?"

"I don't know if you're guilty or not." Captain Lonergan spoke with what seemed like surprising fairness for him. "It's not my place to make that judgment. That's for a court to decide. But I do know a lot of circumstantial evidence points toward your being involved in this thing somehow, and if I find any new evidence I'll book you back in here so fast it will make your head spin."

"Is that a threat?" Julie asked hollowly.

"No," Anita answered. "I think Denis is simply being honest with you."

Julie fingered the scarves in her lap. She had thought this whole episode was behind her, but now she wasn't so sure. "Does this mean you'll be actively looking for evidence against me? If so, perhaps I can save you some time by telling you there isn't any. I'm innocent of these charges."

"So you say." The captain pinned her with a sharp glance. "I'm not convinced. I think we'll be seeing you again soon."

Julie rose from her chair with dignity. At the door, she paused and turned, looking first at Anita and then at Captain Lonergan. "It may be rude to say this, but I hope I never see either of you again."

GREG WAS WAITING FOR HER outside the police station. Julie paused, blinking in the glare of the brilliant Hawaiian sun. A warm breeze touched her skin, the familiar trade wind, and she soaked up the warmth of the breeze and the sun, savoring the taste of freedom.

"I thought I'd drive you home," Greg offered, and his hand grasped her elbow gently, guiding her toward a shiny, late-model gray Mercedes parked at the curb.

Julie was momentarily thrown off balance. She had pictured Greg as the public-defender type of attorney, someone more interested in helping people than in amassing a fortune. "Where did you get this car?" she asked as he held the door open.

"It's a rental."

Julie slid into the seat and waited as Greg came around and got in the other side. "Where's your car, Julie? Is it parked at the airport?"

"No, I left it at home this time. I usually grab a taxi from the airport rather than leave my car in the airport parking lot. Sometimes I ride with Tricia and her fiancé."

"Tony?" Greg asked, maneuvering the car smoothly out into the traffic heading for Kalakaua Avenue.

"Have you met him?"

"No, but we talked briefly on the phone last night when I called Tricia. A doctor, he said." Greg drove with one hand on the wheel, sliding on a pair of sunglasses with the other. Julie didn't like the sunglasses. They concealed his eyes, and she had already learned that the best way to read Greg's moods was to observe his eyes.

He glanced in her direction. "This sun must be bothering you. Why don't you put on your sunglasses?"

"I lost the last pair I had weeks ago. Anyway, I seldom wear sunglasses."

"Really? With this sun?" Greg was oddly insistent, and his tone irritated Julie.

"I'm used to it. Does it matter?"

"Even if your eyes don't feel especially sensitive to light, those rays can be damaging."

A little surprised by his concern, Julie didn't reply.

Kalakaua Avenue was crowded with tourists and shoppers. Julie looked out the window as Greg concentrated on edging past a steady stream of hand-carried surfboards, tourists wobbling unsteadily on rented roller skates and the ever-present bicycle-drawn pedicabs.

The beach of Waikiki, much of it hidden beyond shops and hotels, lay to their left. Still some distance ahead, the crowded business section gave way to the quiet suburbs beyond Pearl Harbor, where her condominium was located. "Where to?" Greg asked.

She gave a rapid series of directions and then smiled. "I'll repeat them when you need to know."

Soon they were on the other side of Honolulu, where the busy traffic gave way to quiet streets shaded by clusters of palm trees. As they came to a row of small roadside juice stands, Greg pulled over abruptly beside one. Turning toward her with a smile, he said, "I'm succumbing to temptation. How about something to drink?"

A teenage girl was manning the stand. She busied herself filling two tall, frosty glasses with fresh pineapple juice while Julie and Greg wandered over to where pineapples and other fruit in stacked boxes waited on one side. Greg thumped a couple of pineapples. "I've always wondered how you tell when these things are ripe."

"It's quite easy." Choosing a succulent-looking, golden fruit, Julie demonstrated. "See, a ripe pineapple will feel like the inside of your wrist when thumped with a finger."

He reached for her hand and ran a finger over her soft wrist. "Hmm, just right."

She pulled back, laughing, and he slipped off his sunglasses and perched them on her nose. They were too large, and she peered over them, surprised to find him studying her intently. A bird swooped overhead, casting a shadow over her, and her happiness faded as quickly as the sun. "I think that juice is ready." She handed the shades back to him with a puzzled frown.

They stood beneath a tall palm tree. A breeze gently rustled its lengthy fronds as they sipped the refreshing juice. "I'd like to thank you for your help, Greg. If you send me a bill for your services, I promise I'll pay it as soon as I can."

Greg brushed aside her offer. "I really didn't do anything. Anyway, I'm on vacation, so it didn't count."

"I don't like being in your debt," Julie insisted.

Greg considered her words for a moment. "I had planned to ask you to have dinner with me tonight, but perhaps you'll refuse if you're afraid of being in my debt."

"I'll take you up on that invitation if you'll let it be my treat," Julie said lightly. "After all, you're a visitor to these islands. As a 'malihini,' you're entitled to a warm aloha greeting.''

"I know what aloha means, but what is a malihini?"

"A newcomer or stranger," Julie explained. "It's an affectionate term we islanders use for those visitors we want to know better."

"I like that. As for dinner tonight, the answer is definitely yes."

TRICIA OPENED THE DOOR when she heard the elevator. "Julie, you're home," she exclaimed, her smooth face lit by a welcoming and relieved smile.

Julie entered the small foyer, pausing to slip off her shoes and slide her feet into her zoris, a pair of one-thong Japanese slippers. It was a custom here in the islands and one Tricia insisted on observing, since it suited her fetish for neatness.

As Greg paused uncertainly in the doorway, Tricia hurried to hand him one of the spare pairs they kept on hand for visitors. He bent over awkwardly, removing his shoes and sliding his feet into the slippers as Julie watched with a smile.

"Welcome to my home," she said.

Greg looked around the living room as they entered, his glance appreciative as he observed the tasteful rattan furnishings and cool, pastel colors that gave the room an atmosphere of quiet restfulness. The condominium was small, just one living area, an efficiency kitchen and small dining alcove, and two compact bedrooms. Yet its high ceilings and wide balconies were obvious luxuries. Julie was proud of her home, despite the drain it had been on her finances when she first purchased it.

Through the floor-to-ceiling windows along one wall of the room was a marvelous view of the ocean, made even more spectacular by the fact that they were located on the fourteenth floor. "Your home is lovely," Greg murmured, and Tricia beamed and offered him a choice of coffee or drinks.

"Nothing, thanks." Greg stood in the middle of the room, studying its contents as if he were appraising it for tax purposes.

Julie stared at him, noting that his eyes lingered on a tall rattan étagère that Julie had converted into a bookcase. Greg turned abruptly and caught her watching him. He smiled apologetically. "Am I seeing things or are those books really arranged in alphabetical order?"

"By author," Tricia said proudly. "I debated whether to line them up by height or colors but decided it would be more appropriate to use a logical method."

Julie couldn't help laughing at Greg's expression. "You should hear her fuss at me when I dare to put one in the wrong slot."

Tricia flushed. "Now, Julie. I'm only trying to keep us organized." She turned to Greg. "We're so busy that we can't afford the luxury of being untidy. But please, have a seat and tell me how you convinced the police Julie isn't a criminal."

"I'd love to but I have to get back to my hotel now. I'm expecting a call." He looked at Julie. "Shall I pick you up around eight-thirty?"

"Fine." She followed him back to the door. "You didn't really have to take off your shoes," she whispered.

"And risk offending Tricia?" He changed back into his own loafers. "I told you, the woman intimidates me. Books in the home in alphabetical order?"

"I appreciate her," Julie defended staunchly. As Greg headed for the door she moved to open it. "Where are you staying?"

"At the Hilton."

"Will you be able to find your way back here, or do you want me to draw a map?"

"No need. I'll remember."

"I'll see you tonight then, Greg. And thanks again."

"Until tonight," he said, taking her hand lightly and holding it for a long moment before reluctantly releasing it.

His gaze was warm, smoky gray and full of promise. Julie felt her heart skip a beat, and as Greg turned away and walked to the elevator, she gazed after him thoughtfully. Now that she was out of jail, perhaps it was possible the initial spark of attraction between them would catch fire. Even as the doors slid quietly closed behind him, she felt her pulses leap with anticipation. Until tonight, then.

Chapter Five

Dusk was darkening the sky when Julie opened the double, French doors that led to a small balcony off her bedroom. Behind her, the room was in its usual state of casual disarray, a handful of silky underwear spilling from a half-open bureau drawer, a thick lilac chenille robe slung across the wicker chaise lounge in the corner, a stack of unopened mail spread out on the bedside table awaiting her attention.

When Tricia complained occasionally about the state of her room, Julie was always quick to point out that it wasn't dirty, only disordered. There was a big difference, and Tricia had learned to accept that Julie was only comfortable when surrounded by the haphazard clutter of her own belongings. Too many nights in sterile hotel rooms had instilled in Julie a strong appreciation for the freedom to spread herself a bit in her own home.

Nothing about the disorder of the room behind her showed in her own personal appearance. She had dressed with unusual care, lingering for more than an hour in a tub of scented bubbles, scrubbing with perfumed soap until every trace of her night in jail was washed away. After thorough conditioning and a session with her blow-dryer, her hair was restored to its usual shining blond curves, barely skimming her shoulders with graceful elegance.

Since Greg was her lawyer, she told herself, it was important to impress him with her professional poise and self-confidence. After lengthy deliberations in front of her closet, she finally settled on a deceptively simple, straight-cut silk chemise in a rich jade green that lightened her hair to silvery-blond and lent a soft glow to her complexion.

Beneath the dress she wore only a silk camisole that left her soft breasts unconfined and lace-trimmed tap pants covering the sheerest of pantyhose. Lingering thoughtfully over her jewelry, she chose a tiny pair of pearl earrings and a matching pearl ring.

The view from the lanai was wonderful. To the east were green mountains and below was the restless sea with its gentle combers that broke on the fringe of white beach. The sky had a pinkish tinge, glowing with the last fiery light of the sun as it slid over the horizon. Above her, a set of wind chimes whispered softly in the evening breeze.

She was looking forward to her evening with Greg, but in her mind it was a social occasion. During her long bath she had come to the conclusion that she couldn't impose on Greg any further. If she needed more legal advice, she must find a lawyer here in Honolulu. To that end, she had investigated the telephone book, only to find that Honolulu boasted more than ten pages of lawyers. How on earth did she choose from such a vast array?

She sighed, breathing deeply and inhaling the scent of her neighbor's blossom-filled trellis. As night fell, a tapestry of colorful lights appeared on the horizon, strung out along the coast. The warm trade winds increased their gentle assault from the northeast, and behind the city the Koolau range of mountains took on a purple cast as the shadows deepened.

Greg would soon be arriving. She returned to her room and picked up the phone, punching out the number for her mother's home in Los Angeles. Time for a quick call to see what the doctor had said.

It was picked up on the second ring. "Mom, it's me, Julie."

"Hi, darling. Are you calling from Tokyo? Isn't that frightfully expensive?"

"I returned home earlier than Tricia expected. How are you?"

"Fine," her mother said cheerfully. "Rose and I were just talking about you. Now that I don't need the surgery, we want to plan a trip to Hawaii soon."

"I don't believe it. How soon? Tricia told me the doctor had good news."

"The best. A little medicine and I should be better than ever. The doctor did warn me to take it easy and not get myself worked up about anything, but I told him I had a carefree life these days."

Any thoughts Julie might have entertained about confiding in her mother disappeared immediately. Not for anything would she worry the older woman with news of her arrest. Anyway, by the time her mother's visit could be arranged, the whole thing would probably have blown over.

They chatted for a few moments longer, her mother sounding happy and relaxed. As Julie carefully replaced the receiver, she experienced a pang of anxiety. What if her mother somehow found out she had been arrested? Surely only the local news was carrying the story.

Greg arrived promptly at eight-thirty, and Julie was waiting for him. Tricia was in her room talking on the phone to Tony, so Julie answered the door herself.

Greg was startlingly handsome—freshly shaved, his broad shoulders encased in a dark dinner jacket, his thick hair brushed back casually. In his hands he carried a shiny florist's box.

Julie stood aside and he entered the foyer. "How lovely you look." His eyes paid a silent tribute of their own as he surveyed her from head to toe. Setting the box on a narrow table behind him, he opened it and deftly drew out a circle of lush white blossoms. Holding them up, he waited for her to incline her head toward him before slipping them on.

"These reminded me of you."

The scent of plumeria filled her nostrils. His hands brushed gently against her breasts as he adjusted the lei, and her heart began beating with long, slow thuds. Greg looked down at her and then suddenly his hands were cupping her face, tilting her chin upward. His face was very close, and she stood helplessly as his lips brushed hers in a light, butterfly kiss. "Aloha," he murmured and then, releasing her, he stepped back quickly.

Julie fingered the velvety blossoms, their petals cool on her heated skin. "Thank you. They're perfect. But I should have given them to you. You're the newcomer." The words seemed inadequate for such a touching gesture. Greg was a surprising man, and his unexpected gift left her off balance.

"Tricia out?" he asked as they descended in the elevator.

"No, she's staying home tonight." Jake, the night watchman, was in the lobby, and he grinned at them approvingly as they crossed to the imposing front entrance.

"Tight security?" Greg inquired.

"Not really. We can't afford around-the-clock help here, so our homeowners' association voted to hire a night watchman only. But we've never had any trouble. We keep an eye out for each other. Jake lives here in the building, so even when he's not on duty we can call on him if there's an emergency."

In the car, Julie said, "I made reservations at a restaurant that specializes in Hawaiian cuisine. I thought you'd like that."

"I would. Just tell me how to get there."

The restaurant was situated above Honolulu, with a spectacular view of the curve of Waikiki and Diamond Head. Indoor fountains murmured quietly into small ponds, and a variety of orchids and an array of potted Chinese palms enticed the eye. Once seated in high-backed wicker chairs, they were enclosed in a world of their own, effectively screened from the nearby diners.

"This is nice," Greg approved, his dark-suited arm with its snowy-white cuff and distinctive gold cuff links resting quite near her own slender arm on the table. "Why don't I let you order for both of us?"

"Fine." The drinks waiter appeared and Julie suggested *mai-tais*, the house specialty. When the dinner waiter arrived, she ordered grilled skewers of rumaki for starters, to be followed by fresh pineapple, grilled mahimahi and hearts-of-palm salad.

They sipped their drinks until the rumaki, sizzling chunks of chicken livers, water chestnuts and bacon, arrived. Greg selected a skewer of rumaki and ate it ap-

preciatively. "I could really get used to life in Hawaii,"
he commented. "The food alone is worth the visit, not
to mention the spectacular scenery."

"And the beaches and the weather and all the other
nice things," Julie added with a light laugh. "It does
tend to have that effect on people. I knew the first time
I visited here that I would have to return to make my
home."

Greg seemed curiously intrigued by her comment. His
eyes narrowed as he scrutinized her with special care.
"Is that why you chose your work with the airline?"

"Not really. I think I mentioned to you before that I
love travel and some day would like to run my own
agency. Unfortunately, starting my own travel business
would be risky and expensive. This job is sort of a
compromise—and it's good preparation for what I
eventually hope to do."

Greg leaned back in his chair, grasping his drink and
eyeing her over the rim of his glass. The shaded lamp in
the center of their table cast his face into shadow, making it difficult for her to read his expression. "You
weren't very friendly on the plane," he said, changing
the subject abruptly.

Julie felt her skin flush a bright red. It was true, but
what reason could she give Greg for her aloof manner?
She had an idea he wouldn't be pleased to hear she had
pegged him as a man on the make.

"When I'm on the plane," she said at length, "I'm
supposed to maintain a professional manner. I can't be
overly friendly with any one passenger."

"I see," he murmured, and she was afraid that he saw
far more than she intended. The arrival of the waiter
was a timely interruption. As clear glass bowls of mint-

garnished pineapple chunks were set in front of them, Julie managed to avoid meeting Greg's gaze.

"You mentioned you were working on some business for a client in Tokyo?" If he could change the subject, so could she.

"My client has business interests in Japan," Greg explained.

"I can certainly attest to your expertise as an attorney. It must have taken some doing to get me out of jail so quickly. After my interrogation by Captain Lonergan, I wasn't certain I'd breathe free air again."

"All in the line of duty," Greg said quietly. He regarded her steadily, his eyes growing serious and dark. That gaze of his seemed to see so much, Julie realized. As a lawyer Greg had probably learned to sum people up quickly, making instant decisions about character and honesty. His eyes were uncannily observant, and she was certain it would be difficult to fool him or hide one's feelings from him.

When their main course arrived, Greg surveyed the sizzling platter of grilled mahimahi with satisfaction. The fish was prepared to perfection, flaking easily and tasting of fresh lemon and a delicate blend of spices.

Greg ate his meal with relish. He had the wonderful ability to concentrate on and savor even the smallest pleasures of life. Julie admired that. So many people diluted their enjoyment of life by living in the past or anticipating the future. Julie preferred to focus on the present, an attitude that meant she knew how to play and work with equal intensity.

"I've answered all your questions," she said as fragrant cups of steaming Kona coffee were set beside them. "Now it's your turn to be on the witness stand."

"What would you like to know?"

"Why did you become a lawyer?"

Amusement gleamed briefly in Greg's eyes. "I never really had a choice." As Julie lifted her eyebrows, he continued, "Oh, I may look like a man of decision, but my father is a brick wall. He was a lawyer, and so was his father, and his father before him. Glen, my brother, and I never considered any other profession."

"What if you hadn't liked the work?" Julie grinned. "I can't see you doing a job you didn't like just to please someone."

"You're right. Fortunately the issue didn't arise because I love the law. It's a challenging field and a great responsibility, as well. My father never lets Glen and me forget that when we're handling a case we're dealing with people's lives. If we're careless or make a mistake, we could cause others to suffer and that would be unforgivable."

"An admirable attitude," Julie said.

Greg stirred his coffee and waited a moment before replying, apparently lost in thought. At last he looked up at her, and his eyes seemed to be communicating wordlessly. "Not just an attitude, Julie. You could say that sums up the way I hope I live my life. Never causing anyone else to suffer and making sure that those who do are brought to justice swiftly and fairly."

"Now who's crusading?" Julie couldn't resist teasing him, he seemed so serious. Most men she met were afraid to be serious, choosing instead to fill their conversation with intellectual-sounding trivia or trendy chatter in an attempt to impress her. She had never met a man who seemed as comfortable with serious topics as Greg. His intensity almost frightened her. He had an uncanny ability to get right to the heart of an issue and an unshakable determination to uncover the truth. She was suddenly grateful she had no secrets to hide from him, no dark corners of her life he would feel compelled to unearth.

"Now that I'm safely out of jail," she said quickly, "what do you plan to do with the rest of your vacation in Hawaii? You've already got a good suntan, so are you perhaps a weekend sailor or a surfer?"

"No surfing," Greg said, slanting a relaxed smile at her. "I do sail occasionally, though." Taking a quick swallow of his coffee, he added, "But I thought you still had some work for me. You mentioned this afternoon that you wanted to make a point with the police department."

Julie frowned. "Yes, but I've realized I can't impose on you any further. You came to my rescue very gallantly, but you deserve to enjoy the rest of your vacation in peace."

"I do appreciate your concern," he said gently. "Since I'm now free to do as I please, would you be interested to find that it would please me very much to spend my time with you? I realize you may have other plans, but I'd like to see more of you."

Julie was inwardly delighted, but she managed to school her expression into a semblance of casual interest. "That sounds nice." She hesitated, not knowing quite how to put her thoughts across to him. "Look, Greg, I don't want you to feel responsible for me. You've been extremely helpful and kind, but I assure you I can handle things on my own now. If I need the services of a lawyer, I'll find one locally."

For a second Greg's eyes flashed angrily; but his reply, when it came, was even and detached. "I'm sorry if I failed you in some way."

"That's not what I meant." Exasperation sharpened her tone. "I want to make it clear you mustn't feel you have to help me. You're here for a vacation, and I'd hate to feel I kept you from it."

"Then where's the problem?" Greg's mouth relaxed into a smile again. "Promise me you'll spend some time with me, and I promise I'll let you know any time I feel you're cadging free legal advice."

Julie hesitated, measuring his mood, trying to gauge the emotion she saw in his eyes. "Okay, but I'll probably drive you crazy; I have to admit the whole thing is still weighing heavily on my mind."

"In what way?"

"I'd like to know more about why I was arrested, and I'd like to make sure it doesn't happen again."

Greg reached across the table, capturing one of her hands in his own firm grasp and holding her gaze captive, as well. "Why don't we spend the day together tomorrow? We can talk over what happened. If we put our heads together, maybe we can make sense out of the whole thing."

"I doubt it will ever make much sense." Julie shook her head ruefully. "It's too bizarre."

"Maybe after a night of sleep, you'll be thinking more clearly. Perhaps you'll even remember something that could help the police."

"Remember something?" Julie was confused.

"Oh, perhaps you heard or saw something that pertains to the case."

"How could that be?" Julie withdrew her hand from his, feeling an odd sense of loss as she did so. "You sound almost as if you still suspect me, Greg."

"I only meant that you might recall seeing some other woman at the Imperial on Friday evening. A woman wearing sunglasses and a beige raincoat."

"Sunglasses? That's the first I've heard of that." Julie drummed her fingers on the table. "Did you find out anything about Jon Derickson?"

"Such as?"

"Who he is. Where he's from."

"Only that he's a spy who cons women into helping him." Greg's gaze narrowed. "I have a lot of sympathy for his victims."

"I wish I could help solve the case, not only because it must be pretty important to our country but because it would clear my name. The problem is, I don't know anything, Greg."

"You're tired. Why don't we go over this again tomorrow?"

As the silence lengthened between them, the noises of the restaurant gradually seeped into Julie's awareness. Silver clattered against china, and a woman laughed nearby. Music wafted from the far corner of the room. Odd, she hadn't noticed before. "You're right," she said at last. "Tomorrow would be a better day to talk about this. Right now, I need to relax."

"How about a walk on the beach?" Greg suggested.

"Okay."

Julie settled the check—over Greg's protests. "My treat," she insisted. "Remember? It isn't polite to haggle over the dinner check, so be quiet."

They left the restaurant, going out to the parking lot at the side. Propane-fueled torches lent their soft flicker to the glowing hotel lights strung out along the coast.

In the car, Greg concentrated on his driving. "Ever wonder what these islands must have been like before the invasion of Western-style civilization?"

"Only Oahu is heavily populated." Julie gestured at the panorama of sparkling lights in front of them. "Some of the other islands are still almost completely unspoiled."

The beach at Waikiki was quiet and almost deserted. From a nearby hotel Hawaiian music drifted on the breeze. The surf murmured softly nearby, and more of the sputtering torches cast a warm, golden glow on the surging waves of the restless sea.

Julie kicked off her shoes when she stepped from the car, lifting her arms as the wind blew her dress against her body. Beside her, Greg paused to take off his shoes and roll up his trouser legs. He had removed his tie, and his white shirt was unbuttoned, making him seem more approachable, less intense.

They strolled in silence down to the water's edge, letting the warm waves lap smoothly around their ankles as they walked hand-in-hand through the surf. A nearly full moon shone through the palm trees, lighting their way. The whisper of the rolling waves was like music, and overhead palm fronds rustled gently in the breeze. The silence between them was comfortable and strangely intimate.

"Where shall we go tomorrow?" Greg asked finally.

"The beach?"

"Here?" Greg asked. "Won't it be crowded?"

It pleased her that he wanted to be alone with her. "We could drive up along the coast road to Waimanalo Park. I'll fix a picnic lunch. The drive is beautiful, and the beach is especially appealing."

"I'll take care of lunch," Greg insisted. "I'm already in debt for dinner." He paused, grasping her elbow and pulling her even with him with gentle insistence. His hand felt warm on her arm, and she noted without surprise that her pulses were pounding. She was reluctant to end the contact.

He crooked a finger under her chin to lift it. Their eyes met and held, and her breath caught in her throat as he wound his fingers through the strands of her hair and pulled her gently toward him. She waited for his kiss, closing her eyes and then opening them to find that he was looking at her. A muscle twitched along his jaw, and his fingers tightened their grasp.

"Greg?" she asked softly.

Gradually his hold on her relaxed. Julie pulled away slightly and looked at him more closely. His face was grim and set, and he appeared to be unmoved by her nearness. "Shall we walk some more?" she asked, feeling uncomfortable in the face of his silence.

He nodded, and they strolled along the damp sand. A thread of tension stretched between them. He wasn't touching her at all now, but Julie was almost painfully aware of him. She had been so sure he was going to kiss her, in fact she was positive he had intended to do so. Yet something had stopped him.

She stole another sidelong glance at him and found that he was watching her. It was unnerving to be the object of such intense scrutiny. He looked at her as though he hoped to read her thoughts.

An impish urge made her determined to make him laugh. "Are you always so serious?" She noted his embarrassment with satisfaction. So he didn't like to be caught staring. Lifting her arms to soak up the breeze, she twirled a few steps ahead of him, smiling at him over her shoulder. "I always want to act crazy when I'm around serious people. Take Tricia, for instance. At times she brings out the worst in me."

He stopped, shoving his hands in his pockets. The wind tugged gently at his shirt, whipping it slightly open to reveal a tantalizing view of firm, tanned skin. A wave washed up around his feet and splashed his trousers, and Julie laughed again. "You look much less intimidating out here." She moved closer to him.

He lifted his eyebrows. "I wasn't aware that anything intimidates you, Julie."

"You did, on the plane yesterday. You were always watching me, every time I turned around. Even Tricia noticed."

"I'm sure you're used to it." Greg took a few steps toward her, dodging the path of an advancing wave.

"And you, are you used to it?" Julie felt daring. Out here on the beach, with a cloak of velvety darkness, she could ask questions she wouldn't usually ask.

"Am I used to what?" Greg regarded her warily.

"Being stared at," she said simply. "You're quite good-looking, you know. I did a double take the moment I saw you."

She had startled him. It was obvious in the surprised widening of his eyes and the way he shifted his body. He was quiet for a moment, and then he threw back his head and laughed, a warm, mellow sound that filled the darkness around her. "You're full of surprises, Julie. I like that."

"Do you?" She considered him thoughtfully. He was barely two feet away from her now. Barefoot and windblown, he looked more at ease than she had yet seen him. She liked him this way, without his professional manner, simply a man enjoying himself.

"I think I'll surprise you again," she murmured, and then before she could reconsider, she stepped close to him and placed her fingertips lightly on his arms as if to restrain him. It was easy to slide her hands from his arms to his shoulders and then around to rest on the nape of his neck.

Lifting her face, she focused on his mouth. Slowly, delicately, she kissed him. It was a gentle kiss and yet it wasn't timid. She nibbled tantalizingly on his lower lip and then grew bolder, opening her mouth and inviting his exploration.

At first Greg didn't move. His arms stayed down by his sides, and she felt his neck muscles tense beneath her fingers. When his breathing quickened, she pressed herself closer, continuing her tender assault on his mouth.

Greg groaned deep in the back of his throat, and then his arms were around her, gathering her close, his palms dragging across her back, warm and sure through the thin silk of her dress.

She felt the need in him and the leashed hunger. Whatever thoughts he might have been holding back earlier that evening, his feelings now were honest and uncontrolled. At length she drew back, not because she wanted to but because she sensed that they had both revealed more than they intended.

"I've been wanting to do that all evening." Julie's laugh was husky, not as cool and light as she had meant it to be. "Aren't you glad I did?"

"God, Julie." Greg joined in her laughter. "I've never met anyone quite like you."

"Thanks." A glint of amusement brightened her eyes. "I like you, too."

GREG DROVE HER to her condominium without saying much. Now that they were in the car, she felt constrained, perhaps even shy. She wasn't sorry she had kissed him. Yet it was difficult to tell what Greg was feeling. He seemed to sense her tension, for as they neared her street, he smiled warmly at her.

"What time shall I pick you up tomorrow?"

Julie considered his question. "Around nine? Or is that too early?"

"Nine's okay."

Greg insisted on accompanying her to the entrance. "I always see a lady to her door. I guess that comes from living in a big city like Los Angeles."

"I never worry about being alone at night in Honolulu. Nothing much ever happens around here. At least, it didn't until my arrest." She smiled wryly.

Jake let her into the lobby, and she turned to look at Greg.

"Thank you for a very nice evening, Julie." Greg touched her hand briefly and smiled. "I'll see you in the morning."

"Good night."

Jake had called the elevator, and she arrived at her floor moments later. For once, she had her key ready.

As soon as she opened the door, Tricia came into the foyer. "Julie, come quick. I was just about to call Jake when I heard your key."

"What is it, Tricia?" Julie followed Tricia into the living room.

"I think someone is watching our apartment," Tricia whispered. She clutched her robe closer about her body. "I went out on my balcony a few minutes ago and there he was. A man, in the bushes down below." She motioned toward her bedroom. "Come on. I'll show you."

The two of them went into Tricia's room. She had left the light off, and her balcony doors were still open, the drapes whipping back in the ocean breeze. She led the way out onto the balcony and pointed. "There he is, See?"

Julie leaned against the railing and looked down. A low hedge of bushes surrounded the back terrace of the building and lined the path to the beach. For a moment she saw nothing, and then a movement made her glance back to her left. Yes, there he was.

From this height it was impossible to see much of the man. Moonlight glinted on something in his hands, something, Julie noted as she peered more closely, which might be binoculars. Tricia was right; he seemed to be looking up at her window. Yet how could she be sure from this distance? There were many other balconies on this side of the building.

"I'm going to call Jake." Tricia turned back into the bedroom, and Julie heard her pick up the phone. "He's going around to check," she called a moment later.

Julie watched intently. Seconds passed, and then Jake appeared, moving around from the right, his flashlight bobbing on the sidewalk. From her vantage point she could see a movement in the bushes, and then a dark figure detached itself stealthily from the hedge and glided around the left side of the building. "Over there, Jake," she called, waving frantically, but he was too far away to hear her.

A second person joined Jake on the sidewalk, and Julie recognized Greg. Swiftly she went into Tricia's room. "I'm going down to talk to Jake. Greg's with him."

Tricia nodded. "I'll wait here."

The elevator seemed to take forever to arrive at their floor. Downstairs, she found the lobby still empty. Peering through the glass, she saw Jake and Greg coming up the outside steps.

"Did you catch him?" she asked as they came in, directing her question at Greg.

"Who?" Greg shrugged. "We didn't see anyone."

"There was a man in the hedge. Here, I'll show you." Julie led the way back around the building and showed them the corner where the man had been hiding. "He had something in his hands. Binoculars, I think."

"What makes you think he was watching your apartment?" Greg asked Julie.

"Well, I don't know for sure. Tricia seemed to think he was watching our balcony."

"You're on the fourteenth floor, Julie," Greg pointed out reasonably. "How on earth could she tell what balcony he was watching? Look behind you."

Julie turned and glanced up at the building. Greg was right. The back of the building was lined with balconies, many of them lit up.

"Are you sure you saw something, Miss Smith?" Jake clubbed the bushes apart with the heavy stick he usually wore dangling from his belt and then shone his flashlight at the ground. "Didn't leave any telltale signs," he muttered. He straightened up. "Hope it's not some Peeping Tom. We've got a lot of beautiful women living in the complex." He grinned over at Julie.

"Probably a jealous husband gathering evidence on his wife," Greg teased.

"What a sordid thought," Julie protested lightly. "I suppose you handle a lot of divorce cases."

They walked back to the front of the building, seeing no one else outside. "I didn't expect to see you out here," Julie said to Greg. "I thought you'd left."

"He was about to drive off when I came outside," Jake broke in. "I told him we had a trouble call from your place. I thought he'd want to know, since he just brought you home."

"I'm glad I was still here." Greg grasped Julie's hand and walked closer beside her. "But I don't think there's anything to be concerned about."

"I'll keep an eye on things out here tonight," Jake promised.

Julie shivered, feeling vaguely threatened by the whole incident. Until yesterday her life had been simple, and now here she was, one night in jail already behind her and worried about being spied on from the bushes by strange men.

"Try not to fret about this, Julie," Greg said as he bid her good-night. "I'm sure it wasn't anything important."

"See you tomorrow, Greg." She attempted a smile and then watched as he strode to his car and left.

Jake came into the lobby behind her. "What's the new boyfriend's name?" he asked.

"Stafford. Greg Stafford." Julie shook off her somber mood and smiled at Jake.

"Will we be seeing a lot of him?"

"I hope so, Jake. I hope so."

GREG STOPPED AT THE FIRST PHONE BOOTH he spotted on his way home and waited impatiently until someone picked up the phone at the other end of the line. "What kind of clumsy idiots do you have on surveillance tonight?" he demanded.

Walt's voice sounded slightly sleepy. "What's up?"

"Julie just spotted a man in the bushes behind her condo spying on her with binoculars. Who's the clown? I'd like to dress him down myself."

"Bushes? Binoculars? Not our operation. We've got two men in a van down the street from the building. They're watching who goes in and out of the building. Did you get a good look at the guy in the bushes?"

"I didn't see him."

"Oh."

"Apparently Miss Hyde saw him, though."

"Or she's pretending she did." Walt sounded as if he believed the latter. "We'll keep a closer eye on the place. It could have been Derickson. That's assuming there was anyone."

"Julie doesn't seem to know anything about the disk," Greg said. "We spent the evening together, and I didn't get her to tell me anything."

"Any idea when we can search her place?"

"She'll be with me all day tomorrow, but I'm not sure about Miss Hyde. I could call Julie and see if she wants to include Tricia in our plans for a beach picnic."

Walt chuckled. "Sounds like you're getting real cozy. Call Smith now and let me know."

After Walt hung up, Greg hesitated. He didn't know what to think about Julie at this point. On the surface her story looked so straightforward that it was impossible to believe she could be involved in a crime. Yet he, of all men, should know that people were not always what they seemed.

He was torn between his personal feelings and his professional judgment. He liked Julie a lot. She was warm and funny, and he felt good just being with her. But did that count for anything? You couldn't trust your personal feelings. He had learned that lesson early in his career. Remembering that incident sobered him considerably, and he forced himself to dial Julie's number.

"Julie. Greg."

Her voice brightened. "That was a quick drive back to your hotel."

"I was wondering if Tricia and Tony would like to go with us tomorrow."

"To the beach?" She didn't hide her surprise.

"I guess I feel badly about making fun of Tricia's neatness. She's a friend of yours, a very loyal friend. Maybe with a little effort I'll feel more comfortable with her." His explanation sounded lame to his own ears.

"That's very thoughtful of you. Now I feel terrible that I didn't think to ask her. But it's too late. She and Tony are planning a visit with his sister and her family tomorrow."

His answer was quick. "All day?"

She laughed. "Definitely. They live on Kauai Island. Tricia and Tony will be flying over early and not returning until late tomorrow evening."

"Too bad. Oh, well. Maybe some other time. Good night, Julie."

Julie put down the receiver with a puzzled frown. What a strange call. Greg had sounded totally preoccupied, and Julie was certain she had heard the roar of traffic in the background. Why had he felt it so important to call her before he reached his hotel room?

Chapter Six

Clad in a pair of khaki cotton trousers and a loose cotton shirt whose sleeves were rolled up to reveal muscular, tanned forearms, Greg was leaning casually against the doorjamb when Julie answered his ring the next morning. Even as she smiled at him, her gaze took in the warm intimacy of his look, the glint of half-amused pleasure darkening his eyes.

The white shorts she was wearing revealed the smooth, tanned skin of her long legs, and her pale-pink cotton-knit top hugged her breasts with subtle emphasis. Greg's eyes expressed his approval, leaping with the fire of barely disguised masculine desire. "You look like an ad for a vacation on the beach. Something for the mainlanders to dream about all winter long."

"Pure flattery, Mr. Stafford, but I love it." She flashed a pleased smile. "Let me gather up my beach gear and I'll be ready to go."

"Pack something to change into later this afternoon." Greg's voice followed her as she crossed the living room to her bedroom. "That way we can go out to dinner."

Julie paused in her doorway and surveyed her room with a groan. Men, she thought expressively. Imagine expecting her to go from shorts to bikini to dinner dress, all out of one not-too-roomy beach bag. Not to mention the sand that would undoubtedly be coating her hair.

Nevertheless, she grabbed a red-and-white striped T-shirt dress, added a pair of flimsy red sandals and, for good measure, threw in some shampoo and a couple of bright red barrettes. She would manage somehow.

After stowing her things in the trunk of the Mercedes, Greg slid into the car beside her. "Since you're my tour guide, do you want to drive?"

"I'll give the directions. You drive."

Greg slanted a mocking smile at her before reaching for his sunglasses. "Look in that bag," he directed, pointing to a white plastic sack on the dashboard ledge.

Julie reached for it and peeked inside. "Sunglasses," she said, lifting them out of the bag. Noting that they were an expensive designer brand, she slipped them on. Although their huge size and octagonal shape were not what she would have chosen for herself, she felt warmed by his thoughtfulness.

He was watching her carefully, and she tried to sound enthusiastic. "Lovely. They block out the sun's rays but still allow me to see quite well."

"Do you like that style?"

"Perfect." She smiled at him reassuringly.

"No, I'm serious. Would you choose that shape for yourself? They seem a bit oversized to me."

Puzzled by his insistence, she chose her words carefully. "Greg, I love them because you picked them out for me. Now hadn't we better head for the beach?"

For a moment she thought he was going to say more. Then he turned toward the wheel, slipped on his own glasses and started the engine. She was aware that her answer hadn't pleased him. Yet his gift confused her. She had told him she seldom wore sunglasses, and he had indicated he thought she was foolish not to. But following it up by actually giving her a pair seemed to be carrying his concern a bit far.

He stopped the car a block later and parked in front of a neighborhood deli. "The concierge at the hotel told me this was a great place to buy picnic supplies."

"He's right. Just passing it makes my mouth water."

Julie picked out the delicately roasted chicken that was the owner's specialty, while Greg added a tortellini salad and a carton of Greek olives. Together they chose a bottle of chilled Italian white wine of Tuscan origin and ended by adding a package of orange-flavored butter cookies to their basket.

It was still well before noon when Greg headed the car in the direction of Makapu. Soon they were driving along the windward coast road, a route that climbed over ancient lava flows beside the surging Pacific. Traffic was light, and Greg easily followed Julie's simple directions.

When they reached the famous Blow Hole, Julie asked Greg to pull over to the side of the road. Against the brilliant blue-green background of the sea and trees, water was geysering through an underwater vent, arcing in a shimmering prism of mist.

Far out in the Pacific, the turquoise water gradually shaded to darker hues of blue and indigo. On the inviting beaches, gentle waves broke against white sand. Julie opened her door and got out, standing for a moment to enjoy the feel of the wind whipping through her hair and the sound of the surf crashing below. Greg joined her. His arm slid around her waist and he leaned close. "I see why you've adopted these islands as your home," he murmured in her ear.

Julie drew a deep breath and looked up at him, startled to find his face only inches from hers. For the briefest second, she relived the night before, overwhelmingly tempted to let her lips brush against his, to linger in a deepening, urgent caress. . . .

Steady, she warned herself. You're rushing things. She was powerfully attracted to Greg, yet despite her friendly and outgoing nature, she wasn't a person to rush into intimate relationships, preferring to know as much as possible about a man before making a physical commitment.

Stepping away from him, she shrugged off his arm in what she hoped was a casual manner and forced her voice to sound calm and impersonally friendly. "I was thinking how much more this beauty means to me today," she confessed. "There's nothing like a night in jail to make a person appreciate the simple pleasures in life."

"And do you?" Greg asked quietly, his voice barely audible above the surf. "Appreciate the simple things?"

"Yes, always," Julie said. "But especially now."

"I thought maybe you were the type of person who craves excitement," he said. When she turned to face him, she was taken aback by his speculative scrutiny.

"Not particularly," she said coolly after a brief pause, moving back to the car.

They drove on in silence. Julie glanced at Greg from time to time wondering what she had done to give him such an impression of her character. His comment had put a certain distance between them again.

Despite Greg's surface friendliness, she sensed his distrust. There was nothing in his manner she could pin down, no specific action on his part that told her exactly where the problem lay. Yet she knew something wasn't quite right between them.

Instinct told her that Greg was fundamentally an honest man, a man of honor and integrity, two old-fashioned virtues that nonetheless seemed natural in him. If he was suspicious of her, he must feel he had good reason to be, and that bothered her intensely. It seemed so unfair for someone as uncomplicated and aboveboard as she was to be under the shadow of suspicion.

IT WAS A PERFECT DAY for a drive along the coast. To their left were the towering Koolau Mountains, their rough slopes a dramatic contrast to the restless sea on their right. Although sunlight already glistened brightly on the cresting waves, a cool breeze promised a day of moderate temperatures.

Twenty minutes later, Greg stopped at a roadside stand. "I'd like to try some of that pineapple," he suggested, his mouth curving in a smile that emphasized the cleft in his chin. "I didn't bother with breakfast."

The fruit stand was one of many that dotted the coast road, a ramshackle building that dispensed a variety of island juices and souvenirs as well as pineapple. Sitting at a picnic table beneath a shady stand of ironwood trees, they ate fresh slices of the juicy yellow fruit.

The hard speculation had disappeared from Greg's eyes, and he was friendly once more, questioning her about her work as a flight attendant and laughing with her when she described some of her more unusual and trying passengers. Determined to learn more about him, she asked a few questions of her own, but he changed the subject abruptly. "I'm an everyday lawyer, Julie."

He shrugged his shoulders. "Nothing particularly interesting about my work."

"What about your family?"

"I have only the one brother," he replied. "We share the law practice in Los Angeles. Glen is married, and has provided me with several nieces and nephews. My parents are ecstatic. They spend most of their time being doting grandparents now that Dad has retired from law."

"They sound nice," Julie said wistfully. "I always wanted a brother or sister."

"Glen and I were lucky," Greg said. "We always got along well and we still do."

Julie savored her last bite of pineapple and then looked across at Greg. "It seems odd you haven't been to Hawaii more often. Living in Los Angeles and traveling to the Far East, I would have thought you'd be very familiar with the islands."

Greg took a bite of pineapple and chewed deliberately, avoiding her gaze. "I don't take time off very often," he said.

"Then I really do feel awful," Julie exclaimed. "Here you are finally taking a vacation, and I spoil your first day by needing to be bailed out of jail."

"No problem." Greg rose from the table abruptly. "I like to work."

"But why were you so interested in my case?"

Greg didn't look at her for a moment. Instead, he seemed to be lost in thought, gazing at a spot far out on the ocean. When he did look at her finally, his smile was a little too smooth, his eyes dark and unfathomable. "You're a very attractive woman, Julie. Maybe it wasn't your case I was interested in."

ONCE THEY WERE BACK on the road, Julie had time to consider his last statement. His answer hadn't been what she expected. Indeed, she didn't think she liked it one little bit. There was no way she was going to believe that Greg was so bowled over by her good looks and charm that he had decided to give up his vacation to involve himself in her problems.

Could it be, rather, that he was eager for the legal experience he would gain from a case involving international espionage? Not a particularly flattering explanation, but probably much closer to the truth.

"We'll stop for lunch at Waimanalo Beach Park," Julie explained as they neared their picnic destination. "Lots of the native islanders consider this one of our nicest beaches."

Surveying the grassy knolls and tree-shaded picnic tables, Greg nodded his approval. The beach was clean and white, a pleasant rolling surf beckoning invitingly to swimmers and sunbathers.

They chose a table near the beach, unpacking the car quickly. "Lunch first?" Julie suggested. "Then we can swim."

Greg uncorked the wine and poured it into the two disposable wineglasses. "I love picnics." Julie pushed her hair back out of her eyes and swung her legs over the picnic bench until she was seated facing him. "I have a specially equipped basket I bought in Tokyo last year. I probably use it at least once a week."

Greg lifted his glass in her direction. "What shall we toast?"

"To proving my innocence," Julie suggested quickly. Picking up her glass, she clinked it gently against his before taking a sip and regarding him over the rim.

Greg's gaze captured and held hers for a long minute. So intense was his scrutiny it seemed to strip her bare of all defenses, leaving her breathless and shaken. At last he brought his glass to his lips and said carefully, "To finding the truth."

The chicken was superb, a crispy golden brown on the outside with a moist interior. As they ate, Greg and she compared notes on their hometown of Los Angeles. She soon realized that he must come from a very affluent family. The neighborhood where he had lived and the schools he had attended suggested a background quite different from her own modest upbringing. He seemed not to notice that she had grown quieter as he quizzed her about her school days. "Were you a cheerleader?" he asked.

"No. I had a part-time job during high school, working in a fast-food restaurant. That didn't leave much time for the usual school activities, but I still had a lot of fun."

"How about clubs? A crusader like you must have supported a lot of causes."

"I'm ashamed to admit I didn't get involved. My mother was more like a grandmother in a lot of ways, and she kept me on a tight leash. The thought of my marching in protest against something would have killed her."

"Just the opposite in my family. We were expected to be passionately devoted to what we believed."

"Then I envy you. It taught you to stand up for your beliefs."

"You did a pretty fine job at police headquarters yesterday. You seemed like an old hand at the game."

Not liking the turn of the conversation, Julie took a long cooling sip of her wine. "What made you think that?"

"For one thing, you seem so bent on making an issue out of your arrest."

"Wouldn't you?" Julie demanded hotly. "Think of what this could do to my reputation. My career. Having a police record is nothing to joke about."

"If the accusations aren't true, they can't hurt you. Someone made a mistake, that's all."

"How did they make such a mistake?" Julie's eyes revealed her hurt. "That's what I want to know. I've never done anything suspicious. I have lots of friends, with a variety of life-styles, but I've never knowingly maintained a relationship with someone who was involved in anything illegal."

"Are you sure?" Greg's gaze suddenly pinned her down, fixing on her with a hawklike scrutiny that made her realize what a formidable foe he must be in a courtroom.

For a long moment her gaze locked with his in an intimate duel. "I'm positive," she said finally. "But I'd like to make sure that everyone else believes that, as well. I don't want this thing hanging over my head like a storm cloud, capable of bursting any moment. If the Honolulu police or those federal agents think I'm somehow involved in this crazy case, I've got to convince them otherwise."

"That won't be easy," Greg stated quietly.

"I know." Julie reached over and touched Greg's hand lightly. "I don't want to bother you with this anymore, Greg."

"We agreed we'd talk things over today, Julie." Greg's hand grasped hers warmly, his thumb moving to caress her wrist. "I want to help you."

"I also think you seem unusually interested in this particular case."

Greg gazed out at the ocean. The silence between them was broken only by the crash of the surf and the laughing calls of a few children farther down the beach. When he turned his gaze back toward her, he said, "Hell, yes, I'm interested. Any lawyer would be. I'd also like to help get that disk back. From what the police told me, it's vital they find it."

"The famous disk," Julie said, sighing. "Dare I make a confession and admit I know nothing about computers?"

"It's a small disk, highly sophisticated."

"And it was taken from a navy ship by this Derickson?"

"With the aid of his cousin, a sailor on the ship. The cousin confessed the next morning and led them to where Derickson was supposed to be staying. It was a small inn, the Masuda, on the outskirts of Tokyo."

"What about this woman, the one who they believe is me?"

Greg hesitated a moment. "This woman arrived at the Masuda around seven on Thursday evening. She asked for Derickson and went up to his room. A few minutes later, she called down to the desk and told the clerk she was expecting a phone call and wanted it put through to Derickson's room. She gave her name as Julie Smith."

"So there was more to it than a raincoat and a scarf—" Julie stopped abruptly as the full meaning of his words registered. "Someone used my name."

"You think so?"

Julie's head shot up and her eyes flashed fire. "I certainly wasn't at this Masuda Inn, if that's what you're implying."

"There can't be that many women named Julie Smith in Tokyo," Greg pointed out reasonably.

"It could happen," Julie snapped. "Smith is a fairly common name, and Julie isn't exactly special, either." She didn't give Greg time to reply. "But it looks to me as if someone deliberately used my name. I'm being framed—don't you see?"

"Who would want to frame you, Julie?"

"I don't know," she said helplessly. "All I know is that I wasn't at the Masuda Inn that night. I've never been there. But at least this whole thing is becoming a bit clearer. I can see now why the police confused me with this other woman."

Greg made no direct response, but continued with his rundown of the facts. "Federal agents followed the woman all day Friday. They were hoping she would lead them to Derickson, but instead she went to the Imperial. The only Julie Smith registered at the Imperial Hotel was you, Julie."

"We all stayed at the Imperial, the whole flight crew, Greg. I checked in with everybody else on Thursday night, and I went to bed early."

"But you can't prove it. By your own admission, you spoke to no one and saw no one after room service delivered your dinner."

"But the bed...didn't the maid report I'd slept there? I'm sure these federal agents could check something like that."

"It's an old trick to establish an alibi, Julie. Check into a hotel and then leave after you ruffle the bed, order conspicuously from room service and dampen some towels. It happens more often than you may think.''

"Other people may do things like that," Julie said hotly. "But *I* did nothing of the sort."

"The police had a fairly convincing case, as you can see."

"Then why did they let me go?"

"The evidence was circumstantial, Julie."

"That's why Captain Lonergan said he expects to see me again soon," Julie mused. "He still thinks I'm guilty." She shivered convulsively despite the warm rays of the sun. "I thought this was all over, but now I'm worried again. I know I promised not to cadge free legal advice, but I would like to know if you think I need to retain a lawyer."

Greg drained the last swallow of his wine. "Why don't you wait a few days, Julie? I'll be right here in Honolulu if you need help. Meanwhile, keep thinking about what you did in Tokyo those two days. If you remember anything at all, tell me."

"Thank you," she murmured gratefully. "It's nice to know I have somewhere to turn."

WHEN THE REMAINS OF THE PICNIC were cleared away, Julie collected her colorful beach bag. "I'm going to the bathhouse to change," she explained to Greg as he stowed the wicker basket in the trunk.

He straightened up and looked in the direction she was pointing, toward the small building that housed dressing rooms for men and women. "I'll do the same," he agreed. "Meet you back here in a few minutes?"

"It won't take me long."

Julie slung her bag over her shoulder and headed off across the sand. She had removed her shoes, and now the sand crunched pleasantly between her toes, warm and smooth. The conversation with Greg had left her feeling unsettled, vaguely uneasy, and she tried hard to recapture her earlier contentment.

The area around the bathhouse was deserted, and Julie walked around to the women's side, relieved to find that it was reasonably clean. The interior was hot; the high, shuttered windows permitted minimal circulation of air. It was dark, too. The lone light bulb overhead did little to dispel the dim shadows.

Two long benches were provided for holding sunbathers' paraphernalia. The floor was slightly damp, a residue of footprints indicating that someone had used the showers along the back wall recently. On Julie's left was a long row of sinks, and on her right a row of stalls for the toilets.

Setting her beach bag on one of the benches, she fished out her white bikini and then started to remove her top. A vague feeling of uneasiness made her pause and glance around the room.

Don't be silly, she admonished herself. Quickly she stripped off her shorts and top. She was reaching to slide off her bra when her feeling of uneasiness returned.

Her breathing sounded loud and ragged in her ears. She held her breath for a moment, but the only sounds were the distant rumble of the surf and the high-pitched cries of children she had heard earlier. The laughter grew louder, as if they were heading in the direction of the bathhouse, and she relaxed. It was stupid to worry—though it did pay to be careful. You heard about such awful things happening.

Stepping quickly out of her silky panties, she pulled on her bikini in record time. There wasn't much to it, actually, only a tiny string bottom and two triangles that hugged her full breasts. Such bikinis were worn everywhere in Hawaii, and she knew her own body looked good. For a blonde, she tanned well, and the snowy-white fabric emphasized the honey tones of her skin.

She was folding up her shorts and adding them to the stack of underwear and other clothes in her bag when she heard a rustling noise. She quickly straightened up, her heart pounding erratically as she listened for it again. Nothing. Not a sound.

For a moment she was tempted to grab her bag and run, yet the thought of how ridiculous she would look tearing out of the bathhouse stopped her. Then she heard a childish giggle outside the door and turned to see a little girl of perhaps five enter the room.

"Ooh, it's dark in here." The child's curly brown hair exactly matched the lively brown of her eyes.

"That's because you've been out in the bright sunlight. If you stand perfectly still and wait a minute you'll be able to see just fine." Julie's voice held a bubble of amusement.

"You're awfully pretty," the child said, studying Julie carefully. "Not like my mommy; she's fat."

"Thanks." Julie laughed. "But don't let your mommy hear you say that."

"I won't." The little girl giggled. "She's still down on the beach. I just came up here because I need to go to the bathroom."

"If you want, I'll wait for you," Julie offered, remembering her earlier uneasiness and reluctant to leave the little girl alone.

"I'd like that." The little girl went into a stall and Julie waited, her hand on her bag, wondering why she'd reacted so oddly only moments earlier.

Suddenly the skin on the back of her neck prickled and she turned quickly. Again she had the feeling she was being watched. Scanning the far wall, she thought she saw the shower curtain that hid the last cubicle move slightly.

Julie's eyes narrowed and she grew angry. Now that she wasn't alone, now that she had a child to protect, she felt braver. Marching over to the curtain, she hesitated a moment. Probably some young Peeping Tom, she decided, and with a swift yank she pulled open the curtain.

Her heart stopped. Even as she stared, she was sure her heart would never begin beating again. There was a loud drumming in her ears, but she didn't make a sound.

A man was standing inside the shower and a gun was pointing directly at her face. She tried to speak but not a squeak would come out.

"Don't scream," he warned in a husky whisper. Even in her frightened state she detected a faint accent, as if English was not his native tongue.

He was a small man, wiry and of indeterminate age. His dark trousers and long-sleeved shirt looked odd on such a hot day, especially inside a shower stall. Julie wondered suddenly if she was going mad. Was she imagining this? Perhaps her recent bout in jail had unbalanced her mind.

But no, he was speaking again. "Where's the disk?" he asked, and Julie fought back a sudden hysterical urge to laugh.

"The disk?" she whispered faintly, managing to speak at last. Slowly her mind began functioning again, and she measured the distance between them, fighting the temptation to turn and run from the deadly, cold black weapon in his hand. No chance of outrunning that; and anyway, she had the little girl to consider.

"Tell me," he ordered. "What have you done with the disk?"

"I don't have it." She stalled for time, trying desperately to think what she should do.

There was a triumphant gleam in his eyes. "Derickson's got it?"

"I don't know anything about it."

"Don't play games with me." He thrust the gun against her throat.

"I'm not playing games." She searched her mind for the forgotten points of a long-ago lesson on handling disturbed plane passengers.

"Where's the disk?" he repeated.

She heard the sound of the toilet flushing behind her and panicked. The little girl. Any moment now she would come out into the room. The man might be frightened into pulling the trigger. As Julie recalled the trustingly childish face, she knew she had to do something.

"I can't talk now." She spoke in a conspiratorial tone, playing for time until the child could escape.

He looked startled, and as he hesitated she quickly scanned his face, noting a small scar on his left temple and estimating him to be in his late forties. "We're watching you every second," he warned.

Julie shivered spasmodically at the threat in his voice. "Who?" she whispered.

He looked at her incredulously and then gave her a knowing smile. "You're smarter than Derickson's other women. But you won't outsmart us. If you've got the disk, we'll get it. And we'll get you, too."

With a hard shove he forced her out of his way, throwing her back against the wall. As she fell she struck her shoulder and felt a sharp pain that took her breath away. Then he was gone, running out the door, pushing past the little girl who had just stepped from the stall.

"Hey, there's a man in the bathroom," the little girl said, and then she saw Julie lying on the floor. "Did he hurt you?" she cried, and ran over to Julie, starting to sob loudly.

"No, no," Julie managed to reassure her as she struggled to her feet. "I'm fine. Let's get out of here, okay?"

Julie led the little girl out of the bathhouse, pausing only long enough to pick up her beach bag. Outside, they both blinked in the bright sun. Julie glanced around, looking for the man, but he was nowhere in sight. Off in the distance she spotted Greg's tall figure as he leaned against the car, staring out at the ocean.

"There's my mommy," the little girl said suddenly, and took off, running down the beach toward a woman who was trying with limited success to manage two other young children.

Julie stood still for a second longer, gulping deep calming breaths of air, until she saw that the child had safely reached her mother. Then she headed for Greg, half running. As she neared the car, he turned, his gaze sharpening as he noted her breathless haste and frantic expression.

"Greg," she gasped.

He caught her hands as she half fell against him. "What is it, Julie?"

"A man . . . a man."

"Where?" Greg demanded, his gaze making a quick survey first of her and then of the beach. "What happened? Are you hurt?" Even through her dazed panic she caught the quiet anger in his voice and reveled in the protective assurance of his embrace. Whoever that man had been, whoever was watching her, he couldn't hurt her as long as Greg was here.

"ARE YOU SURE he mentioned the disk, Julie?" Greg's voice was quiet as he asked the question. They were seated at the picnic table, and Julie had just finished relating the whole story.

Her hands curved around the cup of coffee Greg had poured for her from a thermos he'd had filled at the deli. "I told you, he asked me where the disk was located."

Greg frowned at her, raking a hand impatiently through his hair. "How could he have connected you with the disk? It doesn't make sense."

"You're telling me," Julie said feelingly. "Why is everybody asking me about this disk?" she moaned.

"But who was he?" Greg murmured.

"How would I know?" Julie's voice threatened to rise to the level of a shriek, and Greg reached across to clasp one of her hands.

"Steady, Julie," he soothed. "Now let's go over this again, shall we? What did he look like?"

"Short. Thin. Mid to late forties," Julie said quickly. "He had an accent of some sort and a small scar on his temple."

"An accent?"

"You know, foreign. He spoke English very slowly, as if he had to concentrate on his words." Julie took another sip of coffee. "What would make him think I know something about this disk?"

"Perhaps he saw your picture in the papers."

"There have been pictures of me in the paper?" Julie slammed her mug down on the table.

"This morning's paper had your photo and the story of your arrest."

"What picture? Where did the paper get it?"

"Probably during your arrest at the airport. Some photographer could have gotten a tip-off there was going to be an arrest. Spies are big news any time, especially beautiful female ones."

Julie glared at him and he shrugged. "Sorry, just teasing."

"If he thought I had the disk, why didn't he grab me? Why question me and then leave?"

"Why ask me?" Greg looked at her intently.

"Does that comment mean you don't believe me?"

"You have to admit your story sounds a bit far-fetched."

"No more ridiculous than my being arrested in the first place," Julie retorted. "Obviously someone else thinks I've got the disk, too. It looks like I'm being framed, Greg. Don't you see that?" When he didn't say anything, she added, "And where were you while all this was happening?"

Greg eyed her sharply. "I went to the men's bathhouse right after you did. It only took me a moment to change. I've been waiting here for ten minutes or so."

"Didn't you see a short, thin man loitering around?"

"I can't see the door to the women's side from here, Julie. I didn't see anyone lurking around outside the building."

"Shouldn't we call the police?" Even as she said the words, Julie felt dread at the thought of renewed contact with the police. Yet she felt she was being drawn into something dangerous.

"Of course we'll report this," Greg agreed. "But I don't expect they will believe you."

"Why not?"

"You don't have any proof there even was a man in the bathhouse, Julie."

"Yes, I do," she said suddenly. "The little girl." Quickly she told him about the little girl who had been in the bathhouse. "She saw the man knock me down."

"Where is she now?"

"Somewhere down along the beach, I guess. She's here with her mother and some other children."

"Let's go find her," Greg said abruptly. "I'd like to hear the story from her." He unfolded his lean body from the table and rose to his feet. Julie clutched her coffee mug and eyed him carefully.

"I get the feeling you think I'm lying, Greg. But there was a man in the bathhouse. And now I'm sure someone was watching my condo last night."

"But who, Julie? And why?"

"Do you think the police have someone watching me? I mean, I guess the man in the bathhouse was foreign, but maybe Captain Lonergan has something to do with this. Maybe he's trying to scare me, hoping I'll tell him where the disk is."

Even as she spoke she remembered the man's whispered threat. "We're watching you," he had said. Her hands shook as she lifted the mug to her lips.

"It's not likely," Greg said slowly. He frowned. "We'll talk about this later. Right now, let's go find that child."

It was almost as though it was all happening to someone else. Two days ago she had been an ordinary, everyday person, living an ordinary, run-of-the-mill existence. Then in the last forty-eight hours she had been arrested, kept for a night in jail, accused of being a spy and accosted in a public bathhouse by a man waving a gun. What next? she wondered tiredly.

Rising to her feet, Julie followed Greg as he strode along the beach. They walked for some time, passing the path to the bathhouse, but the woman and her children were nowhere in sight. "They seem to have left," Julie said at last.

"Apparently," Greg said dryly.

"They were here," Julie insisted stubbornly. "A little girl of about five and her mother and several other children."

"If they were here, they're gone now." Greg's voice was clipped.

"What do you mean, 'if'?" Julie stopped, grasping his arm. "They were here, I assure you."

"I'm doing everything I can to help you, Julie."

"I know." She dropped his arm and stared down at the sand. "What does it all mean, Greg? What did happen to that disk? And why does everyone believe I took it? Even more important, where is that other Julie Smith with her damn paisley scarf?"

Chapter Seven

Julie was still shaken from her ordeal at the bathhouse when they arrived some time later at Sunset Beach. The beach itself was crawling with surfers, and off in the distance the huge, white-capped waves that drew surfing enthusiasts from around the world rumbled incessantly.

"Why don't we find a place to have dinner?" Greg cast a sidelong glance at Julie, worried by her white face and shadowed blue eyes. "You look like you could use a rest."

"I need a shower," she reminded him. They had sunbathed at Waimanalo Beach for an hour, but it had been ruined for Julie. She had spent the entire time looking over her shoulder, scanning the bushes anxiously, to determine whether anyone was watching her.

When it was time to leave the beach, she had refused to return to the bathhouse to change, and Greg hadn't pressed the issue. He went to change, while she waited nervously in the car. Her sigh of relief when he rejoined her, his hair still damp from the shower, did not escape him.

Now the T-shirt she had pulled on over her bathing suit was clinging damply to her skin, and she felt awkward about the sand she had already dumped in his luxurious car. She was beginning to wonder why a man as attractive as Greg would want to waste his time on a woman who should be declared a disaster area.

"Can you recommend a good restaurant?" Greg scanned the main street, dodging the crowds of bikini-clad surfers and swerving quickly to avoid a young boy carrying a surfboard almost twice his size.

"There's a beautiful resort outside town," Julie suggested. "Keep going and you'll spot it as we leave the main beach area."

The resort sprawled along the coast, discreet signs pointing the way to the main buildings. It was situated on a peninsula that extended into the sea, bordered on either side by tiny coves with sheltered, sandy beaches. The principal building was long and low, lushly modern, set amidst jewel-like green lawns and flower beds of red and pink and white hibiscus. A terrace stretched along the upper level, its umbrella-topped tables and white-coated waiters an island of brilliant color in a sea of cool greens and blues.

Greg pulled the car alongside the entrance, sliding out in one swift movement and handing the keys to a valet before coming around to Julie's door. "I can't go in like this," she whispered when he held out his hand. As she swung her long legs out of the car, Greg surveyed her lazily, his smile approving.

"I'm sure they're used to women in bathing suits, Julie." He waited until she was beside him before taking her beach bag out of her hand. "I'll see about getting us a place to change before dinner."

Greg's idea of a place to change was definitely classier than hers, Julie realized, as she explored the room a courteous bellboy led her to moments later. Greg had chatted quietly with the desk clerk before saying, "I've gotten you a room, Julie. You can shower and have a rest. Call me when you're ready for dinner."

"But Greg—" Julie started to protest his extravagance.

"Shh," he murmured, placing one finger softly against her lips. "Don't argue. Just enjoy."

Julie gave in gracefully. Now as she crossed the room to gaze out at a glorious view of the ocean, she realized that his prescription was exactly what she needed. If Greg wanted to treat her, why not let him? He hadn't asked to join her in her room. In a way, that surprised her. To most men, such a suggestion would be automatic. His thoughtfulness and sensitivity gratified her.

Investigating the room, which was exquisitely decorated in blues that echoed the colors of the ocean, she found a luxurious bathroom. She turned on the taps over the huge, sunken tub, poured in a handful of complimentary bath salts and went back into the bedroom to the telephone. A quick call to room service, and she was assured that a bottle of chilled mineral water would be delivered quickly. Julie settled down to enjoy herself.

In his own room, Greg was far from relaxed. His chamber, a single on the ground floor, was austere and businesslike, boasting no view of the ocean. Dialing the hotel operator, he asked for an outside line and then called the long-distance operator, giving her his credit-card number. Moments later he heard Walt's voice.

"We found nothing." Walt's blunt announcement greeted his ears.

"Nothing?" Greg felt a surge of relief.

"The place was clean as a whistle. Our boys gave it a careful going over as soon as her roommate cleared out this morning. If that disk had been there, they would have found it."

"I hope they left everything the way they found it. That Hyde woman is a stickler for neatness."

"They know their job. The place was a cinch to break into. No security in the daytime, a simple knob lock that can be opened with a credit card. You're right about the place being clean, though. Our boys said they'd never seen any place so organized."

"Did they find anything connecting Julie with Derickson?"

"No." Walt's tones were clipped, fraught with frustration. "No photographs, no letters, no addresses, no disk, nothing."

Greg hid his relief with a noncommittal reply. "We'll have to keep looking."

"How are you doing?" Walt asked eagerly.

"Okay." Greg's reply was guarded. "We talked some more today, but there's nothing new. She's still proclaiming her complete innocence."

"Damn." Walt paused a moment. "Anything else to report?"

"There was one incident today." Greg gave a brief account of the man in the bathhouse.

"Clever," Walt said when he had finished. "You were right there and you never caught a glimpse of the guy?"

"I wasn't on that side of the bathhouse."

"You have to give her credit for being shrewd. She's trying to con you with that story. This woman has an imagination. First she tells you about some man in the bushes. And now this."

Greg fought against a flare of anger. "Frankly, I believe there *was* a man in the bathhouse. Probably the same man she reported seeing in the bushes last night. I think we should at least consider the possibility."

There was a short silence. "It's pretty unlikely." Walt sounded impatient. "I think Smith is involved. As I see it, there are two possibilities. Either she passed the disk to someone in Tokyo, or she got someone else to transport it for her, intending to retrieve it here in Honolulu. If she still has control of the disk, she could be playing a little game, hoping to raise the price as time runs out. We've already agreed that's a likelihood. It may be Derickson's idea, but I'm leaning toward the theory that Smith is calling the shots herself right now."

Greg swallowed a denial. It was clear Walt still saw Julie as a conspirator, a view he was finding increasingly difficult to share.

Walt continued to speak. "At the moment there's nothing to suggest she got rid of the disk in Tokyo. So far there's been no leak to the press about the President's plans. We're watching things closely."

"You left out one other possibility," Greg interrupted. "Smith may not be involved at all."

"Right now, she's all we've got," Walt stated bluntly.

"Did you check with the airlines to find out her next flight schedule?"

"I fixed that." Walt paused to cough. "We had an official talk with World Airlines and suggested they hold off on any more assignments."

"You got her fired?"

"We can't let her leave the country. You know that. We didn't have enough proof to hold her in jail, so we had a quiet talk with her boss and suggested a layoff for the next two weeks. They were already considering that option. The publicity has resulted in some nasty calls to their company.''

Greg ran a hand through his hair. "What if she's innocent? All of this hinges on my identification of her at the Imperial."

"You saw her, Greg. If you can't trust your own eyes, what can you trust?"

Greg groaned as he hung up the phone. He felt as if events were closing in on him. He leaned his head against the wall and thought of Julie. It looked as if he would lose no matter what happened. If he had identified her wrongly, she would never forgive him. And if he had been right that night in Japan, if she was involved in this sorry mess...His mind balked. He didn't even want to consider the implications of that possibility.

NIGHT WAS APPROACHING as Julie and Greg returned to Honolulu. Dinner had been superb, but when Greg suggested dancing afterward, Julie declined. She was tired, emotionally drained by the events of the past few days. Her mind was whirling with questions, but any time she attempted to bring them into the conversation, Greg sidestepped. There were dark shadows under his eyes.

"You can park over there." Julie pointed as they pulled into the palm-lined car park beside her building. As Greg maneuvered the car into a slot, she reached for her beach bag. "Thanks for everything today, Greg."

He turned, sliding one arm along the seat behind her and leaning forward. "Is something wrong, Julie?" His eyes were serious, sharp and observant as he scanned her face.

"I'm tired."

"Is that all?"

Julie hesitated, then spoke bluntly. "I'm worried about what happened at the beach today. I know you don't really believe me, but the man was there, and he threatened me."

"I never said I didn't believe you, Julie." Greg touched her shoulder, gently restraining her as she moved to get out of the car.

"You didn't say it," Julie said. "But I could see the disbelief in your eyes."

Greg's face became shuttered, closed against her, his expression bland. "Perhaps you misread me."

"I don't think so." She spoke softly but with conviction.

It was quiet for a moment and Greg's eyes darkened and his breathing quickened. "I didn't want anything to spoil our time together. Perhaps I should have taken this incident more seriously. It seems to have upset you more than I realized."

"That's putting it mildly."

"Let's go have coffee somewhere and we'll talk it over," he suggested soothingly.

Julie suspected that his sympathy wasn't totally sincere, yet she badly needed the warmth of another person's presence at the moment. Now that she had been warned she was being watched, she felt like looking over her shoulder all the time. She wasn't sure what she expected to happen, but she had never felt less like being alone. "We could have coffee at my place," she offered.

"Sounds great." Greg was out of the car and around at her door before she could change her mind.

Jake winked at Julie as he let them into the lobby. "Glad to see you again, Mr. Stafford."

When the elevator deposited them at Julie's floor, she fumbled for her key. The hallway was darker than usual, and it took her a moment to figure out why. The light near her door was out, probably a burnt-out bulb. She reminded herself to call the building supervisor the next morning to report it.

Greg waited patiently while she groped through her purse. After several moments, he said, "Want me to help?"

"No, I'll find it," Julie assured him. Seconds later she pulled out the ring of keys and held them up triumphantly.

They walked down the hall to her door, their eyes gradually adjusting to the dim light. As she reached to insert the key, Julie's fingers brushed the knob. Before she could get the key in the lock, the door slid open, yielding to the gentle pressure of her fingers. "That's odd." She frowned and started to enter. "I didn't think Tricia would get home before me. And it's not like her to leave the door unlocked."

Greg moved abruptly behind her, his hand coming out to cover hers, his finger going to his lips, warning her to silence. Stealthily, he brushed past her and opened the door.

The apartment was dark. Julie pressed closely behind Greg. She strained her ears, but no sounds came from within the apartment. Greg flipped the light switch, and the small foyer flooded with light. Then he was moving again, into the living room, where he halted abruptly.

Julie pushed past him and stopped short. "What on earth—?" she gasped, surveying the room in horror.

The place looked as if it had been hit by a tornado. Chairs and tables were overturned, lamps knocked over, pictures torn off the walls.

At the same moment, she and Greg spotted the éta-gère. "Tricia's bookcase," Julie moaned. It lay on the floor, its contents strewn on the carpet.

Julie's eyes went automatically to the console, where her stereo and television were housed, but both were there. Record albums lay scattered across the floor, videotapes and cassettes were discarded with careless abandon on the upturned surface of her coffee table. Yet the expensive electronic equipment had not been touched.

"An odd burglar, to leave my stereo and television," she commented.

Greg wasn't listening. He edged silently across the room and disappeared through the kitchen door. Returning seconds later, he shook his head. Then he headed for the bedrooms, going into each one briefly and then coming back to stand beside her in the living room. "No one here."

Julie automatically started to right a lamp. "Don't touch anything," he ordered. "The police may want to lift fingerprints."

"Are the other rooms as messy as this one?"

"Worse," said Greg tersely.

"My jewelry," Julie whispered and headed for her bedroom. Chaos met her gaze as she opened the door. Her bedspread had been removed, as well as the sheets and blankets, and her mattress dangled off its frame. She sat down and buried her face in her hands. For a long moment she shivered uncontrollably. The events of the past few days had stretched her nerves to the breaking point. Now this had happened. What did it all mean, and where would it end?

Getting up at last, she searched for her jewelry case, finding it abandoned in a heap of tumbled clothing that had been pulled from her bureau drawers. There was not so much as an earring missing. "How odd," she mused.

"What's odd?" Greg stood in the doorway.

She turned to face him, holding out the case for his inspection. "They didn't take my jewelry, either. What sort of burglar breaks in but doesn't take your television or your jewelry?"

"Maybe he was looking for something else of value." Greg didn't reach for the case. "Better put that down," he suggested. "Remember what I said about fingerprints."

Julie put the case back where she had found it. "I'd better check Tricia's room to see if anything is missing in there."

Greg followed her to the other bedroom. The same havoc had been wreaked among Tricia's possessions. Heeding Greg's advice, Julie was careful not to touch anything. It didn't look as if anything had been taken, but only Tricia would know for sure. "Nothing seems to be missing here, either." Julie looked at Greg.

There was a brief silence, and then Greg said smoothly, "Maybe they were looking for the disk."

"The disk?" Julie's eyes widened. "Who would look for it here? The police?"

"Not necessarily the police." Greg looked away from her and took a few paces. He appeared to be lost in thought. "Julie, I've been thinking about that disk. It contains some highly classified material, which the police believe Derickson was going to sell, perhaps to an Eastern Bloc country.''

''Yes,'' Julie agreed, waiting for him to go on.

''Now Derickson has disappeared, and the disk hasn't surfaced, either. Maybe he hasn't sold it to his buyers yet. Maybe they're looking for him, trying to find the disk.''

''But why look here?''

''Obviously they think you have the thing.'' Greg's voice hardened.

''The man at the beach today...'' Julie stopped, thinking quickly. ''He was foreign, Greg. I think you're right. You told me yourself that my picture has been in the paper. Anyone could have seen that story.''

Greg looked at her long and hard. His face was grim and strangely cold. ''If you're caught in the middle, Julie, you're in a very dangerous position. You can't play games with people like these.''

''What do you mean by games, Greg? I don't know what this is all about.''

He looked tired suddenly. ''Okay, Julie. I believe you. Now let's call the police and report this. They'll probably send someone out.''

He went to the living room and Julie heard him pick up the phone. A moment later she joined him. He was speaking quickly into the phone. As she entered, he turned and cupped his hand over the mouthpiece. ''They need to speak to you.''

''Ms. Smith.'' Captain Lonergan's voice grated on her ears when she picked up the receiver.

''Yes,'' she said warily. ''You work long hours, don't you?''

''Crime never stops. Your lawyer says you've had a burglary.''

"Someone's broken in, but I can't tell if anything is missing yet."

"Not even that disk?"

Julie's fingers tightened on the receiver. "You're not making much sense, Captain. Perhaps we have a bad connection."

"We'll send someone over right away to make a report."

"Is this routine procedure?" Julie asked. "Somehow, I've always had the idea that the police only rush to the scene of major crimes."

"But then, you are of major interest to us, Ms. Smith." There was a click as Captain Lonergan hung up.

JULIE WAS IN THE KITCHEN attempting to locate the coffee when she heard Tricia and Tony arrive. Greg had looked around the room first and then told her it was okay to make coffee. "Don't touch the cabinets," he warned. "Just the coffee maker."

The kitchen dismayed her most of all. Flour and sugar had been dumped all over the floor that Tricia kept in shining condition. Boxes of crackers and cereal had been ripped open, and even the contents of the small freezer unit had been cast out on the floor. Such wanton destruction chilled her.

As she entered the living room, she could hear Tricia's shrill protests of horror. "This time you've gone too far, Julie." Tricia turned angrily when she saw Julie.

"What do you mean?"

"Look at this mess. I can put up with a little disorder, but this is ridiculous. What did you and Greg do, have an orgy?"

"Tricia, calm down. I didn't mess the place up, a burglar did."

"A burglar." Tricia's face paled and she sat down abruptly on the sofa. She shot right back up with a grimace, wincing as she pulled a sharp-edged ashtray from beneath her.

"I don't think they took anything," Julie soothed. "We've called the police. They should be here any minute."

Tony hovered anxiously. His red hair and wealth of freckles made him look like an endearing five-year-old, but in reality he was a capable medical resident at the local hospital.

"Julie's making coffee," Greg said. Tony nodded, looking grateful that someone was offering a way to deal with Tricia's rising hysteria.

"You must be Tony. I'm Greg Stafford. We've talked on the phone."

Another wail came from Tricia and she began sobbing. "Look, Tony. My book...bookcase. It will take me hours to put everything back in its right place."

Julie hurried to the kitchen. The doorbell rang a short time later. Locating a package of Styrofoam cups amid the debris on the floor, she gingerly pulled it out without disturbing anything else. Taking enough cups to serve the police, as well, she hurried into the living room with the coffee pot. It occurred to her that the police officers might be reluctant to accept a drink from her if they recognized her from the day before, and she had to suppress a grim smile.

Two uniformed men were in the room, standing with Greg behind the sofa. Tricia had regained her composure and was sitting next to Tony, holding his hand. One of the officers addressed Julie. "The place looked like this when you got home?"

"Yes. We've only been here a few minutes."

"Half an hour," Greg corrected her in a low voice.

"We'll have a look around, and then we may need to ask some questions." The other officer got out a notebook, and the two men started to work.

"Help me lift this." Tricia stood up and headed for the bookcase.

Julie hurried to stand beside her roommate. "Have a seat and wait, Tricia."

Tricia tugged at one end of the bookcase but was halted by a sharp reprimand from a police officer. "Don't touch anything until we're through here."

Tricia subsided back on the couch, her expression mutinous. Greg came up behind Julie, putting his arm around her waist. "Do you have any ideas who might have done this, Tricia?" he asked.

"Absolutely not." Tricia rubbed her fingers against her temples and leaned against Tony. "This has been the craziest week. First Julie was arrested and then this. I'm going to be afraid to wake up in the morning for fear of what might happen."

Two more men arrived, identifying themselves as the fingerprint team. They stretched a long plastic strip across the front door with a sign indicating that this was a crime scene and not to be disturbed. Joining the others in the living room, they briskly unpacked their equipment while exchanging remarks with the officers who had arrived earlier.

"I hope the neighbors don't think I'm some kind of jinx and ask me to sell," Julie whispered. Greg reached for her hand and squeezed it gently, his clasp warm and caring.

The officers worked quickly. Within a half hour they had finished in Julie's bedroom and were part way through the living room. "May I use the phone in your bedroom?" Greg asked Julie.

"Of course." Julie watched him leave the room, wondering who he was calling. It was none of her business, she supposed.

GREG'S TEMPER SOARED as he dialed Walt's number a few minutes later. "Why did you make such a mess of her place?" he demanded. "I thought you promised not to leave any trace."

"What are you talking about?"

"I mean your boys tore up Smith's apartment when they searched it this morning."

"Hey, slow down. You're all mixed up. I sent two of the best. They assured me no one would ever know they'd been there."

"They lied. It's a shambles. Her furniture is a mess, her things are dumped all over the floor and the front door was left open. Since when did our agency conduct searches this way?"

"Never." Walt sounded indignant. "Now listen here, Greg. I sent two men over this morning. They entered the place around ten and stayed less than an hour. They didn't find anything, and they didn't leave any clues they'd been there. Looks like we're dealing with a new dimension here. Maybe a random burglary?"

"Nothing's missing. This was a brutal search."

"How did Smith take it?"

"Like anyone would who finds their apartment ransacked. She didn't run around looking for a disk, if that's what you mean."

"Probably means she's stashed it somewhere and is laughing at all of us now. The closer we get to the deadline, the higher the price will go. Maybe we should offer money ourselves."

Greg bit back a sharp retort. "How about your surveillance van? Did they report anyone entering the building?"

"They didn't see Derickson." Greg heard papers rustling and then Walt continued. "No, according to my notes they didn't have anything unusual to report. There are a lot of people in that condo, Greg. We can't get an identification on everyone going in or out of the building. Our people are looking specifically for Derickson. He never came near the place today. Who do you think did this?"

"I don't know for sure, but I've got some ideas. Why don't I come to your room at ten? We'll talk then."

"I'll be here," Walt agreed.

Greg replaced the receiver and walked over to Julie's balcony doors. He pulled back the drapes and glanced out at the ocean. Turning back toward the bedroom, he studied it carefully. The room must be lovely when it wasn't suffering from the effects of a burglary. He could picture Julie in this setting, her soft blond hair and friendly blue eyes a perfect foil for some of the clothes that now lay in heaps on the floor.

Picking up an earring from the floor, he held it in his palm. It was a tiny pearl that he remembered her wearing the night before, nestled against the delicate curve of her ear. He sensed that Julie was deeply vulnerable despite her outward poise, and he admitted to himself that he was almost totally convinced of her innocence now.

Feelings he had struggled to avoid all day rose to the surface of his mind. He believed in the critical importance of his mission. He had to recover that disk. Yet he couldn't accept that Julie was intentionally involved in this thing. She wasn't the type of woman who could be fooled by the Dericksons, the con men, of the world. Nor under any circumstances could he believe Julie was a spy or a traitor.

Pulling open the doors of the balcony, he stepped outside and breathed in deep, soothing gulps of the fresh ocean breeze. He had to make a decision. Either he halted his growing feelings for Julie, stifling them with ruthless purpose or he took a chance, relied on his own instincts and decided to trust her.

For a moment he wavered, forcing himself to touch the lighter in his pocket. He hated the thing, and yet he kept it as a potent reminder that his gut instincts had once let him down. He'd been younger then, less experienced, more apt to take people at face value. Sure, he'd failed then. But that was the past. It was over. Ten good years had gone by in which he'd proven time and again that he could trust his feelings.

He reached a decision. His jaw tightened, and he opened the door to the living room. From now on he was operating on the assumption that she was telling him the truth. And that meant he had work to do. Somewhere out there were the people who were responsible for this situation. It was up to him to find them.

JULIE AND TRICIA both insisted that neither Tony nor Greg needed to spend the night. The police had inspected the door lock before leaving, demonstrating how easily the simple knob lock could be opened. "A credit card was all that was needed,'' one of them explained. ''You'd better get a locksmith out here to install a dead bolt.''

Greg appeared reluctant to leave. He waited until the police had gone and then checked the lock himself. ''You might as well leave it unlocked. This type of lock is worthless against a break-in.''

''Jake is on duty tonight.'' Julie followed Greg to the door. ''We'll be fine for one night, and I'll call a locksmith first thing in the morning.''

Greg wrote the number of the Hilton on a slip of paper, adding his room number, as well. ''Promise you'll call if you need me?''

''I promise.'' Julie rather enjoyed the sensation of having Greg worry about her. The day had shaken her up more than she revealed.

''How about tomorrow, Julie? I was hoping you'd have lunch with me and then spend the afternoon showing me around Honolulu.''

''Tomorrow.'' Tricia came into the foyer, her arms laden with a stack of books. ''Tomorrow Julie is busy. We'll probably be up most of the night clearing up this mess. Then we'll have to call the insurance adjustors. I can't even start to estimate what it's going to take to get everything back in shape before our next flight.''

''When is your next flight?'' Greg stared hard at Tricia.

''I called them yesterday. Julie and I fly to Tokyo again on Wednesday. Of course, if she wants to run off with you, I can probably manage by myself....''

Julie intervened hastily. ''Why don't I call you after lunch tomorrow, Greg? I do need to stay here and help Tricia in the morning.''

She sensed his disappointment. He looked as if he wanted to protest, though he accepted her statement readily enough. "I understand. If you need any help, I could come around in the morning."

"I wouldn't dream of imposing on you any further, Greg." Julie waited until Tricia had left the room. "I am sorry. I've enjoyed our time together so far, despite all the disasters."

"So have I, Julie." Greg stroked her cheek with one finger and then cupped his palm at the back of her head. She went into his arms willingly, feeling a little breathless. Her lips parted as they met his, and the warmth of his mouth started a fire inside her, a slow burn that gradually spread as he increased the pressure of his lips on hers.

His hands dropped to her shoulders and then, with roughly tender insistence, caressed her back, leaving a smoldering trail wherever they touched. His lips left hers long enough to press lightly against her cheeks and jaw, and his breath was hot and moist against her skin.

Julie moaned, a soft sound far back in her throat. She rested her palms against his chest, feeling the soft rise and fall of his breathing, sensing the quickened pace of his heartbeat. Their lips met again, teasingly, delicately and then in a mutual joining of need and tenderness.

Slowly Greg lifted his head, looking questioningly down into her face. "Julie?" His voice was filled with wonder, and his arms continued to hold her with a kind of fierce tenderness.

Reluctantly she pulled away from him. It would be so easy to ask him to stay. Yet she didn't. She knew instinctively that the time was not yet right.

He let go of her. "Good night." His voice was low, husky with leashed passion. Then he was gone.

TRICIA WAS WORKING at a furious pace when Julie returned to the living room. "Several records are broken," Tricia moaned. "And wires are hanging out of the back of the television." She stacked a pile of records on the coffee table, then stopped working and looked inquiringly at Julie. "Who do you think did this? And why?"

Julie shrugged uncomfortably. "Greg seems to think they were looking for something."

"Looking for what? You don't think this has anything to do with that government property the police claim you took?"

"Apparently that computer disk is still missing."

"Surely no one thinks you have the thing?"

"Thanks for your staunch defense, Tricia," Julie said, smiling gratefully. "But the police are still suspicious of me."

"You think the police did this?" Tricia looked so outraged that Julie had to hold back another smile. "Why, that's not legal. The police have to get a search warrant, don't they?"

Julie busied herself repositioning a lamp shade. "Actually, Greg suggested there may be more people involved. Perhaps the people who wanted the disk in the first place. Spies from some Eastern Bloc country, he suspects."

Tricia gasped. "But this is awful, Julie. What are you going to do?"

Julie sank down on the couch. "I don't know. There doesn't seem to be anything I can do at this point." She debated briefly with herself and finally decided to tell

Tricia what had happened at the beach. Even the sketchy details she outlined seemed to terrify Tricia.

"How did you ever get mixed up in something like this?" she said when Julie finished.

"That seems to be the question everyone is asking. Captain Lonergan thinks I had an affair with this man named Derickson. Frankly, I think I'm being framed. But what I can't figure out is why, and by whom."

"What does Greg say about all this?"

"He's rather vague." Julie paused, thinking back over what he had said that day. "One minute he acts as if the whole thing isn't important. Then he starts asking questions that sound almost as if he thinks I'm guilty."

"But he likes you. A lot. I can tell." Tricia nodded emphatically. "I've seen the way he looks at you."

"Yes, but..." Julie hesitated. "I'm not sure he wants to like me. He seems to hold himself back."

The shrill ring of the phone took both of them by surprise. Julie reached for the receiver. "Hello?"

There was silence on the other end. "Hello." Julie repeated the word with an edge to her voice.

"Julie Smith?" The voice was low, masculine, faintly accented.

"Who is this?"

"Tell me where you've hidden the disk." The quiet command came over the phone like a gunshot, sending a surge of adrenaline through her body.

"Who is this?" She repeated the question, anger giving her the strength she needed.

"You know who this is. You know what we want." The voice was deadly calm, almost without inflection.

"No, I don't know. If you're the person who tried to frighten me today, you've got the wrong woman. I don't know anything about the disk. I was arrested by mistake.''

A harsh laugh caused her to grip the phone tightly. ''We intend to get that disk, Miss Smith. If you're thinking of holding out for a better price, you're making a deadly mistake. Tell your friend Derickson we won't stand for any more delays. Either he delivers or he'll never see you again.''

Julie slammed the receiver back into its cradle as if it were a poisonous snake she'd been holding in her hand. Tricia's eyes were wide. ''Who was that?''

''A man.'' Julie forced the words out between frozen lips. ''A man asking for that disk again.''

''Oh, no, Julie.'' Tears filled Tricia's eyes. ''Whatever are we going to do? We can't even call the police, because they think you're a criminal.''

''I'm going to call Greg. He made me promise I'd tell him if anything else happened.'' Moments later Julie had Greg's hotel on the line. After the phone in his room had rung several times, the hotel operator came back on.

''He doesn't appear to be in his room. Would you care to leave a message?''

''No.'' Julie hung up. Greg had had ample time to return to his room. Where was he?

Tentacles of fear squeezed her chest. She felt alone, abandoned. The caller had been in deadly earnest. From out there in the night somewhere a nameless person menaced her. Perhaps more than one person. She couldn't go to the police; they didn't believe her. There had to be something she could do to stop all this. But what? Until the disk was found, the danger wouldn't end.

Chapter Eight

Lonergan was waiting in the hotel lobby when Greg returned from his meeting with Walt. "Can we talk in your room?" He smelled of stale cigar smoke, and his face was haggard with weariness.

Greg groaned inwardly. His meeting with Walt had been exhausting and highly unsatisfactory. He wasn't in the mood to fence with the captain. Besides, it was nearly midnight. "Isn't it rather late?"

"It's important."

In the face of Lonergan's insistence, there was little Greg could do. They went to his room without talking. Once there, he opened a small refrigerator and pulled out a single-serving bottle of Scotch. "Can I offer you something? A beer?"

"Nothing for me."

"What did you need to talk to me about?" Greg poured the Scotch into a tumbler and downed it in one gulp. If he was reading the captain right, he was going to need it. "It's been a long day, so let's make this quick."

The older man looked around the room and then settled into a chair by the window. "Have you gotten anything out of Smith, yet?"

Greg fought a burst of anger. "If I had, you'd know about it. We're sharing all our information with you."

"You didn't tell us about the man in the bushes last night."

"What man?" Greg hoped he was successful at covering his surprise. As far as he was aware, no one had felt it necessary to share that incident with the police staff.

"You know what I'm talking about."

"Miss Smith's roommate reported seeing a man in the bushes." Greg chose his words carefully. "We have no proof the man has any connection with this case."

"And no proof that he even existed." Captain Lonergan pulled out a cigar. "Do you mind?" He fumbled for a match.

"Actually, I do mind," Greg said coolly. "I don't like the smell."

Captain Lonergan's eyes narrowed. He put the cigar back in his pocket. "You should have told us about that man. We found out about it when one of our boys talked to the night watchman."

"It wasn't important." Greg shoved his hands into his pockets and went across to the window. The drapes were still open, and he could watch Lonergan's reflection in the window without actually being forced to look at the man.

"Looks like she's trying to gain your sympathy." Lonergan's tone was sneering. "Looks like maybe she's succeeding."

Greg whirled. "Is that an accusation of some sort?"

Lonergan looked him over consideringly. "Should it be?"

Greg hesitated. From the first he had sensed this man was antagonistic. Jealous, perhaps. To a certain extent he even understood why. The captain had put in a number of long, hard years in order to achieve his present position on the police force. He wasn't used to taking orders. He was the boss now. It probably galled him to have to knuckle under to a federal agency. Maybe he even hoped to solve this case by himself. It wouldn't be the first time someone had used a case like this as a stepping-stone to a bigger position in one of the intelligence organizations.

The phone rang, and Greg reached automatically to pick it up. "Greg, it's me, Julie."

Greg froze. From the corner of his eye he saw Lonergan lean forward, making no attempt to hide his interest. "Yes?"

He could tell that his cool reply startled Julie. Her voice wavered, and she hesitated over her next words. "I hope I'm not bothering you. It's just that I promised to let you know if anything happened." She paused. "Someone called me tonight about the disk."

He was instantly alert. "Who?"

"I'm not sure. I don't think it was the same man who was in the bathhouse today. But this one could also have been foreign. He threatened me, Greg. He threatened to kill me."

Greg muttered a low oath. "Tell me what he said, Julie." At the mention of Julie's name, the captain half rose from his chair. Greg cursed himself inwardly for having revealed his caller's name.

"He asked me where I hid the disk. I told him I didn't have it, that the police had arrested the wrong woman."

"And?"

"He gave me a message for Derickson." Julie's voice wobbled. "He said to tell him that if he didn't get the disk, he'd never see me again."

Greg was silent, debating his next move. "I'll come over."

"No...No, don't," Julie protested. "That's silly. No one can get in. The entrance is guarded, and Tricia just barricaded the door with a chair." She laughed slightly, and Greg could picture her mouth, knowing its soft curves were turned up at the corners. His pulse raced.

"All right," he agreed finally. Seeing that Lonergan had strolled closer, obviously eager to overhear Julie's side of the conversation, he added, "I want to know more about this. Tomorrow, okay?" When she agreed, he said, "And if he calls again, let me know. No matter what time it is. Promise?"

"I will. I tried to call you a while ago, but you weren't in your room."

Greg thought fast. "I stopped for coffee on the way home."

"Tomorrow, then." She hung up.

The minute Greg replaced the receiver, Lonergan pounced. "The girlfriend, right?"

"That was Julie Smith."

"That's what I said. She is your girlfriend, isn't she?"

"You know the situation," Greg retorted grimly.

"Yes, I do." Lonergan took a few steps closer. "I do, indeed. You're falling for the girl. She's clever. Probably told you another story about some man in the bushes, didn't she?"

Greg refused to answer. After a moment the captain continued. "I wanted to tell you to watch yourself, Stafford. Be careful you don't fall for a pretty face and a nice body. That girl is trouble."

Lonergan left, slamming the door behind him.

BY NOON the next day, the apartment was restored to a semblance of order. Tricia had contacted their insurance agent, and he had promised to send an adjustor out at one. Although Julie had worked as hard as Tricia, her mind had been elsewhere. She kept waiting for the phone to ring again, dreading another threatening call.

Talking to Greg had made her feel a little better. Yet he had seemed odd on the phone, almost as if he was afraid someone was listening to their call. Had someone been with him?

As if Greg had read her mind, the phone rang. Tricia answered it and called for her a moment later. "Julie, it's Greg. Remember, you're not free until after the adjustor comes."

Julie grabbed the phone. "Hi, Greg."

He was laughing. "I see Tricia is back in control of herself."

"She's worked so hard I'm afraid she may collapse, but our place looks better this morning."

His voice took on a serious note. "Any more phone calls?"

"No, thank goodness. I'm sorry if I called too late last night. You weren't asleep, were you?"

"No." Did she imagine that he hesitated over the word?

"I've been thinking about what you said last night, Greg. About those people, the Eastern Bloc agents. Do you think the man who called was one of them?" In the cold light of day, the words sounded terribly melodramatic.

"It's very possible, Julie. And if so, they'll try to contact you again." She sensed a difference in his voice, a new assurance and authority. He hadn't talked to her in quite this way before, as if he was taking her innocence for granted. She wondered if she was imagining it. Or had she only imagined his earlier suspicion?

"What can I do, Greg? Do you think I should go to the police? They still think I'm the one who has the disk. I doubt they'll believe a word I say."

Greg was silent for a long time. "Not yet, Julie. We need some proof of who these people are. Let's wait a little longer. If you want, I'll check with Lonergan again to find out if they know anything more about the case."

Julie considered his suggestion. "Okay, I'll wait. But I'm frightened, Greg."

"When may I come by for you?"

"After two, I suppose. I'm sorry. Where did you want to go?"

"I thought we might go kite flying."

"What?" She started laughing. "Are you serious?"

"Certainly. You'll love it. You're the adventurous sort. I went shopping this morning and found a couple of fantastic Japanese numbers."

"I haven't flown a kite since I was about ten," Julie protested. "I'll get the strings all twisted."

"Nonsense. Be ready at two."

Tricia passed her as she hung up the phone. Her arms were loaded with a stack of newspapers. "Hurry up, Julie. Get back to work."

"Is that yesterday's paper?"

"I guess so." Tricia looked down and flipped through the stack. "Yes, here it is. Sunday's paper. I didn't have time to read it, but it's old news now."

"Let's hope so," Julie agreed fervently. She took the newspaper from Tricia and opened it, kneeling down to lay it on the floor. It was worse than she expected. Her own face stared out at her from page two. She was being led from the terminal building to a waiting police car, flanked by the two federal agents.

Tricia leaned over her shoulder. "My God, Julie. That's you."

"I'm afraid so." She snapped the paper shut and took it into her bedroom. Closing the door, she turned to the story again. The accompanying article wasn't long. It didn't have to be. The headline said it all: "Local woman arrested for espionage." The first paragraph described her ordeal at the airport. The next paragraph was a brief biography, giving her place of employment and a few facts about her background.

With a grimace, she shoved the paper into the bottom drawer of her bureau. Maybe someday she'd want to look at it again. Right now she was praying the Los Angeles papers hadn't picked up the story.

TWO HOURS OF RUNNING up and down the beach convinced Julie that kite flying was far from a kid's game. Greg had taught her how to maneuver the strings, and soon her rainbow-hued butterfly kite was soaring proudly through the sky.

Greg's kite was more elaborate, a fierce dragon with a long tongue that unfurled as he manipulated the strings. Greg was an excellent teacher, easygoing and immensely patient. He consoled her when her kite plunged to the ground, driven by a sudden gust of wind, then challenged her when she threatened to give up. "Keep trying, Julie. You'll see. It's easy when you get the hang of it."

When he turned his attention to his own kite, her eyes were hypnotically drawn to him. He carried himself with innate assurance, every movement of his body exuding power, grace and vitality. Barefoot, head thrown back, a wide smile relaxing his mouth, he radiated enthusiasm and a healthy zest for life. Yet even now Julie sensed that beneath his carefree exterior ran an undercurrent of alertness, of keen observation and sharp concentration.

At his suggestion, they chose the beach behind the condominium for their kite flying. Some of her neighbors came out on their balconies to watch, and she wondered if they were talking about her. *Julie Smith, the one who was arrested for spying. They let her go. Wonder if she really did it? She spent the night in jail. She's an airline stewardess. Probably an enemy agent.* Yes, she could imagine what they were saying. What did it matter if she was innocent? Her picture had been in the paper, hadn't it? That's what people would remember.

"Julie," Greg shouted.

"I'm exhausted," she called, above the sound of the pounding surf. "How do I bring this thing down?"

"You can't. It's your master now. When you stop, it will carry you into the skies."

"I'd feel right at home," she reminded him.

They guided the kites downward eventually, maneuvering to keep them from falling into the water. "I saw my picture in the paper." Julie was rolling up her kite strings when she spoke.

Greg looked at her sharply. "Don't let it bother you, Julie. People won't remember. They'll be talking about someone else by tomorrow."

"This is all so new to me." Julie subsided on the sand at a safe distance from the water's edge. "My life has been so ordinary until now."

"You don't fit the role at all." Greg sat beside her, shifting until he was half lying, resting on one elbow.

"What role?"

"Spy. Traitor. Victim. None of those could possibly describe you." He watched her thoughtfully, quietly, as though he enjoyed doing so.

"You didn't feel that way at first. You were very suspicious of me."

"No, I wasn't," he denied. When she lifted her eyebrows and smiled, he added, "Well, I was cautious."

"Are you always so cautious?" Julie sifted sand through her fingers, not meeting his gaze. "Or was it just me?"

"It wasn't personal. I would have acted the same had it been anyone. A lawyer can't afford to be wrong about his clients."

"And you don't meet a lady spy every day, do you?" Julie slanted a grin at him.

He looked away. "Not every day, no."

"Why are you being so nice to me, Greg? I appreciate it, but I don't want your pity."

Greg's hand covered hers, warm and sandy. "I like you, Julie. Very much. I'm with you because I like being with you." His voice was gruff. "You're not the sort of person who inspires pity. You're far too self-reliant for that. So don't even think such a thought."

Julie felt embarrassed. She was pleased to have him say he liked her. Yet she felt as if she had driven him to it with her mention of pity. "It's getting late. Shall we go in?"

They took the kites to Greg's car, putting them in the trunk before going upstairs. Tricia must have heard the elevator, for she had the door open before Julie could get her key inserted in the lock. "Julie, the most awful thing has happened."

"What now?" Greg stepped into the foyer quickly.

Tricia looked at Julie. "Remember that man the police insisted you knew? Jon Derickson?"

"Of course I remember the name."

"Well, you really do know him."

"I do not." Julie stared at Tricia in bewilderment.

"You must have forgotten when you met him. You spent some time with him in Japan once."

Greg's breathing grew shallow. Julie looked at him, catching a strange expression on his face. "I don't know that man. What on earth has happened to upset you?"

"You got a present from Jon. An expensive present." She pointed toward the living room.

Greg strode in, with Julie following close behind him. A basket of flowers was sitting in the middle of the coffee table. There were at least a dozen flowers, exotic black orchids. Orchids so expensive that one alone was a gift to be treasured.

"Look at the card," Tricia demanded. "I didn't mean to be nosy, but it's pinned right on the ribbon on the side of the basket, and it's not in an envelope."

"Who delivered them?" Greg moved closer to inspect the basket.

"It was an old man. He didn't mention the name of a florist. Jake called up from the lobby, so you can check with him."

"I will." Greg's voice was harsh. "Mind if I take these with me, Julie? We might be able to trace who sent them."

She leaned over and looked at the card. The words blurred before her eyes momentarily, and then she focused. "Thanks, Julie, for all you've done for me. These orchids are a tribute to the perfect moments we spent together in Tokyo. Yours forever, Jon Derickson."

"This is absurd." Julie looked at the other two. "Who's doing this to me? And how would a stranger get my address, anyway?"

"Easy enough for a pro with Derickson's contacts. Or anyone with money for a couple of bribes in the right places. Do you recognize the handwriting?" Greg's voice was cool, practical.

Julie inspected it closely. The card was written in blue ink, the handwriting small and carefully formed, totally unfamiliar to her. "No." She shrugged her shoulders helplessly.

Greg picked up the basket, his face grim. "I'm going to find out what's going on, Julie. I promise you that."

"Don't tell Captain Lonergan about these. This is the sort of thing that would convince him I'm guilty."

"He'd have to be pretty damn stupid to fall for a trick this obvious." Greg strode to the front door. "I see you didn't get new locks yet," he said as Julie came up behind him.

"Not yet. We were so busy this morning we didn't have time to get around to everything."

"Keep the door locked at all times and put the chain on when you're inside." Greg's face softened when he saw her worried expression. "I'll tell Jake to be extra alert tonight."

"Let me know if you find out anything."

"You can count on it."

AT TEN THE NEXT MORNING, Julie emerged from the shower and dressed in a cool linen dress of lemon yellow. A large white collar framed her face, highlighting her golden tan. She slid her feet into delicate high-heeled sandals and added gold earrings and a watch to her ensemble.

Makeup couldn't hide the shadows under her eyes, though. She had awakened once in the night, her sheets tangled around her, her heart beating rapidly. Feeling foolish, she had nevertheless gone out to see that the front door was tightly locked. It had taken her an hour to fall back asleep, and then her sleep had been troubled.

Her first order of business for the day was to telephone the airline office. Tricia had told her she was assigned to the next day's Tokyo flight, but she wanted to make sure. It was too much to hope that her arrest wasn't going to affect her reputation at work. All she could do was to explain what had happened and hope for the best.

The receptionist didn't return Julie's friendly greeting. "We were about to call you. Mr. Wallis wants to speak to you personally. Let me put you through to him."

Julie's heart thumped irregularly. Mr. Wallis was a vice-president. A request from him could only mean he wanted to discuss her arrest. His first words confirmed that.

"Ms Smith, we're alarmed about the publicity you've been given by the papers. After careful consideration we have decided that you should be removed from flight status temporarily until this matter is resolved."

"The matter is resolved, Mr. Wallis. It was a false arrest. The case is closed."

The vice-president cleared his throat audibly. "This isn't anything personal against you, Ms Smith, but we have made the decision to suspend you for two weeks."

"Suspend me?" Julie considered the implications of such a move. "Without pay?"

"Well, of course. That's part of the suspension package. If you're not doing any work for us, we can't very well pay you."

"You can't do this. It's not fair."

"We have to think of our passengers. Would you want to fly with someone suspected of . . . this?"

"Of what?"

"Of spying. Tokyo Rose may sound romantic, but not when she's pouring your coffee at thirty thousand feet." There was a short pause. "I'm sorry. I have a call on another line, Ms. Smith."

Julie was still holding the receiver when the dial tone buzzed in her ear. She dropped the phone and grabbed her purse. "Tricia," she called. "I have to go to the airline office. If Greg calls, tell him I'll be back by noon."

"An assignment? Without me?" Tricia came out of her bedroom.

"Trouble. The airline is suspending me for two weeks without pay over this arrest business."

"We'll go on strike. I'll organize the other attendants. Maybe the pilots will support us, too. They can't do this to you."

Julie laughed. "Tricia, you are a gem but I don't need any help. I'm not going to lie down like a doormat and let anyone walk over me."

JULIE HAD TROUBLE finding a parking space at the airport. World Airlines headquarters were located in an office park that serviced several airlines. Circling the lot three times, she finally slid her tiny Toyota into a slot meant for motorcycles.

Mr. Wallis's secretary surveyed Julie with avid interest before buzzing his office to see if he was available. "He says he's too busy to talk with you right now."

"I don't want to get you in any trouble, but could you call him again? Tell him either he sees me now, or my attorney will be contacting him."

The secretary complied. "Mr. Wallis can see you now, Ms. Smith," she reported a moment later.

Mr. Wallis was standing when Julie entered. A tall man, whose thick brown hair was streaked with gray, he held out his hand and managed a smile. "I really don't have much time, Julie, but I knew you deserved more than that phone call earlier. Please sit down and I'll explain how we reached our decision about your case."

"First I'm going to explain my rights to you." Julie seated herself. "I have an exemplary record with World Airlines. Both of us know you have no legal right to suspend me without pay because of a police mistake."

He sat down, leaning back and pressing his fingertips together. "Our first obligation is to our passengers."

"I agree. How is that relevant?"

"That story about you in the paper has upset a lot of people."

"How many people are we talking about? Are there letters? Phone calls? I want facts."

"The number isn't important. It's the image of our company we're selling."

"What kind of image does a company have if it doesn't promote the welfare of its employees?"

"Good point," he conceded. "But nothing is going to change our board's decision to keep you off duty for the next two weeks. One of our members is in touch

with a law-enforcement agency, and they were adamant that your case is still not totally resolved."

Captain Lonergan, Julie realized. Obviously he wasn't through with her yet. He was next on her list of people she intended to confront.

Meanwhile, she had to settle this problem. "I have a compromise to suggest. I will voluntarily abstain from accepting any assignments for two weeks as long as it doesn't show on my record and I receive my pay."

"Without working?"

"That is your decision, not mine. I'm perfectly willing to work."

"We can't..."

"Fine." Julie rose. "My attorney will be in touch with you." She started for the door.

He reconsidered hastily. "How about if we call it two weeks paid vacation?"

Julie eyed him consideringly. It was better than nothing, but agreeing to use up all her vacation to suit their convenience was still a cop-out. "Let's call it one week paid vacation, one week on regular status, whether I work or not."

He stood up. "I accept. It's been a pleasure talking to you, Ms. Smith. Please remember that I'm always available to talk to our fine employees whenever they have a problem."

She managed to escape before giving in to the laughter bubbling inside her.

ONCE OUTSIDE, her laughter died quickly and was replaced by determination. As she left the building, she met Bob Reed on the steps. He threw his arms around her. "Julie, how are you? Carol and I have been so worried. I talked to Tricia yesterday, but you were out."

Julie freed herself from his warm embrace. "I'm fine now, Bob. But I appreciate your concern."

"Silliest damn thing I ever heard of." He shook his head. "Flying with me tomorrow?"

"I'm taking a week's vacation."

"Lucky you. Come visit Carol and me if you have time. She's anxious to see for herself that you're okay."

"I'll call," Julie promised.

THE POLICE HEADQUARTERS BUILDING was crowded when Julie made her way inside a little later. She headed directly for Captain Lonergan's office and was pleased to find him seated at his desk. "Come in," he growled impatiently when she tapped on the frame of the open door. He glanced up, his gaze narrowing as he saw the identity of his visitor.

Julie's heart was beating rapidly and her words tumbled out in a rush. "Why did you try to get me fired from my job?"

He pointed toward a chair. "You got the wrong person, Ms. Smith."

She sat down. "Didn't you speak to a board member at World Airlines and suggest they keep me off flight status?"

"Not me. But it's a good idea."

"Who, then? Lieutenant Massie?"

"Nobody from my staff. Must have been one of those federal agents. Maybe the one who trailed you from the scene of the crime."

Julie sighed. "Let's not start that again, Captain Lonergan. Can I talk to this federal agent?"

"You want to talk to him?"

"I'd like to tell him exactly what I think of him."

Captain Lonergan looked at her hard. Then he burst out laughing. At last he grew silent and leaned forward and shook his finger at her. "Why don't you bring me that disk and end all this game playing? From what happened to your condo yesterday, I'd say you're in real trouble."

Julie rose. "You'll forgive me if I leave, Captain. This sounds like a rerun of a script I found extremely boring the first time."

THERE WAS NONE of the usual spring in her step as she walked down the corridor leading outside. Ahead of her, a door suddenly opened, and Greg emerged. Another man, thin and not as tall as Greg, was beside him. "Greg," Julie called, and began walking faster.

Greg lifted his head, his eyes revealing his surprise. "Julie, what brings you here?" The man beside him vanished back behind the door.

"I should be asking you that." She lowered her voice. "I hope this doesn't mean you've been telling Captain Lonergan about the orchids."

"No," he said quickly. "I was just checking on the burglary to see if they had any leads yet."

"And?"

"Nothing yet. I haven't been able to discover much about the orchids, either. Why not have lunch with me? I can fill you in on the details."

"That would be nice."

They walked down the hall. "You haven't told me what you're doing here," Greg prompted.

"I was fighting job discrimination."

She wasn't sure if she imagined it, but she thought he tensed. "Something wrong about your job?"

"It's not as bad now as it was two hours ago." She summarized her meetings with Mr. Wallis and Captain Lonergan. "At least I have a paycheck now."

Greg put his arm around her. "I'm glad you won that battle."

"Thank you," she murmured. "I really needed the money. But then, who doesn't?"

THEY LUNCHED in a small restaurant in the Chinatown section of Honolulu. Julie left her car parked in front of police headquarters and rode with Greg. "Don't let me forget to pick it up before tonight," she reminded him. "All I need is for Captain Lonergan to ticket my car in front of his office."

"I'll bet he was surprised to see you come barging in." Greg's gray eyes glinted with amusement. "He never thought you would darken his door voluntarily."

"He still thinks I've got the disk." Julie picked at the snowy white pieces of shredded chicken with her fork. "Tell me what you found out about those orchids."

"None of the major florists will admit they sold them, but sometimes customers ask to remain anonymous."

"But this Derickson is supposed to be in Japan, isn't he? I'll bet the police department and those dreadful federal agents are keeping a watch on the airport. Surely they could nab him the moment he arrived in Honolulu."

"The police reports say he's a master of disguises."

"How about Jake? Did he remember more about the delivery person?"

"He said the man arrived at dusk, not long after Jake went on duty. It was only a few minutes before we came in from flying the kites. He said the man, who was elderly, asked directions to your apartment. Jake called upstairs, and Tricia agreed to accept the delivery for you. Jake didn't check outside to see what kind of vehicle the man was driving." Greg grinned at her suddenly. "According to Jake, Miss Smith is a popular young lady who gets quite a few deliveries from the florist, so it was only routine to him."

Julie blushed. "I'm afraid Jake was indulging in a little exaggeration."

"Well, the orchids are certainly an odd development in this case. Nothing is making much sense."

After lunch Julie called Tricia to let her know what had happened with Mr. Wallis. "I didn't lose my paycheck, Tricia, so you won't have to organize that strike."

"Where are you calling from?"

"I'm with Greg. We had lunch and we're going to spend the afternoon together."

"Don't be too late. Tony's on night duty, and I don't like the thought of staying here by myself tonight. Of course, you'll have to be alone while I go on the flight to Tokyo tomorrow."

"Don't worry about me. I won't be late."

BY THE TIME THEY LEFT the restaurant, Greg was feeling restless. He hadn't slept much the night before. His talk with Walt had been unsatisfying, and the confrontation with Captain Lonergan had left him edgy. For much of the night he had lain awake, worrying about Julie, puzzling over the facts as he knew them.

Julie seemed to have relaxed over lunch. She smiled at him as they got into the car. "I hope I didn't spoil lunch by talking about my problems again, Greg. Let me make it up to you by showing you around Honolulu.''

"I don't feel much like sightseeing. How about you?''

"I'd be happy to show you around.'' Her smile was warm and genuine.

For a moment Greg wished he could take her up on the offer. The idea of playing tourist for the afternoon appealed to him. He was tired of constantly being on his guard with Julie, worn out by pretending to be someone he wasn't. His feelings about her were confusing, yet one thing was clear. He liked her. He liked her a lot.

In the beginning he had been so sure she was Derickson's courier. Even now, the facts all pointed in her direction. A woman named Julie Smith had spent the night at the Masuda Inn with Derickson. He himself had followed that woman from the Masuda to the Imperial Hotel. When he had asked the hotel clerk to page Julie, she had answered the summons almost immediately.

Yet his gut instincts were telling him something was wrong. Julie was convinced she was being framed. Maybe she was right. Perhaps someone else had used her name. Perhaps someone else wanted them to think Julie was the guilty party.

If that was true, Julie was potentially in a lot of danger. If Derickson was somehow using her to throw the police and the agency off his trail, then the men who wanted to buy the disk could be confused, as well. That would explain the search of her apartment and the phone call last night.

He felt desperate. He had to do something; but what? Walt refused even to consider his theory. "You're letting the girl con you,'' Walt had warned him the night before. And Captain Lonergan had said much the same thing.

Greg glanced quickly around. Even now, if his theory was right, he and Julie could be being followed. If the Eastern Bloc agents or whoever was buying that disk from Derickson thought Julie had it, they would stop at nothing to get it from her. He felt a sudden need to protect her, to keep her out of sight. "I'd rather go somewhere and talk," he suggested.

When she nodded her agreement, he started the car, heading out into the traffic. "There's a large terrace at my hotel," he continued. "We could go there. It's nice and sunny, and we should have some privacy." *And I'll have a better chance of determining whether we're being followed,* he added mentally.

The lobby of the hotel was virtually empty. As he led Julie out to the terrace, Greg scanned the room as unobtrusively as possible. Once they were seated at a table, he realized that Julie was watching him and attempted to relax.

"Tell me more about your adopted state." He kept his tone light and conversational and smiled at her.

Julie eyed him as if she found his request odd, but she complied. "Hawaii is a chain of volcanic islands—132 in all. Some are no more than bare rocks sticking out of the sea. There are eight major islands, but only six are open to tourists."

"And which is your favorite?" Greg's gaze drifted to her mouth, and he felt compelled to keep her talking. He liked the way her whole face lit up when she was enthusiastic about something. A gentle breeze ruffled her hair, and the light perfume she wore wafted to his nostrils, stirring his senses.

"There's an allure and excitement about this island—Oahu—that grabs you and makes it hard to leave. But I love Kauai and Maui and Molokai...." She ended on a laugh. Gesturing lightly with one slim hand, she explained. "I love all of them, but that doesn't mean I don't enjoy visiting the other forty-nine states—or anywhere else in the world. I've never visited a place I didn't like at least somewhat. Don't you like to travel?"

Greg was caught off guard. He had been so busy watching her that it took him a moment to formulate an answer. "Most of my travel has been on business, so it can get tiring."

"I didn't realize attorneys had to travel so much. Do you practice international law?"

He felt uncomfortable. For a moment he longed to tell her the truth. If he turned to her right now, this moment, and told her that he wasn't really a practicing attorney, that instead he was an agent for the DIA, what would she do? He imagined the scene, visualized the way her face would tense, the shock and distrust in her eyes. He took a deep breath, and when he spoke his voice held none of his inner turmoil. "Not really. I spend a lot of time doing paperwork, like most lawyers. So even when I'm traveling, I'm not acting the part of tourist."

Silence fell between them. "Tell me something, Greg," Julie said at length. "I want an honest answer."

Greg's whole body tensed as he waited for her question. When it came, it was not what he expected.

"Did you intend ever to see me again when you left the plane here in Honolulu?"

He lifted his hand to touch her cheek. "You'd made it pretty plain you didn't want me around." There was so much more he could have said. He wanted to tell her how he'd felt when she turned to look at him on the plane, how difficult it had been for him to remember his mission. From the first he had wished things could be different, that he was simply a man who had found a woman he really liked. Liked wasn't the right word. He cared for Julie in a way he'd never cared for any woman before. And it had happened so fast he'd hardly realized it until it was too late to go back.

Julie turned her face until she could press her lips to his palm. "You knew better than that."

His pulse pounded furiously and his senses responded madly to her soft caress. Yet he managed to look vaguely amused. "You could read my mind?"

"Umm...." Julie reached across and touched his face, her fingers sliding along his throat, brushing just beneath his collar, tangling in his hair.

Greg gave in to the moment he had known was inevitable. He pushed aside his worries, his duties, his confusion. "Now you tell me something," he said thickly. "Would you have said yes if I'd asked?"

"Apparently I never had a choice." Julie smiled wryly. "It seems that fate stepped in."

"You have a choice now." Greg's breathing slowed. "I don't think I really brought you here to talk, Julie."

"I suspected as much." Her smile was soft, hesitant; and yet she didn't back away.

He reached for her hand and brought it up until her palm was resting against his heart. Perhaps he couldn't be truthful with her about everything, but his feelings were real. With no thought for anything except this moment, he whispered, "Let's go somewhere a bit more private."

Chapter Nine

Julie waited while Greg collected his key from the desk. They didn't talk on the way to his room. Once inside, Greg turned and eyed her unsteadily. "Julie. are you sure?"

"Yes," she said simply. She had never been more sure of anything in her life. From the moment when she had first seen Greg on the plane, she had known there was something different about him. She had grown to admire Greg, to respect his fundamental honesty and integrity.

Under other circumstances she might have waited. But she was certain that what she felt for him was solid and enduring. She knew instinctively that this relationship was meant to last. As soon as this mix-up with the police was sorted out, their feelings would have room to grow. Meanwhile, it was enough this afternoon to take what he was offering.

His touch was warm, compelling, sure. Guiding her into his arms, he lowered his mouth to hers. There was a sense of urgency in his kiss that communicated without words. She felt it, too—that need to give and accept, to share and explore, to know and to be known.

He uttered her name on a husky groan and then kissed her until she was breathless. She could sense the fire in him, the barely restrained surge of passion. From their first meeting she had felt that he was holding himself in check, afraid of revealing too much of himself. And now she sensed that some barrier inside him had broken and that he was ready to pour out the full intensity of his feelings.

She opened herself to him, holding back nothing. His tongue probed the recesses of her mouth and she returned the kiss, curving her arms around his neck, pressing her breasts against the solid muscles of his chest.

At length, his mouth broke away from hers. He buried his face against her neck, his lips caressing, his tongue darting up to tease the soft outer shell of her ear. "Julie," he muttered thickly, and his body trembled against hers.

"I know," she whispered. She leaned back slightly, putting her hand beneath his jaw, lifting his face until she could look into his eyes. They were dark gray now, their deep velvety centers surrounded by warm gray circles that reminded her of the surf outside their window.

His gaze captured hers, memorizing and exploring every feature of her face. She responded by moving closer, her hands reaching to open the buttons of his shirt. Greg watched her, his eyes unfathomable, as she tugged his shirt loose. He drew in a deep breath when her hand touched his bared skin, and then he was gripping her tightly.

His hand moved to her breast, spreading heat wherever he touched. She was on fire for him, with a hunger that was new to her. She was only vaguely aware of the moment when he carried her to the bed. Then they were undressing each other, taking time to explore and touch and caress, yet with a building intensity that could not be denied for long.

As Greg shed the last of his clothes, he stood for a moment beside the bed. Julie drank in the sight of him. He was everything she had ever wanted in a man. She lifted her gaze to his and surprised such a look of wonder and desire that her breath caught in her throat. How could she ever have thought this man was hiding secrets, when his very soul was laid bare and he was entrusting it into her care?

He couldn't take his eyes off her. Julie was aware that he was following her every movement, noticing every detail. "You're perfect," he said hoarsely. "Everything I could ever want...."

As he hesitated, she pulled him toward her. "I know," she said, placing her finger against his lips when he would have interrupted. "I know exactly what you mean."

GREG STIRRED FIRST, feeling the soft caress of Julie's hair against his chest. Her eyes were closed and her breathing even and restful.

His last lingering doubts about Julie were gone now. Unless she personally confessed to him herself, he could never believe she was guilty. A spasm of self-hatred went through him. He would never forgive himself for involving her in this mess. Obviously he had made a mistake. Followed the wrong woman. Identified the wrong suspect.

She opened her eyes slowly, her generous mouth curving into a tremulous smile. "What time is it?"

Time. The word shot through him like an arrow. *We're running out of time, Stafford. Get that disk. We only have a few days left.* "We have plenty of time," he said softly, in defiance of his mental demons.

She leaned up on one elbow. "Do you have a cigarette?"

He laughed and slid out of the bed. When he returned with two cigarettes and his lighter, she had slipped on his discarded shirt and was sitting up. Her hair was tousled, her cheeks flushed, her long legs curved sensuously from beneath the garment. To Greg, she had never seemed more alluring or provocative.

He handed her a cigarette and leaned over to light it for her. As their eyes met, he remembered the first time he'd performed this act for her in the airport tunnel. He could tell she was remembering, too.

She leaned back and he slipped into bed, lighting his own cigarette. She took the lighter from his hand and ran the tip of a polished nail over the ornately carved initials. "You've had this a long time," she mused.

"Hmm."

"A woman gave it to you."

He hid his expression behind a curl of smoke.

"She didn't know you too well," Julie observed.

He lifted his eyebrow, smiling. "Oh?"

"Does it have sentimental value?"

"Not in the way you mean. I hate the thing. It reminds me of a painful lesson that I never want to forget."

"She betrayed your trust?"

"Not in love. In...business. She lied about something important. I believed her and defended her, and the results were disastrous."

She stared at the lighter for several moments and then brought it to her mouth, gave it a light kiss and threw it in a curving arc across the room. It landed neatly in the wastebasket.

He watched her action with a feeling of amusement. "Just like that?" he asked.

She nodded. "Remind me I owe you a new lighter."

THEY SHOWERED and dressed, then dined on the roof of Greg's hotel, watching the flood of twinkling lights along the curve of Waikiki Beach. As they lingered over coffee, Julie checked her watch. "I have to leave now," she said regretfully.

"Not tonight."

"Tricia's afraid to stay alone."

"Where's Tony?"

"He's on duty." She reached for her purse. "Don't forget I have to pick up my car at the police station."

"We'll spend tomorrow together." Greg's voice was firm, stating a fact rather than asking a question.

"Tomorrow afternoon." When he started to protest she stopped him. "I need to call my French-language tutor and schedule a lesson. We'll spend the rest of the day together. Let's meet at the Polynesian Bar at noon. They serve fantastic lobster."

"Okay, but I'll be counting the minutes." Greg reached for her hand and brought it to his mouth. She loved the quiet insistence of his voice and the warmth of his lips as they moved on her soft palm.

CAPTAIN LONERGAN WAS COMING out of the building as Julie unlocked the door of her compact car in front of the police station a short time later. Greg spoke to him first. "Good evening, Captain."

The short, bulky man flashed one of his grim smiles. "How are you, counselor? And you, Ms. Smith? Enjoying this beautiful moonlight?"

Julie made a slight face at Greg after acknowledging the greeting. When the captain was out of earshot, she turned to Greg. "Did you get the feeling that he found us amusing?"

Greg frowned, staring after the man. Then he turned back to Julie with a smile. "Probably wishing he could spend time in the moonlight with you, Julie."

"Greg..." Julie laughed. "I can't imagine the captain ever taking time off for any fun."

Greg followed her home in his car and then insisted on riding to the fourteenth floor with her. It took several minutes for Tricia to move a chest from in front of the door after Julie had identified herself. "I didn't want to take any chances," Tricia explained.

"Anything else happen today?"

"Nothing. Hello, Greg. Can I fix you some coffee or a drink?"

"You're not on duty," Greg reminded her.

Julie glanced at him reprovingly. "Thanks for seeing me home, Greg. We're to meet tomorrow for lunch?"

"Unless you'd like to make that breakfast instead." He gazed down at Julie and started to pull her into his arms. Tricia beat a hasty retreat, calling out as she went, "Bye, Greg."

Greg looked down at Julie. "I don't know if I can wait until tomorrow to see you again." His eyes grew serious. "Take care of yourself, Julie. Don't open the door to anyone."

Julie drew back slightly. "You're so serious, Greg. You frighten me."

"I don't mean to frighten you." He pulled her back against him. "Just be careful."

TRICIA WAS PACING the floor when Julie entered the living room. Her eyes gleamed with excitement. "You're going to be proud of me, Julie."

Julie put down her purse. "You finally agreed to set a wedding date?"

"I went to see Mr. Wallis and refused to handle the Tokyo flight without you."

"Tricia, you shouldn't get involved in my troubles." Julie felt slightly sick. Seeing that Tricia was looking hurt, she reached over and hugged her swiftly. "But I do appreciate it. What did he say?"

"He grumbled a lot and finally said he'd reassign me for these two weeks. I'm taking the local runs. Tomorrow I handle the Hilo flight."

"That's a terrible assignment," Julie groaned. "No first class, and you have to grab the drinks out of the passengers' hands almost as soon as you serve them." She did a quick imitation, pretending to hand a glass to an imaginary passenger. "Good morning, Mr. Tourist. Here's your drink. Now swallow it like a good boy and hand it right back or I'll pour it down your throat."

Tricia giggled. "I know what a rush that flight is, but I thought it was important to take a stand."

Julie eyed her fondly, but there was a sinking sensation in the pit of her stomach. The glorious time she had spent with Greg faded into the recesses of her mind.

Nothing had changed. She was still under suspicion. A cloud of suspicion that was threatening to envelop her . . . and everyone connected with her.

GREG AWOKE to the sound of a knock on his door. He groaned and rolled back over, trying to recapture the dream he'd been having. He had been holding Julie in his arms, and they had been on a moonlit beach....

"Who's there?" He reached for his robe. He'd intended to sleep late, and he was almost certain he'd put the Do Not Disturb sign on the doorknob before he went to bed. A glance at his watch told him it was almost ten-thirty.

"Walt," a voice replied. Instantly alert, Greg strode across the room to open the door.

The older man pushed his way into the room, his manner agitated. "Greg, I've got something for you."

Greg settled into a chair and motioned for Walt to sit down across from him. "What is it?" he asked, suddenly wary. He knew his partner well enough to realize that only something important would bring him here personally. They had agreed the day before to avoid making contact if at all possible.

"She's been paid off."

"Who?" He knew even as he spoke that he was merely buying time. It was perfectly obvious Walt was referring to Julie, and Greg held his breath as he waited for Walt's next words.

"The Smith woman." Walt spoke impatiently. "Remember, it was your suggestion that we watch her bank account? Her banker agreed after a little persuasion on my part to alert us to any unusual activity in that account. First thing this morning a deposit was made. Ten thousand dollars. Cold, hard cash."

Greg leaned forward abruptly. "Are you sure?" Even as he asked the question he was reeling from the blow Walt had dealt him. Not Julie. A sense of déjà vu overwhelmed him. Not again. He couldn't have been so completely taken in by a woman a second time. And why did it hurt so much more than that earlier occasion?

Walt seemed unaware of what his announcement had done to Greg. "We're positive. One of the tellers took the money from a woman when the bank opened this morning. There was a large crowd, since it's a local payday. When she fed the account information into the machine, it triggered a red flag and was brought to the attention of a vice-president."

"Could the teller describe the woman?"

Walt shook his head. "We keep running up against snags in this damn case. The teller only remembered that the woman was young and wearing jeans. Aside from that..."

"Come on, now. Julie is rather distinctive looking." Greg slammed his fist against the arm of the chair. "Her hair is a gorgeous shade of blond. I can't believe another woman didn't notice."

"Well, she didn't. We showed her a group of photos, and she couldn't identify Julie as the customer making the deposit. She said she didn't observe the woman well enough to remember. But what else do you need, man? Give me another explanation for this deposit in the Smith woman's account."

Greg glanced down at the floor, trying to make sense of it all. He reached in the pocket of his robe for his cigarettes and pulled one out. Fumbling for his lighter, he suddenly remembered. He stood and went over to the dresser, lighting his cigarette with a match provided by the hotel.

"Lose your lighter?" Walt sounded surprised.

Greg glanced over at the wastebasket. "Yes, it's gone," he said. "I didn't care for it any longer. I'm getting a new one." For a moment his hand tightened into a fist and then he released it, breathing deeply, calming himself.

He sat down again and held out his hand. "Let me see that deposit slip. I'm still working on my theory that Smith has been set up in this whole deal."

Walt snorted in derision. "That's the flimsiest theory I've ever come across. Who ever heard of someone throwing away ten thousand dollars?" He handed a copy of Julie's bank transactions to Greg. "As you can see, she's not much of a saver. Although she's never in trouble with the bank, she keeps a pretty low balance. Ten thousand dollars is a lot of money to drop into an account in one day."

"Did any of our operatives follow her to the bank?"

"Well, no." Walt shifted uncomfortably. "I know you reported last night that you weren't seeing her until noon today, so I assigned Keith to the job. He saw the roommate leave and followed her a short way. Smith must have left during that time, because half an hour after Keith returned he saw her entering the lobby of her building. She had a sack of groceries, so he didn't think anything of it. The time frame is perfect. I think we've got what we need this time."

"Not yet. We still don't have that disk." Greg thought quickly, trying to work out a plan. "I'm meeting Julie for lunch at the Polynesian Bar today at twelve. I want you to send a backup tail, and make sure you keep track of when she leaves her condo. I have a feeling that she's going to be in a lot of trouble before this day is over."

As soon as Walt left, Greg dialed Julie's line. He had no choice now. He had to tell her the truth. He'd already waited too long as it was. She was in danger, of that he was certain. But together they would find out what was happening before it was too late.

A busy signal sounded on her line, and he replaced the receiver. As he hurried to the shower, he thought of what her reaction to his true identity would be. *Coward, tell her in person,* he admonished himself. As hard as it would be to see the pain in those blue eyes, he owed her that much.

AN HOUR AFTER SHE SAW TRICIA off for her flight, Julie returned from the grocery store and stowed away the perishables. She was trying to decide what to wear for lunch with Greg when the phone rang. She picked it up warily, still unnerved by the events of the past few days.

A well-modulated feminine voice spoke. "Julie Smith, please."

"Yes?"

"This is Brenda Clark. I was a passenger on your flight...."

It took Julie a moment to remember her. The young woman who had seemed so troubled. It was strange that she should be calling. Julie replied cautiously. "Yes, Ms. Clark? I remember you. You flew with me both ways, I believe. Is anything wrong?"

"Everything." The statement was delivered flatly and unemotionally. "I was wondering if you could meet me somewhere for a talk."

"I have a luncheon engagement." Julie hesitated. "What did you want? And how did you get my phone number?"

There was a pause. "I...I paid someone to locate you for me."

Julie gasped. "What was so important about speaking with me?"

"You have such a kind face." Brenda's voice broke, and Julie could hear her struggling to regain control. At length she continued. "I'm in terrible trouble. Please. I need to talk to someone. I'm desperate."

"I can give you the crisis hot-line number. I'm not trained to help..."

"No." Brenda's voice rose on the protest. "No, I want to talk to you. You seemed to understand me on the plane. I won't take long. If we could just meet somewhere fairly close to your home."

Julie hesitated, checked her watch and then gave in reluctantly. She'd never been able to turn down anyone who needed her. "I can meet you in half an hour in the Rose Garden at Kapiolani Park. There are some outdoor tables there. I can only talk for half an hour before I absolutely must leave. Maybe I can refer you to my doctor or a professional who could help you."

"Yes, okay." Brenda sounded relieved. "Will a taxi driver know where the Kapiolani Park is?"

"It's well-known and a main tourist attraction. On Kalakaua Avenue." She couldn't resist adding, "Are you sure you'll recognize me this time?"

After she hung up, Julie dialed Greg's number to tell him she might be a few minutes late. He didn't answer, and she hurried into her bedroom to dress, promising herself that no matter how much Brenda Clark needed to talk, she would give her one half hour and no more.

Greg would be leaving the islands soon, returning to Los Angeles. She had no intention of missing a chance to spend the afternoon with him. On impulse she grabbed the phone book, flipping through the yellow pages to find the number of a cab company. Underlining the number quickly, she dialed the company and ordered a taxi. It seemed a shame for her to take her own car. When she met Greg, they would use his car.

Instead of leaving by the main elevator, she walked to the end of the hall and rode down a side elevator to the entrance where she had asked the taxi to pick her up. The driver was standing outside the cab waiting and she slid inside. "Kapiolani Park, please. The entrance near the Rose Garden."

The driver was young and wore a brightly flowered shirt hanging open over his muscular chest. "You a visitor?" he asked.

"No." She leaned back to discourage conversation and thought about Brenda Clark. She had been right about one thing: the woman had been upset. Tricia had dismissed her worries about their passenger, but Julie had sensed immediately that the woman was distraught. And at the airport, she remembered, Brenda had looked as if she might faint during Julie's arrest. If she had already been upset, perhaps the stress of seeing someone arrested had been too much for her.

Julie scarcely noticed as the cab swept through the downtown area. When the driver slammed on the brakes in front of the park entrance, she caught herself just in time to keep from catapulting forward. He apologized quickly; she nodded abstractedly in acknowledgment as she paid him.

The park was busy but not as crowded as during the height of the tourist season. Its lush tropical greenery had been designed as a tribute to the wife of Kalakaua, the last king of Hawaii.

Following the labyrinth of paths, Julie located the fragrant Rose Garden. As her eyes scanned the area, she located a cluster of outdoor tables near a refreshment stand. At the farthest one, a woman sat hunched over.

From this distance it was impossible to tell if she was Brenda Clark, but Julie walked toward her. "Ms. Clark?" she asked.

Brenda Clark turned around, her eyes enormous. Like Julie, she was wearing a pair of jeans. But hers were low-slung, and her blue knit cropped top barely skimmed her breasts. In her hand she clutched an expensive leather handbag, which reminded Julie of the mink she'd worn on the flight. "I almost gave you up. Thank God you've come."

As Julie pulled out a seat she consulted her watch. Actually, she'd made excellent time, but she supposed that it passed slowly when you were in as much agony as this young woman appeared to be. "What can I do to help?"

"I'm in terrible trouble."

"You told me that on the phone. What kind of trouble?" Mentally, Julie ran through a list of things that might be troubling her.

"I don't know where to begin." Tears filled Brenda's eyes, but she brushed them away impatiently.

Julie smiled soothingly. "Just start anywhere. If I don't understand, I'll ask questions."

Brenda bowed her head. "Perhaps if I tell you a little about myself you'll understand why I got involved in what I did."

"That's a good place to start," Julie agreed patiently. Inwardly, she sighed. It appeared as if Brenda's story might be lengthy.

"My father is Dewitt Clark."

Julie smiled blankly, aware that Brenda had expected her to recognize the name. Brenda continued. "He's super rich. He's the majority shareholder of a *Fortune* 500 company, and he breeds world-class thoroughbreds. I'm an only child. My mother divorced him when I was young, and he got custody.''

Brenda paused, and Julie glanced surreptitiously at her watch. As if sensing her impatience, Brenda hurried on. ''He was always good to me, but he expected me to be something great. When I finished high school in Switzerland and came home, he outlined his plans for me. I was to be a terrific success. I had three choices: medical school, law school or a business degree. Since I had barely been able to pass high school, even with special tutoring, I just stared at him.''

''Surely he could understand.''

''He doesn't want to understand. He has to believe that his daughter is the best. I did manage to get accepted by a college and really tried hard, but after two semesters, I flunked out. My dad didn't give up. He hired more tutors, and I tried another school.''

Julie's sympathies were aroused. It was a familiar enough story. Successful parents wanted their children to exceed even their own accomplishments. ''And then what happened?''

''I flunked out again and ended up with a nervous breakdown. After two years of intensive therapy I recovered somewhat. That was when I met . . . this man.''

''Yes.'' Julie tried not to sound impatient, but she wondered when Brenda would get to the point.

''I met this man in Hong Kong. I was on a shopping trip there with some friends. This fabulous man introduced himself to me in a restaurant one evening. He asked me out, and after two dates we made love.''

Here Brenda paused, pulling out a tissue and dabbing at her eyes. Her voice quavered when she continued. ''Julie, it was fantastic. It was the first time in my life someone really paid attention to *me*. I couldn't believe it. He didn't know who I was or who my father was. He liked *me*, Brenda Clark. I was ecstatic.''

''But it didn't work out.'' Julie was beginning to guess at the ending to the story. Brenda had a youthful naiveté that made it painfully obvious that she could be easily hurt.

''We arranged to meet again, and I went home, feeling like a different person. We saw each other several times after that, twice in Tokyo and once in Singapore. During the next year, I enrolled in vet assistants' school. When my dad made fun of me, I just laughed. Nothing he said seemed to hurt anymore. Someone special loved me.'' Her voice suddenly cracked, and Julie reached over and patted her hand.

''What happened next?''

''He called me to meet him in Tokyo again. He even sent me tickets.'' She laughed. ''I exchanged them for first class, naturally. I had never been so happy in my life. Here was a man wanting to give to me, instead of always taking.''

''I remember how excited you looked on the way over.''

''And what a wreck I was on the way back.'' Brenda began to sob in earnest.

''Let me get you something to drink from the refreshment stand,'' Julie suggested hastily.

''Coffee.'' Brenda was searching for another tissue.

Julie hurried away. As she waited her turn at the stand, she debated what she was going to do about the girl. Brenda needed professional help of some sort, of that Julie was certain. Perhaps she could put her in a taxi, Julie mused. Then she could direct the taxi to take Brenda to a local counseling clinic.

Brenda reached for the coffee when Julie returned and took a sip. "I'm okay now. I'd like to finish my story."

"Look, Brenda." Julie chose her next words carefully. "Perhaps you should talk to a counselor about this. Someone who can really help you. I'd like to do something for you, but I'm not trained to help." Julie reached for her purse and started to rise. "Let me call you a taxi."

"No, you can't do that." Brenda half rose from her chair. "You don't understand. You're involved in all this."

"But how?" Julie stared back at Brenda, dismayed and uncertain what to do next.

"The man I'm talking about..." Brenda paused and took another sip of coffee. "He's the man the police are looking for."

Julie stared at the other girl in growing shock. "Jon," she said at last, in a strangled whisper. "You're talking about Jon Derickson. You're the woman with the disk. The one who's been using my name."

Brenda nodded her head and started crying again. "Julie, I don't have the disk any longer. You do. I hid it in your condo." She hesitated and then added, "It's between the mattress and the box spring at the foot of your bed."

Julie clutched her arm, her eyes blazing. "How dare you! We're going straight to the police, and you're going to tell them what you've told me."

"Give me a minute more," Brenda wailed, tears running down her cheeks.

"Start talking," Julie said coldly. "You'd better tell me what's going on. What made you use my name?"

"It was Jon's idea. When we left the airport he acted odd, and I was worried. I kept asking him what was wrong, and he told me he had a business problem. We went out to eat and, over dinner, I pleaded with him to tell me what was wrong. At last he gave in and told me he needed to get a computer disk out of the country."

Brenda stopped to blow her nose. "He told me it was a disk that contained information about his company; that it was only important to his rivals and that he wanted to guard his company secrets. I didn't know until I read about your arrest in the paper that Jon was asking me to be a spy."

"Go on," Julie pressed her after a few moments during which Brenda had continued to sob quietly.

"I finally agreed to help him." When Julie made a sound of disgust, she added in a defensive tone. "It sounded important. I didn't know it was a crime."

"Tell me what happened next. Get to the part about using my name."

"We left the restaurant. Suddenly Jon grabbed my arm and pulled me into an alley. He said we were being followed. I started to cry and Jon got mad at me. I couldn't stand that, so I told him I'd do anything to help. He came up with this idea of my pretending to be someone else. He promised me that that way I wouldn't get into any trouble with that rival company."

"So you decided to pretend to be me? Didn't you think about getting *me* into trouble?"

"It didn't occur to me until later. Right then, I was so afraid of Jon. He told me to think of a name, any name, real quick. The only name I could think of was yours. I had read it off your name tag on the plane."

"There were other attendants on the flight."

"But your name, Smith. It seemed so easy. Julie Smith."

"And Jon agreed to that name?"

"Yes. He said it sounded okay. I told him I had talked to you. I told him you were staying at the Imperial . . . when I was talking to the other attendant about Tokyo she told me that. Jon decided I was to go by taxi to the Imperial and register under my real name. That way, if anyone was looking for me, I'd have an alibi."

"But if you weren't doing anything wrong, why would you need an alibi? Didn't that make you suspicious?"

"Julie, I didn't know what was going on. I just went along with Jon because I was so confused and shocked."

"Okay." Julie kept her voice as calm as she could. "This all happened on Thursday night?"

"Yes, but I didn't stay in the room. After I registered Jon took me to a department store. He told me to buy clothes that looked like yours. I bought the beige raincoat, and then I bought the paisley scarf because I knew my hair was such a different color no one would ever think I was you. Then we went to the Masuda Inn, where Jon was staying."

"And to establish your fake identity you told the desk clerk you were Julie Smith and that you were expecting a call."

"How did you know?" Brenda looked up at her sharply.

"I've been filled in on what I allegedly did. Now tell me about Friday."

"Jon and I started fighting late Thursday night. I begged him to tell me what was going on, and he got angry. Then I threatened to walk out and go back to my room at the Imperial. He hit me...."

The tears gushed out again, but Brenda struggled to regain control. "Afterward he apologized and begged me to forgive him. I didn't know what to do. His anger scared me. I was afraid that if I didn't do what he said, he'd really hurt me."

"So he gave you the disk?"

"He gave it to me and then told me how I was to pass it on to his contacts in Honolulu. Early Friday morning, someone called Jon at the inn. He told me he had to leave. Then he warned me I might be followed and suggested I ride the subways and trains all day long. That way if anyone was following me it would be hard for them to keep track of me."

"You had to know you were involved in something illegal. Why didn't you go to the police?"

"In Tokyo?" Brenda's eyes widened. "I don't speak Japanese, even though I know my way around Tokyo pretty well. I wouldn't go to the police. They might not have understood. They might have put me in jail or something. All I could think about was getting back to the United States."

Julie digested this information in silence, trying to decide what she should do next. It would be best to keep Brenda talking, she realized. "What did you do Friday?"

Brenda took a deep breath. "After riding all over Tokyo, I went back to my room at the Imperial. Jon told me before I left that he wanted me to fly back to Honolulu on the Saturday-morning flight. So I called to check on my reservation."

"Did you see Jon again?"

"No." Brenda shook her head and clenched her fingers around the strap of her purse. "No, I haven't seen him since he left the Masuda Inn on Friday morning."

"Apparently, you were followed on Friday, Brenda." Julie tried to remember what Greg had told her. "I think one of the federal agents followed you."

Brenda leaned forward worriedly. "I wasn't certain anyone was following me. But there was this tall man. I noticed him because he wasn't Japanese, and I thought it was strange that I kept seeing him everywhere I went. He never seemed to be looking at me, but I saw him on the subway several times, and he always got off at the same stop as me. I was so frightened by the time I got back to the Imperial Friday night that I went straight up to my room as quick as I could."

"But you couldn't be sure he was actually following you?"

"No." Brenda paused. "But the same man was on our flight that morning."

"The agent was on our flight?"

"I don't know if he was an agent, but the tall man I saw in Tokyo was on our flight." Brenda reached across and clutched Julie's arm. "Oh, Julie. When I saw you being arrested I almost fainted. I knew I was in terrible trouble. I wanted to step forward and talk to the police, but I was too frightened. Then they said in the paper that you were a spy. That was the first time I realized exactly what Jon had wanted me to do."

She looked at Julie with pleading eyes. "Please help me straighten this out. We've got to get that disk out of your apartment and hand it over to the police. Only, I'm scared that I'll go to prison forever."

"The disk may already be gone. My condo was ransacked."

"I know." Brenda leaned forward eagerly. "That was the day I first went to see you. I got your address through the airline—it's not hard if you're willing to pay. I was going to talk to you then and tell you the truth. But when I reached for your doorbell, I realized your door was open."

Julie's eyes widened. Brenda let go of her arm and kept talking. "I called out your name. No one answered, so I went in and saw that terrible mess. I guessed that the people I was supposed to deliver the disk to must have thought you had it and had already been there. That's when I decided to hide the disk there. After all, they wouldn't come back looking for it a second time, would they?"

Julie stood up decisively. "We've got to tell the police about this. Come on, let's go find a taxi."

At the word "police," Brenda shrank back. "I need to see an attorney first. I'm afraid."

"Attorney," Julie exclaimed, glancing at her watch again. "I've got a date with my attorney. We'll go there together, and he can decide how we should handle this."

They found a taxi in front of the park entrance. "The Polynesian Bar," Julie told the driver. "And please hurry. We're late."

As they swung through the streets, Julie thought over what Brenda had told her. The missing pieces of the puzzle were beginning to click into place. "Who were you supposed to deliver the disk to?"

"I'm not sure. Jon told me to leave the disk in a locker at the airport. I was supposed to buy a copy of the *Wall Street Journal* at the airport newsstand and then go into the coffee shop and sit at one of the back tables. When a man came up to me, I was to give him the key to the locker. That was all."

"But you didn't deliver."

"No. I ran as fast as I could. I've been changing hotels every day."

"Was it you who sent me those orchids?"

"Yes. I talked to my dad on the phone that day. I realized that he wouldn't give me any help. He'd be horrified if he knew about this mess. I decided to make sure the police believed it was you so they wouldn't look for another suspect. I thought that would buy me some time while I tried to decide what to do."

"Didn't you ever stop to think what all this was doing to me?" Julie tried to contain her rising anger.

"I was so sure that somehow I would think of some way to make everything right. All I needed was time. So I decided to keep making you look guilty. But I haven't been able to think of any solutions. In fact, things keep getting worse." Brenda reached into her purse. "I got you in more trouble this morning. That's when I knew I had to call you."

"What?" Julie inhaled deeply. Was there never to be an end to this?

Brenda handed Julie a deposit receipt.

Julie studied it and started to hand it back. "Ten thousand dollars. What's that supposed to mean?"

"I deposited it in your account this morning."

Chapter Ten

It took Julie at least three blocks to recover. She swallowed hard. "You deposited money in my bank account?"

Brenda nodded. "When I was in your condo the other day I saw your checkbook lying on the floor. I picked it up, and that's when I got the idea to get rid of this money."

"What money?" Julie asked wearily.

"The money Jon left for me so I'd be in this with him. He put an envelope in my purse as he was leaving the Masuda Inn in Tokyo on Friday morning. I thought it was a little note like the one he wrote to me the last time we were together. After rushing through Tokyo all day I was too exhausted to look at it. Anyway, I was so angry at him, I didn't want to read his note."

"Get to the point." Julie was getting tired of Brenda's lengthy explanations.

"On the plane Saturday morning, I remembered the note. I opened it in the bathroom. He told me I was in this up to my neck, so I'd better not think of going to the authorities. The money was to make sure I kept my mouth shut." Brenda paused and looked at Julie. "The money made me really frightened of going through customs. I didn't dare declare that I was bringing that much cash into the country, so I hid it in the lining of my purse. This morning, I remembered your deposit slip, so I just went to the bank and put it in your account.''

"Clever." Julie was still in shock. "So now I've got the disk and I've been paid ten thousand dollars for my efforts. If Captain Lonergan finds out about this, he'll chortle with glee.'' She twisted the deposit receipt nervously. "What made you decide to tell me the truth this morning?''

"I told you, I didn't really want to get you in trouble. I was only trying to buy time.'' Brenda sniffed and groped for another tissue. "But you were so nice to me on the plane, and you looked so shocked at the airport the other night. I don't want anything awful to happen to you. I'm not a bad person. I've just made a lot of stupid mistakes.''

"You can say that again.'' Julie wasn't moved by Brenda's tears.

Brenda insisted on paying for the taxi when they reached the hotel where the bar was located. "After this is over, I'm sure my father will give you a reward for helping me.''

"I didn't realize I had a choice.'' Julie pointed her toward the revolving glass doors, and they entered the lobby. The clock on the wall showed twenty minutes past twelve, and Julie shoved Brenda toward the Polynesian Bar.

When they reached the entrance to the bar-and-grill, Julie scanned the brightly decorated booths. Greg was sitting near the atrium, an enclosure filled with tropical plants and birds.

She turned to Brenda. The other woman was wearing a look of pure terror. "What's wrong?" Julie grasped her arm.

Brenda was breathing erratically, trying to speak. "There. That man." With almost superhuman strength she grabbed Julie's hand and pulled her away from the doorway.

"What on earth is the matter with you now?" Julie spoke angrily, but inwardly she was trembling. She was beginning to doubt the other woman's sanity.

"He's in there."

"Who? One of the men who wants the disk?" As Brenda's mouth worked tremulously, Julie tried to speak calmly. "Who is in there, Brenda? Tell me what's got you in such a state."

"The man. The tall man. The man who looked like he might be following me in Tokyo."

Julie stood stock still, her breathing suspended. "Where is this man sitting?"

"In a booth." Brenda caught her hand. "I'll show you. I don't think he'd recognize me, but I don't want to take any chances."

Julie walked beside her. They slid along the wall into the bar and stood behind a carved teakwood screen. Brenda peered around it and counted. "He's in the fourth booth, the one right beside the atrium. He's dressed in a . . ."

Julie's whisper was hoarse. "In a light green polo shirt?"

"How did you know?"

"That's Greg. My attorney."

GREG GLANCED AT THE CLOCK on the wall for at least the tenth time. Twelve-thirty now. He tried to still the churning in his stomach. Julie had mentioned that she had trouble being on time for things. Something must have come up. Perhaps she'd stopped to shop somewhere, as she had in the Tokyo airport.

His hands clenched into fists, and he forced himself to concentrate on what he was going to say to Julie when she arrived. He tried to imagine her reaction. He wanted to hold her in his arms and tell her he loved her before he explained what his role in this deadly game had been.

There were two separate issues here. For now he had to deal with the fact that he'd been less than truthful with her. He had lied and deliberately, cold-bloodedly, deceived her.

He could see those clear, warm blue eyes turning cold and icy, an angry flush staining those glowing cheeks. What would she say when he told her it was he who had paged her at the Imperial Hotel and then notified the authorities to arrest her in Honolulu?

At twelve forty-five he slid out of the booth and went over to a pay phone. He kept his eyes averted from a man in a brown suit sitting in a booth in the far corner. It surprised him that Walt had personally taken on the duty of backup man. He wondered if that meant Walt had guessed the truth about Greg's feelings for Julie and didn't trust him.

Greg allowed Julie's phone to ring twenty times before he reluctantly hung up. God, where was she? He fought back the fear that the men after the disk might have broken into her condo. Keith was supposed to be watching the building.

Keith. Why hadn't he thought to check with Keith about what time Julie had left the condo? He fished in his pocket for more change and dialed the police dispatcher to have Keith beeped.

He waited by the phone, grabbing it as soon as it rang. No one in the bar looked at him except Walt. Apparently, no one noticed that the pay phone had rung.

"What's going on at Smith's apartment?" Greg asked as soon as Keith spoke to him.

"Nothing. I thought she was supposed to meet you for lunch at noon."

"She was."

"She hasn't left here. I'm in a phone booth across the street. There's no way I could have missed seeing her leave in the last two hours. Anyway, her car is still in the parking lot."

Sudden alarm gripped Greg. "She's not answering her phone. Something's happened to her." He hung up before Keith could say anything else.

Walt glanced up in surprise when Greg headed straight for him. Sliding into the booth, Greg announced, "Something's happened to Julie."

Walt lifted his pale brown eyebrows as Greg outlined his conversation with Keith. "It's obvious to me," Walt growled. "She's on to us. I was afraid of this. My gut reaction was to move in when we learned about that bank deposit, even though I knew you didn't agree." He slid out of the booth. "Let's go over there."

Greg stood beside him and gripped his shoulder tightly. "She's in danger, Walt. Don't you see that?"

Walt treated him to a frosty glare as they moved toward the door. "You got problems with my handling of this case, Greg?"

"I've got problems with *my* handling of it. You forget, I'm the one who set her up."

"What's that supposed to mean?" They had reached the cashier's booth. "I'll pay for our drinks," Walt said. As he waited for his change he surveyed Greg with a puzzled frown.

Once outside, he added, "We'll take my car. She's too familiar with yours."

When they were settled inside, Greg turned to the older man. "Either this is my show from now on or I'm on my own. I firmly believe that I was wrong about Julie Smith being the woman I followed in Tokyo." He paused, running his hand through his hair. "Oh, I know everything tallies, but that has bothered me from the beginning. It was too easy. Too neat. We've been set up."

Walt regarded him skeptically, but he thought over Greg's remarks for a moment. "Let's assume you're right. That would explain why Smith has seemed so genuinely shocked over the man watching her house and her encounter with the gunman at the beach." He chuckled grimly. "If nothing else, it does me good to think the guys after that disk are as mixed up as we are."

"Where does that leave Julie? And who has the disk? Obviously it hasn't been turned over yet."

"No, that's what gives me hope we can solve this case. Since you're now in charge, what's our next move, Stafford?"

"Let's go to Julie's place."

When they arrived, they hurried through the lobby and rode the elevator to the fourteenth floor without speaking. Greg was tense, alert, worried over what he might find in Julie's apartment.

The door was locked when they arrived. Greg breathed a sigh of relief when he realized that Julie hadn't yet managed to have the dead-bolt locks installed. It took only seconds for him to open the lock. The two men glided inside in silence, working together in the efficient manner they had developed over the years.

Greg flattened himself against the wall and slid into the living room. Its serene beauty was untouched. Nothing appeared to be out of place. He strode across the room and moved into Julie's room. She wasn't there.

Walt joined him as Greg searched the closet and the balcony. "Any sign of her?" the older man asked.

"Not in here."

"The other bedroom and the bath are clean. Ditto for the kitchen. She's not here." Walt glanced around Julie's bedroom, noting the frilly satin teddy spilling out of a drawer and the two blouses draped over a corner of the bed. "Another search?"

Greg grinned in enormous relief that there were no signs that Julie had been harmed. "No, just Julie's usual. She's the casual sort."

"The rest of the place looks like it's ready for a white-glove inspection."

"Her roommate, Tricia Hyde, is the cleanliness freak. She's working today. The Tokyo run, I guess." Greg sighed. "Where the hell is Julie? She wouldn't have stood me up unless something important came up."

"Maybe the airline decided to disregard us and let her fly again. She might have tried to call you after you'd left your hotel. Why don't you call the airline?"

"Good idea." Greg reached for Julie's bedside phone and noticed the yellow pages lying open beside it. Curious, he glanced down. A number was underlined under the heading for taxis. "Wait, I've got something here. She called a taxi."

Walt came over to stand beside him. "Maybe. That could have been underlined some time earlier."

"The pen's here." Greg retrieved it from the center of the book. Thank God for Julie's carelessness. It was the first solid lead they'd had. He started to call and then changed his mind. "Let's go to the cab company's main office. They might hedge on the phone."

"I've got some photos of Smith." Walt patted his pocket. "I picked them up from Lonergan this morning to show the bank teller. Like you said earlier, Smith's a good-looking woman. The driver is sure to remember her." As they started toward the door, he added, "Don't you think it's a little odd that Smith sneaked out in a taxi when her own car was parked in its regular slot?"

Greg didn't answer. He was fairly certain he knew the answer to that one. Julie had been planning on spending the day and maybe the night with him. She wouldn't have needed her own car to go anywhere. Something had happened to make her change her plans. Something he couldn't bear to think about.

TEN MINUTES after Brenda had identified Greg as the man she had seen in Tokyo, Julie was sitting alone in the lounge of the ladies' powder room just off the Polynesian Bar. She had forced Brenda to go into the bar and let herself be seated at a booth.

When the other woman protested, Julie insisted. "He won't recognize you. You had your hair covered, and you were wearing sunglasses. The moment he leaves the bar, run in here and get me. I'll be thinking about what we're going to do next."

Julie collapsed on a chair in the powder room. She was as confused as she ever remembered being. One part of her wanted to go right into the bar and talk to Greg. After all, it didn't make sense for *Greg* to have been following Brenda in Tokyo.

Carefully she thought over the situation. Greg was an attorney. He had gotten her out of jail, advised her on her legal problems. He had simply been in Tokyo on business, as he said.

Yet he had told her that someone had followed the woman in the beige raincoat—Brenda, as she now realized. Could Greg have been that person? And if so, what did that make him? A federal agent? The thought was inconceivable.

But was it? If it was so ridiculous, why didn't she go back into the bar and tell him exactly what she was thinking? The answer was simple. She couldn't be sure. For the first time, she doubted Greg. Perhaps he wasn't the man he had seemed to be.

She stood up and began pacing the room nervously. Two well-dressed women—tourists judging by their conversation—entered the room, and she sank back down in one of the soft armchairs and pretended to be reading a letter she pulled from her purse.

The electric bill. Overdue, she realized. But what did that matter? She might not be involved in such mundane matters much longer. Unless she got to Captain Lonergan while Brenda was still willing to confess her part in this, Julie might well be spending the rest of her life behind bars.

God, the disk was in her condo, and ten thousand dollars had been deposited in her account. It was a slick setup. When this story got out, who would believe her? Everything depended on Brenda, and she'd been gone a long time now. It was past one. Maybe she ought to slip outside and see what was happening.

The two tourists left the powder room. Julie stood up to leave. At that moment the door swung open and a white-faced Brenda was shoved through it. Behind her were two men.

Julie recognized one of them as the man who had been in the bathhouse. The scar on his face was more visible in the brightly lit powder room. He was holding a gun against Brenda's throat. He and his companion were both dressed in business suits.

"We meet again, Miss Smith," he said.

Julie's voice quavered. "You seem to have a hang-up about women's rest rooms."

He ignored her. "We're leaving here now. You walk in front with Rolf. Talk to him like he's your best buddy, unless you want to see me put a bullet through this woman." Despite his thick accent, his meaning was perfectly clear.

"They grabbed me, Julie," Brenda moaned. "Don't let anything happen to me."

Julie thought fast. "Everything is fine, honey." She turned to the man holding the gun. "This woman knows nothing about what you want. Let her go and I'll come with you quietly." She gave Brenda a sharp look, hoping she would understand that she was to play her part so she could escape and go to the police.

"And let her go to the authorities?" the man sneered.

"She wouldn't do that." Julie addressed Brenda. "Honey, you promise just to go home and not mention this. I'll call you this evening and explain. I got in a little trouble gambling again and I have a debt to pay. You don't want to get involved in this."

"I didn't see a thing," Brenda insisted. "I promise I won't mention it to anyone."

"Don't listen to her, Sven." The other man, the one called Rolf, had spoken. Julie noted the contrast between the two men. Rolf was at least a head taller than Sven and decidedly overweight. His hands were white and as soft as bread dough.

Before Sven could say anything, the door started to open. Rolf leaned his back against it to hold it shut. Sven shoved the gun closer to Brenda's throat and whispered, "Miss Smith, call out that you're cleaning the rest room. Tell them it's closed."

Julie eyed the gun and then obeyed. "Where's another rest room, then?" a woman's voice demanded. When Julie didn't answer, the voice continued. "I'm going straight to the hotel management and report this. There's a law saying you have to have a public rest room."

When her voice faded away, Julie felt her arm being grabbed. "Hold your head high. Laugh and talk," Rolf said from behind her. Now he was holding a gun, as well, and she felt a sharp jab against her ribs.

The lobby had to be at least ten miles across, Julie thought. She tried to think of something she could do. She wondered how Brenda was holding up. It didn't seem possible that two women could be held at gunpoint in the lobby of a public hotel without anyone noticing, and yet it was happening.

Bright sunlight glinted off a high-rise hotel across the street, temporarily blinding Julie as she stepped outside. Behind her, she glimpsed Brenda being pushed along in front of Sven. "This way," Rolf commanded.

Julie balked. "Where are you taking us?"

He shoved her forward and she stumbled slightly, noting that several pedestrians gave them an odd look. She debated whether she should scream, but then she heard Brenda whimpering. "You're hurting me," Brenda cried, and Julie tried to turn to look at her.

"The guns have silencers. Sven will kill her right here if you give any trouble, Miss Smith." Rolf poked his own weapon sharply against Julie's ribs as if to remind her of their deadly intent. "We will stop at nothing to get that disk."

Prodded and shoved along, Julie and Brenda walked down a path that led to a car park. Stopping in front of a tan vehicle, Rolf loosened his grip slightly to open the back door.

Julie sprawled onto the back seat as the man gave her a vicious shove. Brenda followed, and then Rolf crowded in after them, while Sven went around to the driver's seat.

"Put your hands behind your back," Rolf ordered. Julie complied and felt a thin cord cutting into her wrists as he bound them together. Within seconds she was shoved to the floor, her face pushed into the carpet. Brenda landed beside her moments later, and a blanket was thrown over them. "I have the gun pointed toward you," Rolf said. "No matter what happens, don't make a sound or you're dead."

As the vehicle moved across the paved surface, Julie felt a wave of despair wash over her.

THE FEMALE TAXI DISPATCHER was in her late thirties and had no intention of helping any law officers. She glanced at Walt's federal identification badge and then shrugged. "I don't have to tell you anything without a court order."

"You're not in any trouble, lady. If you want to stay that way, you better act a little helpful. My friend at police headquarters, Captain Lonergan, might be interested in knowing you've got something to hide."

Greg's eyes lit with amusement at Walt's attempt to play the part of a hard-boiled cop, but his mind returned swiftly to Julie's predicament. "Did you take a call for a high rise on Konoloho Drive this morning?"

She scowled, then glanced at the sheet in front of her. "Yeah, for eleven."

"Who was the driver?"

"Nick. Cab number sixteen."

"Call him in. Immediately," Walt snapped.

"He's got a paying customer," she said pointedly.

Walt took out his wallet and removed five twenty-dollar bills. "Paying more than this?"

She pocketed the money and then reached for the mike attached to a radiophone. After several fruitless attempts at calling, she turned back to Walt. "Nick's probably gone to lunch."

"It's nearly two."

"Late lunch."

"Where does he usually go?" Greg asked.

"Hot-dog stand in Ala Moana Park." She pointed to a large map on the wall. "His girlfriend works there. I'll give her a call and tell her to have him wait until you arrive."

JULIE HAD NO IDEA how long they had been driving. The ride seemed interminable in some ways, but it had probably taken only ten minutes or so. The car turned onto a graveled surface and crunched along for several hundred feet before coming to a stop.

Rolf and Sven began speaking rapidly in a foreign language that was not familiar to her. It sounded harsh, guttural, but she couldn't pinpoint exactly what it was. Rolf got out first and then leaned over to grab Julie's arm. She felt the gun again, this time poking against her waist. "Hurry up. Get out," he ordered.

As Julie stumbled out of the car, she blinked in the harsh sunlight. They were in front of a large house, a mansion, actually. She thought she remembered having seen it before, but they moved along the side too quickly for her to get more than a glimpse of the front. She heard Brenda and Sven behind her. When they reached the rear of the building, a door was flung open and another man greeted Rolf in the same foreign language.

Rolf pushed her up the steps, jabbing her with the gun every time she slowed down to look around. From the stair landing, Julie glimpsed the front part of the house and saw several uniformed maids carrying trays toward a table covered with a white cloth. From the masses of flowers circling the room, Julie guessed they were preparing for some social occasion. A reception or cocktail party, perhaps?

Rolf shoved her into a large sunny bedroom on the second floor and pushed her face down onto the bed. Squirming against a colorful Hawaiian quilt, Julie attempted to lift her head. "What are you going to do with me?"

He ignored her. Brenda stumbled into the room seconds later and then she was lying on the bed, as well. Brenda's head was at the other end of the bed, her feet alongside Julie's face. Sven walked around the bed and leaned over Julie.

"Miss Smith." Sven's voice was low and menacing. "Rolf and I must attend a social function in a few minutes. While we're gone, we want you to reconsider your decision not to tell us where the disk is located. We're willing to make a deal with you."

Rolf interrupted. "If you deliver the disk to us, we'll let you and your sniveling friend here go free."

"And if I don't?" Julie lifted her head slightly to eye the two men.

Sven shrugged. "Then we will have no further use for you. We'll kill you both."

Rolf came closer to the bed and began stuffing a cloth into Julie's mouth. She gagged and tried to move away. "There's no danger this will choke you," he promised. "You're the only one who can tell us where the disk is." When he finished, he carefully tied another cloth around her eyes.

She could hear him moving around and, from the whimpering noises and the amount of thrashing around on the bed, Julie guessed Brenda was being gagged and blindfolded as well. "Roll over on your side," Rolf commanded, and Julie felt herself being shoved over until she was back to back with Brenda. Julie bit back a cry of pain as her arms were yanked painfully behind her.

It took her a second to realize what was happening. Her hands were grasped, and the thin cords that Rolf had bound around her wrists in the car tightened sharply. Then she could feel Brenda's hands against her own. They were being bound together.

At last the two men left the room. The door was closed softly and then the sound of their footsteps faded away along the hall.

Julie attempted to make a sound, but nothing audible would come out. For a moment panic threatened to overwhelm her. She felt as though she were choking on the gag and forced herself to breathe deeply through her nose. Then she deliberately willed herself to relax, first her tense neck muscles, then her arms and hands. Panic wouldn't help now. She had to think. There had to be some way out of here.

GREG SPOTTED THE TAXI parked beside a small hot-dog stand before Walt did. He had taken over the driving from the older man when they left the cab company. Pulling up beside the taxi, he killed the engine and leaped out.

"Hey, you the cops?" a young native Hawaiian called. He ambled toward them, his flowered shirt flapping open in the breeze, revealing a darkly tanned chest. "I'm Nick."

Walt pulled out his photograph of Julie. "Was this woman a passenger this morning?"

Nick looked at it for a moment. "Sure. Picked her up at that tall high-rise condominium on Konoloho Drive about eleven. Took her to Kapiolani Park. Entrance nearest the Rose Garden. She wasn't too friendly. Didn't smile or talk."

"Damn," Walt muttered. "She must have been making the delivery."

"She was set up again." Greg was equally firm. He turned to Nick and handed him some bills. "Did you see which path she took?"

"Like I said. Straight toward the Rose Garden. She knew her way."

"How would she get a taxi when she wanted to leave the park?"

"Taxi stand down there." Nick pointed. "If a driver doesn't have a fare he gets in line."

Greg let out a despairing breath. "Let's go see if anyone remembers seeing her at the stand."

JULIE HAD MANAGED to conquer her panic, though she hadn't come up with any ideas on what Brenda and she could do next. Tears threatened, but she fought them back and forced herself to grapple with the problem of what she would do when the men returned.

Brenda would break and tell the men where the disk was located as soon as they used force on her. Rolf and Sven would then get rid of them—kill them. Julie had no foolish hopes that the men would let them go free. They looked too shrewd to leave witnesses.

She had to do something. She couldn't just lie here waiting to die. Anything was better than that. Her strength returning, she began to squirm on the quilt again and tried to remember what she'd seen people in her situation do in movies. Two people bound together always managed to untie each other. Impossible.... But was it? She flexed her fingers slowly, easing the numbed tension in her arms and wrists. Brenda moved, too, her fingers brushing against Julie's.

From what Julie could ascertain, they were tied together at the wrists. The cord Rolf had used felt like nylon, a clothesline perhaps. It was slick and slippery and, as Julie wriggled her fingers, she felt it give slightly. She was afraid to move abruptly for fear that anything she did would only tighten the knots.

Slowly and carefully seemed to be the best bet. At first Brenda worked against her, tensing her body and pulling away when Julie tried to maneuver their bonds.

Julie's fingers ached, and her wrists rebelled against being twisted to such a degree. Millimeter by millimeter, Julie eased the slippery nylon cord, tightening the muscles in her hands until she could twist her wrists. At last she was able to feel the knot with her fingers. She slid her long fingernails around it, probing and loosening.

It appeared to be impossible. After what seemed like an eternity, she was forced to take a rest. Her forehead was beaded with sweat, and her neck and shoulder muscles were cramped and screaming. She waited a few minutes, breathing deeply and again willing her muscles to relax.

Then she resumed her efforts. The knot seemed looser now, so Julie tried pushing against it. Perhaps if she could widen the noose around their wrists, she would be able to slip her hands free. Brenda seemed to sense what she was doing, for the other woman pushed and twisted her own wrists.

Julie paused suddenly. Her heart threatened to stop beating and she listened breathlessly. Were those footsteps in the hall? After a moment she realized that the only sound in the room was their own labored breathing. Her movements became feverish as she tried to calculate how much time had passed.

With a desperate effort, she wrenched her hands against the cord and tried to slide them out of their bonds. The nylon bit deeply into the soft flesh of her wrists, but she ignored the pain. She stopped breathing for a moment when she realized her maneuver had worked. It didn't seem possible.

Now she had to free them from their individual bonds. Julie groped behind her, searching with her fingers for Brenda's wrists. When she finally made contact, Brenda drew back. Julie patted her until the woman stilled. Slowly she began fumbling with the cords. This was even more difficult. The rope Rolf had applied in the car was thin and coarse, almost like a stiff twine.

Julie kept working, her long nails sliding under the twine, digging into the knot, pulling, manipulating. As it gave beneath her fingers, she redoubled her efforts. At last, she felt it come loose in her hands. Brenda's hands were free.

For several moments Julie felt the bed bouncing violently under her. "Julie," Brenda whispered hoarsely. "Let me get my blindfold off and I'll help you."

It seemed an eternity before she felt Brenda's fingers fumbling with the cords around her own wrists. Julie gingerly moved her arms around to her sides, wincing at the pain in her shoulders. It took all her strength to reach up and rip the gag out of her mouth. As she gulped long sweet breaths of air, she tore off the blindfold.

"Are you okay, Julie?" Brenda still sounded hoarse.

Julie's own voice didn't seem to want to work. Her throat was dry and burning, and her voice cracked. "Don't worry about that now. We've got to get out of here and find Captain Lonergan." Rubbing at her wrists in an attempt to restore the circulation, Julie added, "Did you see much of the house?"

Brenda's eyes were wide. "Not much. It's two stories and we're on the back, I think." She went over to the window. "There's a tree with branches almost brushing against this window. I think we can reach it if we climb out."

"Let's try." Julie stood up.

They slid the window open. The screen took a little manipulation, but at last Julie was able to unfasten it. She managed to catch it before it fell to the ground, turning it sideways and slipping it into the room. "Let me go first," Brenda urged. "My favorite pastime as a kid was climbing trees."

"Be my guest." Julie gingerly estimated the distance to the ground in case the branch she landed on broke under her weight. Although she had no fears of flying, she had never been one to enjoy climbing far off the ground.

Brenda was as nimble as a cat. She crawled out the window, swung onto a branch and then moved to a lower one, indicating with a motion of her hand that Julie was to follow. Julie moved more cautiously, clutching Brenda's extended hand when she reached the deep foliage of the tree. "Now watch how I slide down," Brenda whispered.

"Wait." Julie pointed to a maid who had just stepped onto the back porch. The maid lit a cigarette and took a deep drag while they watched. After a short time she threw the butt into the grass and went back into the house.

Brenda instantly started down the trunk, clinging to the branches until she was clear of them and then pressing her knees into the bark. It looked fairly easy. Julie started down and had to suppress an exclamation as the rough bark bit through her denim jeans. When she reached the ground, she grabbed Brenda's hand. Bending low, they made a run for the back of the property.

Brenda gave Julie a boost and the two climbed over the wooden fence. They found themselves on a wide boulevard. "Where are we?" Brenda peered around in confusion.

Julie glanced down the street and let out a low cry. "Why, we're only a few blocks from my place. Let's go there and call Captain Lonergan."

"I feel terrific," Brenda said. "I can't believe we got away from there. I'm never going to let anyone walk all over me again. When I worked with the dogs at the kennel, I used to admire the ones who wouldn't let anyone bluff them. From now on I'm going to be like that." Excitement burned in her eyes.

"Great," Julie muttered. "But let's hurry now. Those men will soon discover we're missing."

"And Jon is looking for us." Brenda inserted the comment neatly without so much as looking at Julie.

Julie stopped dead. "What? Did you forget to tell me something?" She pulled Brenda into the protective cover of some bushes.

Brenda nodded. Her chin was trembling in that now-familiar mannerism Julie suspected she could turn on whenever she needed it. "I thought I was safe from him. I didn't stay at any one hotel very long, so I didn't think he could find me. But when I talked to my father, I had to let him know where I was staying because he wanted to call me back."

"Get to the point, Brenda," Julie moaned between clenched teeth.

"Jon had the nerve to call my father and pass himself off as a friend. My dad gave him the phone number."

"But is he actually here, Brenda? In Honolulu?" Julie glanced behind them anxiously and willed the other woman to talk faster.

"He called yesterday and told me not to leave until he got here. He was really nasty. He saw your picture in a Tokyo paper. Evidently, the guys wanting the disk contacted him and told him you wouldn't give it to them. I started crying and wouldn't say anything, so he told me to wait here until he arrived. He made it plain I'd be sorry if I didn't. That's another reason I had to talk to you today."

Julie barely restrained her urge to strangle Brenda. There seemed no end to the trouble this woman had brought on her. But to think that Derickson was on his way to Honolulu this very minute.... She jerked on Brenda's arm. "Hurry up. We've got to notify the police before the Tokyo flight arrives."

Chapter Eleven

After thirty minutes of quizzing taxi drivers at the park entrance, Greg was almost ready to give up. He was actually heading for his car when one of them asked, "Were there two women, maybe? One blond, one dark-haired? Both about the same height and wearing jeans? The blonde had on a red silk blouse, and the brunette had on a little shirt that stopped right here." He pointed to his chest, adding. "The dark-haired one was crying."

Walt shook his head, but Greg intervened. "It's possible. Did you drive them somewhere?"

"No, but my friend Kit did. He's gone home now, but I can call him."

"Tell him there's a hundred dollars for him if he'll get here fast." Greg handed some bills to the man.

Kit arrived within ten minutes. A blond man who would have looked more at home in a lifeguard's chair at the beach than behind the wheel of a taxi, he wore a pair of cutoffs and leather thongs. He recognized Julie's picture instantly. "I drove the lady and her friend to the Polynesian Bar."

Greg glanced pointedly at Walt, then turned back to the cabbie. "And you saw both women enter the hotel lobby?"

"Definitely. The dark-haired woman cried quite a bit, and the good-looking blonde kept trying to calm her."

"What time was this?" Walt asked.

"Fifteen, twenty minutes after twelve. I can find out exactly by checking with the dispatcher."

"That's close enough." Greg turned to Walt after Kit left. "Let's get to the hotel. There's got to be some clue there that will tell us the identity of Julie's friend and why the two women never made it into the bar."

BRENDA DREW BACK when they reached Julie's street. "I'm afraid," she whispered. "I hate that disk. I don't want to ever see it again."

"What about all that brave talk you were just giving me?" Julie wasn't in the mood for any nonsense from Brenda. "If I had my purse I'd get a taxi and go straight to the police station, but it's still in that car."

"We could call on a pay phone."

"Without any change?" Julie started toward the building, but Brenda balked. "Okay, Brenda." Julie turned toward her tiredly. "What's really bothering you?"

"I'm afraid Jon might be there."

"You gave him my address?" Julie almost shrieked.

"No, I swear I didn't. But he could find out the same way I did. Don't forget he's an expert at this."

"But the Tokyo flight isn't in yet," Julie pointed out.

"Well, I'm not sure if he was actually in Tokyo when he called me yesterday," Brenda admitted.

"I think you're just stalling because you're afraid of confessing to the police, Brenda. You won't be in much trouble if we can just retrieve that disk and get it back in the right hands. I'll help you, I promise."

Brenda gave in reluctantly and followed as Julie hurried along the street, keeping in the shadows of the trees. Julie sighed with relief when they walked into the lobby of her building. A bachelor neighbor was coming out the front door. "Hi, Julie," he said. "Looks like you've been having fun."

Julie glanced down in surprise. She had a twig and several leaves sticking to the fabric of her blouse. "Climbing trees," she called after him, and he laughed.

The two women stepped into the elevator and rode up to the fourteenth floor. It wasn't until Julie reached the door of her apartment that she remembered she didn't have a key. "Damn," she muttered. The door lock might be easily broken into with a credit card, but she didn't even have that. "Wait here and I'll go see if Jake will let us in. I hate to bother him, but I've got no choice."

"I'm coming with you," Brenda insisted. They rode back down to the first floor and walked along the corridor to the last door on the right. Julie knocked and they waited.

It seemed to take forever for Jake to come to the door. A smell of something frying wafted from beneath the door, and Julie felt her stomach tighten in response. "I've just realized I'm starving," she whispered. "I haven't had anything to eat since breakfast."

"I ordered some broiled prawns in the bar while I was watching that man for you," Brenda said. "But I was too nervous to eat any."

Julie was instantly alert. "What did he do?"

"He just stared around at the room for a while. Then he got up and went over to the phone. Someone called him back, because it rang a few minutes later. Afterward he joined another man in a booth...."

"He had someone with him?" Julie looked at her sharply. In the rush of being kidnapped, she hadn't had a chance to think about Greg. But this piece of news wasn't promising. Why would he have brought another man along on a date with her?

Brenda continued her story. "They talked together for a few minutes and then went over to pay their bill. I followed them and paid right behind them, but I couldn't hear what they were saying. Then when I went into the alcove where the rest room doors were located, Sven grabbed me. He pointed a gun at my throat and steered me into the ladies' room. You know the rest."

"Those men must have been following me all day." Julie shuddered. "I wonder why they grabbed us in the bar instead of in the Rose Garden. Maybe they thought I'd lead them to the disk."

Jake forestalled any further conversation by opening the door. He didn't look surprised to see her. "Forget your key again, Miss Smith?" Without waiting for an answer, he disappeared into his apartment and returned holding a large ring of keys. "Bring them back as soon as you get your door open, okay?"

There were times when it paid to be careless, Julie realized as she and Brenda went back upstairs. Jake was so used to her locking herself out of her apartment that he hadn't slowed them down with questions.

The condo was quiet and cool when Julie ushered Brenda inside. She headed straight for the phone. "I'm going to call Captain Lonergan." Brenda hovered anxiously by the door as Julie dialed.

After calling emergency, she was connected with police headquarters and Julie was soon speaking with an operator. "Captain Lonergan, please."

After a wait of several minutes the operator came back on the line. "He doesn't answer in his office."

"Lieutenant Massie, then."

Another delay and the operator reported the same results. "Shall I take a message? We can beep Captain Lonergan and have him call in."

"Yes, tell him that Julie Smith called. She'd like him to meet her at her condo as soon as possible. I'm sure he knows where I live. Tell him it's urgent."

As soon as she hung up, Julie turned to Brenda. "You get that disk and bring it to me right now. I'm going to fix a pot of tea and some sandwiches while we're waiting for the captain."

"I need to find your bathroom first," Brenda stalled.

Julie pointed toward the hall and headed for the kitchen. She was reaching for the tea kettle when she heard Brenda scream. Dropping the pot on the floor, she skidded across the floor and ran into the living room. A dark-haired man with a mustache was standing there, the gun in his hand pointed straight at Brenda.

He whirled around to face Julie. "Over against the wall," he ordered.

"Jon," Brenda managed to gasp. "Julie, this is Jon."

Julie stared with resignation at the man who had set this whole chain of events into motion.

GREG WAS READY TO CONCEDE DEFEAT as he and Walt stood in the hotel lobby near the entrance to the Polynesian Bar. They had questioned every employee who had been on duty during the noon hour and none had recognized Julie's picture. "I think we should get back to her apartment," Greg said.

A beeper at Walt's waist sounded. He glanced at Greg and said, "I told Keith to keep me informed if anything happened. I'll call from that booth over there."

He returned a few minutes later wearing a grim expression. "You aren't going to like this, Greg." He was silent for a long moment.

"Well?" Greg prompted.

"Keith saw Julie return to her building a few minutes ago with a dark-haired woman who seems to fit the description that cab driver gave us."

Greg went limp with relief. "But that's great news. Let's get over there right away and find out what's going on."

"Wait." Walt put a restraining hand on Greg's arm. "A few minutes later, a man went into the building who exactly fits the description of Derickson."

Greg felt the blood drain from his face. He stared at Walt, trying to digest what he had said. Sudden decision hardened the lines of his face. "Let's go."

"GIVE ME THE DISK." Jon Derickson kicked Brenda, sending her sprawling facedown on the carpet.

Julie started toward her. "Stop," Jon ordered. "Keep away from her." He leaned over Brenda and held the gun against her temple. Julie froze. Was he going to shoot Brenda, the girl he had made love to only days before? She had to think of a way to stall for time.

"I have the disk," she improvised quickly. "And I want something for it."

Jon gave her an assessing look. "I don't believe you. How did you get involved in this?" He straightened up, moving the gun away from Brenda's head and pointing it at Julie. Taking a step in her direction, he tapped his finger menacingly against the trigger.

Julie swallowed hard and forced herself to speak. "*You* involved me. You used my name and got me arrested. Now I have the disk and you're not going to see it until you pay me off."

Out of the corner of her eye, she saw Brenda moving slowly toward Jon's legs. She kept talking, saying anything that came into her head to divert his attention. "I want lots of money. More than you can pay, probably."

She had all Jon's attention now. "Don't even think of making a deal without me," he warned. "If you try to double-cross me, I'll kill you." From the way his eyes glinted icily at her, she didn't doubt he would.

She didn't dare look at Brenda, who was still inching her way toward Jon. Praying she could hold the man's attention and that Brenda was beyond range of his peripheral vision, she said musingly, "I'm already working on a deal, but maybe I can cut you back in. Let me get a cigarette and we'll talk."

"We'll talk now. Forget the games." He took a step toward her and then paused.

As he hesitated Brenda lunged upward and grabbed his arm. They wrestled violently until the gun spun out of his hands, flying across the room to land by the couch. Julie ran toward it, but Jon was too fast for her.

Struggling against Brenda's grip on his arm, he leaped sideways, pulling Brenda with him and blocking Julie's path. Brenda was kicking him now, screaming and pummeling him with her fists. Julie tried to shove him out of the way, but he struck out at her. She felt the blow land on her shoulder, and then he was trying to grab her, tearing her shirt as Brenda pushed him to the floor. Pulling away, she heard him yell as Brenda climbed onto his back and sank her teeth into his shoulder.

Jon's curses filled the room. Julie tried to recover her balance and make another attempt for the gun. Pulling herself to her knees, she watched in defeated horror as Jon pushed himself up off the floor. He shook Brenda off his back and jumped to his feet. In a moment, his hand was clenched around the grip of the pistol.

Once again Julie was staring down the barrel of his pistol. She stepped back warily. What was taking that police captain so long to arrive?

Jon's hand was unsteady as he pointed the gun first at Julie and then at Brenda. "Up. Get on your feet." He prodded Brenda with his foot and she stumbled upright, joining Julie.

"Now, where's that disk? I've run out of patience." His facial muscles tightened as he spat out the words.

Julie nodded at Brenda. All they could do now was hope Captain Lonergan arrived before Derickson killed them.

"It's in the living room," Brenda gasped, still struggling to regain her breath. "I hid it in a book in the bookcase."

Julie stared at her. Now what was Brenda trying to pull? She had said earlier that the disk was between Julie's mattress and box spring. If she was still trying to play for time, she was braver than Julie had given her credit for.

"Find it." Jon waved the pistol at them.

Brenda went slowly over to the bookcase. "Let's see." She looked it over carefully. "I think it was on the third shelf, third book from the right. No, that's not right.'' She paused thoughtfully. ''Maybe it was the fourth shelf. . . .''

''Get it,'' Jon shouted, going over and pushing her roughly against the bookcase. ''Now!''

Julie watched them without breathing. Oh God, *was* Brenda just trying to stall for time, or had she been lying all along about having put the disk in Julie's apartment? As she waited, she heard steps in the foyer. Sagging with relief, she waited for Captain Lonergan to enter the room.

Jon was cursing and shouting at Brenda and hadn't heard the footsteps. ''Quit stalling,'' he yelled. ''I'm not going to wait any longer.''

The men who entered were not the police. Julie felt like dying when she saw Rolf and Sven come into the room. Sven was holding his pistol. ''Drop your weapon, Derickson,'' he ordered.

Jon Derickson's eyes narrowed and his body tensed. For a moment he paused, as if giving careful consideration to his next move. Then he dropped his gun to the floor. ''I'm just trying to get the disk from these women,'' he explained. His hands were trembling as he turned to face the men. ''I knew we were running out of time and I got here as fast as I could.'' He gestured at Brenda. ''She says the disk is in the bookcase.''

''But, Jon—'' Brenda opened her eyes wide and looked at him ''—you know I gave it to you this morning at your hotel.''

''Why, you little—'' Jon struck her hard across the face and she crumpled to the floor.

For a moment Julie froze, trying to follow what was happening. Brenda's ability to play a role amazed her, and she wondered if the woman had ever been telling her the truth. But at least this was delaying the men, and that was what was needed.

Making up her mind quickly, Julie let out a loud gasp and ran to Brenda. She bent over the woman and then looked up at Jon. "Fool. You've knocked her out. She's the only one who knows where the disk is. Now what are we going to do?"

"Pick her up. Put her on the couch." Sven moved closer and issued orders to Rolf. "And don't just stand there." He looked at Julie. "Get some ice and let's see if we can bring her around."

"I'm going to kill her for this," Jon muttered. He followed Julie into the kitchen with Rolf close behind, watching them both warily.

Julie's hands shook as she scooped ice out of the ice-maker bin and poured it into a pitcher. She filled the pitcher with water and started back to the living room. "No, idiot, not a pitcher of water." For a moment it looked as if Rolf would strike her. "A cloth . . . a cloth with ice in it. We want to bring her around, not drown her."

Julie could see past him into the living room. As her gaze found Brenda, she saw the other woman sit up-right. Immediately, Julie heaved the pitcher at Rolf, catching him on the side of his head.

The hard glass and frigid water dashed against him, and he grabbed for his face. Stumbling to his knees, he dropped the gun. Sven started across the room, but even as he moved, Brenda scrambled to her feet, tackling him from behind and knocking his pistol out of his hand.

Ignoring his flailing arms, Brenda went after Sven's gun, kicking it under the sofa. Julie wasted no time, but dropped to the floor to search desperately for the gun Rolf had dropped. Jon tried to move past her.

Remembering the gun Jon had dropped by the bookcase, Julie yelled, "Get Jon's gun, Brenda." Jon managed to push past Julie, but Brenda was too fast for him.

Brenda grabbed Jon's gun only seconds before Sven tackled her. They landed on the floor, a tangled mass of writhing humanity as Brenda proceeded to bite and kick like a wild animal.

Jon moved toward Sven as if to help him, but there was no way he could get close to the two fighting on the floor by the bookcase. Julie debated whether she should go to Brenda's aid, but it seemed wiser to keep searching for Rolf's gun.

Even as she did so, Brenda broke free of Sven's clutches. In the split second before Jon caught her, she managed to shove the gun she was holding into the space between the floor and the bottom shelf of the bookcase. Then she was fighting again, shouting encouragement to Julie and trying to hold her own against Sven and Jon.

Inspired, Julie scrambled to her feet, kicking the slowly recovering Rolf as hard as she could. Rolf's gun was nowhere in sight, so Julie left him in the kitchen. Once in the living room, she ran over to where the others were fighting.

Jon saw her coming. Julie steeled herself for the blow she knew was coming and, as Jon knocked her to the floor, she grabbed him and brought him down after her. They grappled on the carpet, Jon holding her shoulders and forcing her onto her back. Julie sank her teeth into his forearm. He grunted and loosened his grip.

Brenda was still struggling with Sven. "Kick him," she shouted at Julie. "Bite him."

Julie heaved her body up from the floor and caught Jon off guard. Without pausing, she rolled over onto her back and was waiting for him when he lunged at her again. Just as he reached her, she kicked him in the groin, and he fell back in agony.

Taking advantage of his pain, Julie climbed up on the sofa. Looking around for a weapon, she grabbed a lamp off the end table. Jon staggered and then rose, advancing menacingly toward her.

At that moment, shouts erupted from the foyer, and Julie heard Greg's voice. "Everybody freeze," he ordered in a tone of authority and ruthless anger that Julie had never heard him use before.

Then he was in the living room. Their gazes met and clung across the room. "Julie," he breathed thankfully. "Thank God, you're still alive."

Julie's gaze dropped to his hand and she saw that he was holding a black revolver. Then, too late, she shouted a warning to him. Jon lunged at him and they fell to the floor, the gun Greg had been holding spinning out of his hand. Sven joined the fray, heading for the thin man who had accompanied Greg into the room.

Julie stood on the couch with the lamp in her hands, watching the whirlwind of activity going on around her. She saw Greg pick up Jon and slam him against the coffee table. Jon crumpled to the floor, unconscious.

Sven landed a telling blow on the thin man's chin and then turned toward Greg. Out of the corner of her eye, Julie saw a movement from the kitchen. Rolf rushed into the living room and headed over to help Sven.

Even as Julie tried to make up her mind whether she wanted to join the melee again, the thin man recovered and smacked Rolf.

Julie's eyes darted to Greg. "Julie," he shouted. "Get out of here. It's not safe."

"She's not safe," Sven muttered, aiming another blow at Greg. Greg dodged the blow and delivered one of his own that sent Sven down to his knees.

Brenda lunged into the fight again, throwing her arms around Greg's legs and sending him sprawling to the floor. "Not him, Brenda," Julie cried.

As Sven took advantage of Greg's fall to spring toward him, Julie saw her chance. She leaped off the couch and ran forward, slamming the lamp across the back of Sven's head. He fell like a sack of cement to the carpet.

"Thanks," Greg muttered. "I was beginning to wonder whose side you were on."

"Mine." Julie's eyes flashed. "It's time someone was."

Greg wasn't listening. His gaze swept the floor until he located his revolver. Scooping it up, he turned to face the room. "Stop right now or I'll shoot. Put your hands over your head."

Brenda's eyes widened and she flattened herself against the wall, her hands above her head. "No, not you, Brenda," Julie protested.

A noise from the other side of the living room caught her attention. Greg turned at the sound, as well. Jon was pulling himself up, leaning on the bookcase as he rose. "No, not the bookcase," Greg shouted. "Not Tricia's bookcase." He was too late. The bookcase toppled forward precariously, and the books spilled out in a disheveled heap on the floor.

"Well, missy. This is some kind of party you invited me to." Captain Lonergan strode into the room, Lieutenant Massie and several other well-armed police officers behind him.

"Brenda, get the disk and give it to the captain," Julie said wearily. "It seems I did have it, after all."

POLICE HEADQUARTERS was certainly a different place when you were on the right side of the law, Julie decided an hour later. She was sitting in Captain Lonergan's office, finishing off a steak sandwich and a salad that Lieutenant Massie had ordered for her.

Julie shifted in her seat and then winced, as the bruises she'd recently acquired reminded her of their presence. After the police had arrived, Greg had accompanied them as they took Jon Derickson, Rolf and Sven to jail. Greg's friend, the thin man, had stayed behind to ask questions. Tricia had arrived home shortly afterward. After fussing over Julie like a worried mother, she had inspected her bookcase.

Now Julie was at police headquarters. Lonergan was drinking a cup of coffee and running through a series of questions when Greg and Walt entered the room.

Lonergan leaned forward, smiling. Gesturing toward the two men, he looked at Julie. "I think it's about time for some formal introductions around here. Ms. Smith, I'd like you to meet Greg Stafford, an agent with the Defense Intelligence Agency. And this is Walt Osborn, his partner."

Julie looked at Greg candidly. "I've caught on that you're not a lawyer, Greg."

His voice was low and his eyes seemed to bore into her, as if he was trying to tell her something. "But I am a lawyer, Julie. I just use my legal background for the government."

Julie was careful not to make eye contact with Greg after that. She noticed that he avoided looking at her, as well. She was undecided how she felt about him. Although deeply hurt that he had lied to her, she understood now that he must have had no choice.

The disk had apparently been even more vital than she had realized. "We can't tell you what was on the disk, Ms. Smith," Captain Lonergan had explained only moments earlier. "That's classified information. But you can rest assured that it was important."

"What happened when you reached the Polynesian Bar, Ms. Smith?" Walt asked the question as he sat down. "I'm still not quite straight about when you were accosted by the counterintelligence agents."

"Brenda and I arrived about twelve-thirty. Brenda had just told me her part in all this. She said she wanted to speak to an attorney before seeing the police. Since I had already agreed to meet Greg, I suggested she go with me. When we arrived at the door of the bar, Brenda flew into a panic. She shoved me outside and told me she had seen Greg in Tokyo and that he might have been following her."

Taking a deep breath, Julie continued. "I led her back into the bar behind a carved wooden screen and asked her to show me the man. She pointed out Greg."

"But why didn't you rush to him and tell him your story?" Captain Lonergan asked. "That could have saved everybody a lot of trouble, missy...."

"Don't." Julie stopped him. "Don't ever call me missy again. My name is Julie."

He grinned. "Okay, Julie. And you can call me Denis. Now how about an answer to my question?"

"I was confused. I wasn't even sure at that point that Brenda wasn't making up the whole story. How could she have seen Greg in Tokyo? I just couldn't make sense of it all.''

"I deceived Julie," Greg reminded them. "At that stage, she didn't know if she could trust me."

"He was on your side all along," Walt said, turning to Julie. "He kept telling me he thought you were being framed, but I was too stubborn to listen."

Julie quickly looked at Greg and he smiled at her. She swallowed a lump in her throat. Now wasn't the time for her to ask for more personal explanations.

"What about Brenda?" Julie turned to Captain Lonergan.

"She has agreed to testify against Derickson," the Captain replied. "Her old man is Dewitt Clark. He's on his way here now with a battery of the best defense lawyers money can buy. As long as she cooperates in the investigation, she'll probably get off lightly."

"And Sven and Rolf?"

Walt took over from the captain. "We won't be able to prosecute them, of course. They're on their way back to their home country. As we suspected, they're Eastern Bloc agents, but they have diplomatic immunity. As for Derickson, he'll spend the rest of his life behind bars. You've done us a real service by helping us capture him."

"Poor Brenda," Greg said quietly. "She's only guilty of trusting a man. But I'd like to know where she learned to fight like that. No telling how many stitches it will take to repair the damage she did to those men."

Julie joined in the laughter that swept the room. "Brenda told me she learned it by watching dogs fight. She's been training to be a vet's assistant, and one of her jobs was to break up dog fights at the kennel where she worked."

The phone rang and the captain picked it up. He handed it to Greg. "Washington is returning your call."

The room became still as Greg spoke. "Yes, we have recovered the disk, sir. It didn't fall into enemy hands." There was a pause and he glanced at Julie, his eyes filled with laughter. "As a matter of fact, Miss Smith, our original suspect, has been sleeping on it these past few days."

Julie tucked the remainder of her sandwich into her napkin and dropped it in the wastebasket. "If you don't need me any longer, I think I'll go home now," she said softly to the others in the room.

Captain Lonergan rose. "Julie, it's been a pleasure working with you." He extended his hand.

She shook it and then smiled briefly at Walt. Ignoring Greg's pleading look, she left the room.

She crossed the lobby swiftly and walked outside. It was dusk now, and the evening breezes brushed her hair against her cheeks. She was filled with a sadness she'd never known before. How could she just walk out of Greg's life? She loved him, no matter what he did for a living. It was the real Greg, the man he was inside, the man he had revealed to her, that she loved.

Julie paused at the doorway, turning slowly, wondering if she should go back inside. She was just about to start back up the stairs when she caught sight of him, brushing past two men and taking the steps two at a time. "Greg," she called.

"Julie." There was a wealth of meaning in the one word.

She ran toward him, holding out her hands. He swept her into his arms. "Julie, I was afraid I wouldn't reach you in time. I can't let you walk out on me. I know I deserve it, but I can't bear it." He buried his face in her fragrant hair. "Forgive me, darling. I never wanted to deceive you."

His hands stroked her hair unsteadily, his lips tasting hers, his arms cradling her against his chest. They held each other for a long, healing moment, and she knew she could never tire of this man. With him, her world would be complete. She wished for nothing more. "You're forgiven," she murmured. "I think I understand what happened. But it's time to put that behind us now."

He cupped her face between his hands and looked down at her. "I can't offer you a traditional life, Julie."

"Who needs tradition?"

"I love you." His lips came down to fasten possessively on hers.

With his arms still holding her close, they went down the steps together. "I can't believe I almost walked out on you," Julie said softly.

"I knew I'd see you again."

She tilted her head sideways and saw that he was smiling. "What made you so sure?"

"I know how you feel about being in my debt." His arm tightened around her tenderly.

Puzzled, she stopped and lifted her face. "What do I owe you?"

"A new lighter," he said huskily and bent over to give her a lingering kiss.

Epilogue

The Polynesian Bar was doing a thriving business when Greg settled himself into a booth beside the atrium. A waiter hurried over to take his order. "Something from the bar? Or will you be having lunch?"

"My wife is joining me. We'll order lunch when she arrives."

"Certainly, sir. Would you like a drink while you wait?"

A half hour later, Greg drained his second tumbler of Scotch. Pulling out a cigarette, he reached for his lighter. The waiter approached him again.

"Your wife hasn't arrived yet?"

"She probably stopped to shop somewhere." Greg grinned and paused to light his cigarette. "If she sees something she likes, she stops."

"Ah, an impulse shopper." The waiter nodded understandingly. "Nice lighter."

"Yes." Greg turned the small silver oblong over in his palm. It was sleek, modern, with clean lines. His initials were engraved in one corner. Smooth, angular letters with no ornamentation. "My wife gave it to me."

"She has good taste."

"I like to think so." Greg shrugged. "After all, she chose me." They both laughed.

"Well, if you're sure she's coming..."

"I'm sure." Greg's eyes gleamed with amusement. "It's only a matter of time."

ATTRACTIVE, SPACE SAVING BOOK RACK

Display your most prized novels on this handsome and sturdy book rack. The hand-rubbed walnut finish will blend into your library decor with quiet elegance, providing a practical organizer for your favorite hard-or soft-covered books.

Only $9.95

Approximately 16" x 8" when assembled

Assembles in seconds!

To order, rush your name, address and zip code, along with a check or money order for $10.70 ($9.95 plus 75¢ postage and handling) (New York residents add appropriate sales tax), payable to *Harlequin Reader Service* to:

In the U.S.

Harlequin Reader Service
Book Rack Offer
901 Fuhrmann Blvd.
P.O. Box 1325
Buffalo, NY 14269-1325

Offer not available in Canada.

BKR–1

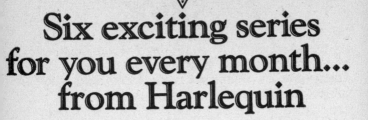

Six exciting series for you every month... from Harlequin

Harlequin Romance·
The series that started it all

Tender, captivating and heartwarming...
love stories that sweep you off to faraway places
and delight you with the magic of love.

◆

Harlequin Presents·
Powerful contemporary love
stories...as individual as the
women who read them

The No. 1 romance series...
exciting love stories for you, the woman of today...
a rare blend of passion and dramatic realism.

◆

Harlequin Superromance®
It's more than romance...
it's Harlequin Superromance

A sophisticated, contemporary romance-fiction
series, providing you with a longer,
more involving read...a richer mix of complex plots,
realism and adventure.

What the press says about Harlequin romance fiction...

"When it comes to romantic novels...
Harlequin is the indisputable king."
—*New York Times*

"...always with an upbeat, happy ending."
—*San Francisco Chronicle*

"Women have come to trust these
stories about contemporary people,
set in exciting foreign places."
—*Best Sellers*, New York

"The most popular reading matter of
American women today."
—*Detroit News*

"...a work of art."
—*Globe & Mail*, Toronto